PENGUIN CRIME FICTION

BEWARE OF THE TRAINS

Edmund Crispin was born in 1921 and educated at Merchant Taylors' School and St. John's College, Oxford, where he read Modern Languages and where for two years he was organist and choirmaster. After a brief spell of teaching he became a full-time writer and composer (especially of film music). Among other variegated activities in the same departments, he produced concert music, edited many science-fiction anthologies, and wrote for many periodicals and newspapers. For many years he was the regular crime-fiction reviewer for the London Sunday *Times.* Edmund Crispin (whose real name was Bruce Montgomery) once wrote of himself: "He is of a sedentary habit—his chief recreations being music, reading, churchgoing, and bridge. Like Rex Stout's Nero Wolfe he leaves his house as seldom as possible, in particular minimizing his visits to London, a rapidly decaying metropolis which since the war he has come to detest." Until his death in 1978 Mr. Crispin lived in Devon, in a quiet corner whose exploitation and development he did his utmost to oppose. His crime novels include *Buried for Pleasure, The Case of the Gilded Fly, Frequent Hearses, The Glimpses of the Moon, Holy Disorders,* and *Swan Song.* Penguin Books also publishes Edmund Crispin's *The Moving Toyshop* and *The Long Divorce.*

BEWARE OF THE TRAINS

EDMUND CRISPIN

PENGUIN BOOKS

FOR NORA, SHEILA AND ELSPETH

Penguin Books Ltd, Harmondsworth,
Middlesex, England
Penguin Books, 40 West 23rd Street,
New York, New York 10010, U.S.A.
Penguin Books Australia Ltd, Ringwood,
Victoria, Australia
Penguin Books Canada Limited, 2801 John Street,
Markham, Ontario, Canada L3R 1B4
Penguin Books (N.Z.) Ltd, 182–190 Wairau Road,
Auckland 10, New Zealand

First published in Great Britain by
Victor Gollancz Ltd 1953
First published in the United States of America by
Walker and Company 1962
Published in Penguin Books 1981
Reprinted 1981, 1983 (twice), 1985, 1986

LIBRARY OF CONGRESS CATALOGING IN PUBLICATION DATA
Montgomery, Robert Bruce.
Beware of the trains.
Originally published in 1962 by Walker, New York
under title: Beware of the trains, sixteen stories.
I. Title.
[PR6025.O46B4 1981] 823'.912 80-28951
ISBN 0 14 00.5834 6

Printed in the United States of America by
George Banta Co., Inc., Harrisonburg, Virginia
Set in Times Roman

CONTENTS

FOREWORD

A SHORT STORY CAN aim either at atmosphere or at the anecdote; those which follow belong, with the exception of *Deadlock*, to the second category. All of them embody the nowadays increasingly neglected principle of fair play to the reader—which is to say that the reader is given all the clues needed to enable him to anticipate the solution by the exercise of his logic and his common sense. He should note, however, that for the solutions of *The Drowning of Edgar Foley, Within the Gates, Express Delivery* and *The Golden Mean* he will require in addition some fragments of technical or near technical information on about the level of the average newspaper quiz.

Excepting (again) *Deadlock*, all the stories made their first appearance in print in this country in the London *Evening Standard*; but the great majority of them have been substantially revised and rewritten for inclusion in this book.

The title *Abhorrèd Shears* has caused some perplexity, and an explanation may perhaps be acceptable here. The relevant lines are in Milton's *Lycidas*:

> *"Comes the blind Fury with th'abhorrèd shears,*
> *And slits the thin spun life."*

The particular Fury referred to is of course Atropos. And atropine, named after her, is the poison which figures in my tale.

E. C.

Brixham.
1952.

BEWARE OF THE TRAINS

A WHISTLE BLEW; jolting slightly, the big posters on the hoardings took themselves off rearwards—and with sudden acceleration, like a thrust in the back, the electric train moved out of Borleston Junction, past the blurred radiance of the tall lamps in the marshalling-yard, past the diminishing constellations of the town's domestic lighting, and so out across the eight-mile isthmus of darkness at whose further extremity lay Clough. Borleston had seen the usual substantial exodus, and the few remaining passengers—whom chance had left oddly, and, as it turned out, significantly distributed—were able at long last to stretch their legs, to transfer hats, newspapers and other impedimenta from their laps to the vacated seats beside them, and for the first time since leaving Victoria to relax and be completely comfortable. Mostly they were somnolent at the approach of midnight, but between Borleston and Clough none of them actually slept. Fate had a conjuring trick in preparation, and they were needed as witnesses to it.

The station at Clough was not large, nor prepossessing, nor, it appeared, much frequented; but in spite of this, the train, once having stopped there, evinced an unexpected reluctance to move on. The whistle's first confident blast having failed to shift it, there ensued a moment's offended silence; then more whistling, and when that also failed, a peremptory, unintelligible shouting. The train remained inanimate, however, without even the usual rapid ticking to enliven it. And presently Gervase Fen, Professor of English Language and Literature in the University of Oxford, lowered the window of his compartment and put his head out, curious to know what was amiss.

Rain was falling indecisively. It tattooed in weak, petulant spasms against the station roof, and the wind on which it rode had a cutting edge. Wan bulbs shone impartially on slot-machines, timetables, a shuttered newspaper-kiosk; on governmental threat and commercial entreaty; on peeling green paint and rust-stained iron. Near the clock, a small group of men stood engrossed in peevish altercation. Fen eyed them with disapproval for a moment and then spoke.

"Broken down?" he enquired unpleasantly. They swivelled round to stare at him. "Lost the driver?" he asked.

This second query was instantly effective. They hastened up to him in a bunch, and one of them—a massive, wall-eyed man who appeared to be the Station-master—said: "For God's sake, sir, *you* 'aven't seen 'im, 'ave you?"

"Seen whom?" Fen demanded mistrustfully.

"The motorman, sir. The driver."

"No, of course I haven't," said Fen. "What's happened to him?"

" 'E's gorn, sir. 'Ooked it, some'ow or other. 'E's not in 'is cabin, nor we can't find 'im anywhere on the station, neither."

"Then he has absconded," said Fen, "with valuables of some description, or with some other motorman's wife."

The Station-master shook his head—less, it appeared, by way of contesting this hypothesis than as an indication of his general perplexity—and stared helplessly up and down the deserted platform. "It's a rum go, sir," he said, "and that's a fact."

"Well, there's one good thing about it, Mr. Maycock," said the younger of the two porters who were with him. " 'E can't 'ave got clear of the station, not without being seen."

The Station-master took some time to assimilate this, and even when he had succeeded in doing so, did not seem much enlightened by it. " 'Ow d'you make that out, Wally?" he enquired.

"Well, after all, Mr. Maycock, the place is surrounded, isn't it?"

"Surrounded, Wally?" Mr. Maycock reiterated feebly. "What d'you mean, surrounded?"

Wally gaped at him. "Lord, Mr. Maycock, didn't you know? I thought you'd 'a' met the Inspector when you came back from your supper."

"Inspector?" Mr. Maycock could scarcely have been more bewildered if his underling had announced the presence of a Snab or a Greevey. "What Inspector?"

"Scotland Yard chap," said Wally importantly. "And 'alf a dozen men with 'im. They're after a burglar they thought'd be on this train."

Mr. Maycock, clearly dazed by this melodramatic intelligence, took refuge from his confusion behind a hastily contrived breastwork of outraged dignity. "And why," he demanded in awful tones, "was I not *hin*formed of this 'ere?"

"You 'ave bin informed," snapped the second porter, who was very old indeed, and who appeared to be temperamentally subject to that vehement, unfocussed rage which one associates with men who are trying to give up smoking. "You 'ave bin informed. We've just informed yer."

Mr. Maycock ignored this. "*If* you would be so kind," he said in a lofty manner, "it would be 'elpful for me to know at what time these persons of 'oom you are speaking put in an appearance 'ere."

"About twenty to twelve, it'd be," said Wally sulkily. "Ten minutes before this lot was due in."

"And it wouldn't 'ave occurred to you, would it"—here Mr. Maycock bent slightly at the knees, as though the weight of his sarcasm was altogether too much for his large frame to support comfortably—"to 'ave a dekko in my room and see if I was 'ere? *Ho* no. I'm only the Station-master, that's all I am."

"Well, I'm very sorry, Mr. Maycock," said Wally, in a tone of voice which effectively cancelled the apology out, "but I wasn't to know you was back, was I? I told the Inspector you was still at your supper in the village."

At this explanation, Mr. Maycock, choosing to overlook the decided resentment with which it had been delivered, became magnanimous. "Ah well, there's no great 'arm done, I dare say," he pronounced; and the dignity of his office having by now been adequately paraded, he relapsed to the level of common humanity again. "Burglar, eh? Was 'e on the train? Did they get 'im?"

Wally shook his head. "Not them. False alarm, most likely. They're still 'angin' about, though." He jerked a grimy thumb towards the exit barrier. "That's the Inspector, there."

Hitherto, no one had been visible in the direction indicated. But now there appeared, beyond the barrier, a round, benign, clean-shaven face surmounted by a grey Homburg hat, at which Fen bawled "Humbleby!" in immediate recognition. And the person thus addressed, having delivered the injunction "Don't *move* from here, Millican" to someone in the gloom of the ticket-hall behind him, came on to the platform and in another moment had joined them.

He was perhaps fifty-five: small, as policemen go, and of a compact build which the neatness of his clothes accentuated. The close-cropped greying hair, the pink affable face, the soldierly bearing, the bulge of the cigar-case in the breast pocket and the shining brown shoes—these things suggested the more malleable sort of German *petit bourgeois*; to see him close at hand, however, was to see the grey eyes—bland, intelligent, sceptical—which effectively belied your first, superficial impression, showing the iron under the velvet. "Well, well," he said. "Well, well, well. Chance is a great thing."

"What," said Fen severely, his head still projecting from the compartment window like a gargoyle from a cathedral tower, 'is all this about a burglar?"

"And you will be the Station-master." Humbleby had turned to Mr. Maycock. "You were away when I arrived here, so I took the liberty——"

"*That* I wasn't, sir," Mr. Maycock interrupted, anxious to vindicate himself. "I was in me office all the time, only these lads didn't think to look there. . . . 'Ullo, Mr. Foster." This last greeting was directed to the harassed Guard, who had clearly been searching for the missing motorman. "Any luck?"

"Not a sign of 'im," said the Guard sombrely. "Nothing like this 'as ever 'appened on one of *my* trains before."

"It is 'Inkson, isn't it?"

The Guard shook his head. "No. Phil Bailey."

"Bailey?"

"Ah. Bailey sometimes took over from 'Inkson on this run." Here the Guard glanced uneasily at Fen and Humbleby. "It's irregular, o' course, but it don't do no 'arm as I can see. Bailey's 'ome's at Bramborough, at the end o' this line, and 'e'd 'ave to catch this train any'ow to get to it, so 'e took over sometimes when 'Inkson wanted to stop in Town. . . . And now this 'as to 'appen. There'll be trouble, you mark my words." Evidently the unfortunate Guard expected to be visited with a substantial share of it.

"Well, I can't 'old out no longer," said Mr. Maycock. "I'll 'ave to ring 'Eadquarters straight away." He departed in order to do this, and Humbleby, who still had no clear idea of what was going on, required the others to enlighten him. When they had done this: "Well," he said, "one thing's certain, and that is that your motorman hasn't left the station. My men are all round it, and they had orders to detain anyone who tried to get past them."

At this stage, an elderly business man, who was sharing the same compartment with Fen and with an excessively genteel young woman of the sort occasionally found behind the counters of Post Offices, irritably enquired if Fen proposed keeping the compartment window open all night. And Fen, acting on this hint, closed the window and got out on to the platform.

"None the less," he said to Humbleby, "it'll be as well to interview your people and confirm that Bailey *hasn't* left. I'll go the rounds with you, and you can tell me about your burglar."

They left the Guard and the two porters exchanging theories

about Bailey's defection, and walked along the platform towards the head of the train. "Goggett is my burglar's name," said Humbleby. "Alfred Goggett. He's wanted for quite a series of jobs, but for the last few months he's been lying low, and we haven't been able to put our hands on him. Earlier this evening, however, he was spotted in Soho by a plain-clothes man named, incongruously enough, Diggett . . ."

"Really, Humbleby. . . ."

". . . And Diggett chased him to Victoria. Well, you know what Victoria's like. It's rather a rambling terminus, and apt to be full of people. Anyway, Diggett lost his man there. Now, about mid-day today one of our more reliable narks brought us the news that Goggett had a hide-out here in Clough, so this afternoon Millican and I drove down here to look the place over. Of course the Yard rang up the police here when they heard Goggett had vanished at Victoria; and the police here got hold of me; and here we all are. There was obviously a very good chance that Goggett would catch this train. Only unluckily he didn't."

"No one got off here?"

"No one got off or on. And I understand that this is the last train of the day, so for the time being there's nothing more we can do. But sooner or later, of course, he'll turn up at his cottage here, and then we'll have him."

"And in the meantime," said Fen thoughtfully, "there's the problem of Bailey."

"In the meantime there's that. Now let's see . . ."

It proved that the six damp but determined men whom Humbleby had culled from the local constabulary had been so placed about the station precincts as to make it impossible for even a mouse to have left without their observing it; and not even a mouse, they stoutly asserted, had done so. Humbleby told them to stay where they were until further orders, and returned with Fen to the down platform.

"No loophole there," he pronounced. "And it's an easy station to—um—invest. If it had been a great sprawling place like Borleston, now, I could have put a hundred men round it, and Goggett might still have got clear. . . . Of course, it's quite possible that Borleston's where he did leave the train."

"One thing at a time," said Fen rather peevishly. "It's Bailey we're worrying about now—not Goggett."

"Well, Bailey's obviously still on the station. Or else somewhere on the train. I wonder what the devil he thinks he's up to?"

"In spite of you and your men, he must have been able to

leave his cabin without being observed." They were passing the cabin as Fen spoke, and he stopped to peer at its vacant interior. "As you see, there's no way through from it into the remainder of the train."

Humbleby considered the disposition of his forces, and having done so: "Yes," he admitted, "he could have left the cabin without being seen; and for that matter, got to shelter somewhere in the station buildings."

"Weren't the porters on the platform when the train came in?"

"No. They got so overwrought when I told them what I was here for—the younger one especially—that I made them keep out of the way. I didn't want them gaping when Goggett got off the train and making him suspicious—he's the sort of man who's quite capable of using a gun when he finds himself cornered."

"Maycock?"

"He was in his office—asleep, I suspect. As to the Guard, I could see his van from where I was standing, and he didn't even get out of it till he was ready to start the train off again. . . ." Humbleby sighed. "So there really wasn't anyone to keep an eye on the motorman's doings. However, we're bound to find him: he can't have left the precincts. I'll get a search-party together, and we'll have another look—a systematic one, this time."

Systematic or not, it turned out to be singularly barren of results. It established one thing only, and that was, that beyond any shadow of doubt the missing motorman was not anywhere in, on or under the station, nor anywhere in, on or under his abandoned train.

And unfortunately, it was also established that he could not, in the nature of things, be anywhere else.

Fen took no part in this investigation, having already foreseen its inevitable issue. He retired, instead, to the Station-master's office, by whose fire he was dozing when Humbleby sought him out half an hour later.

"One obvious answer," said Humbleby when he had reported his failure, "is of course that Bailey's masquerading as someone else—as one of the twelve people (that's not counting police) who definitely *are* cooped up in this infernal little station."

"And is he doing that?"

"No. At least, not unless the Guard and the two porters and the Station-master are in a conspiracy together—which I don't for a second believe. They all know Bailey by sight, at least, and they're all certain that no one here can possibly be him."

Fen yawned. "So what's the next step?" he asked.

"What I ought to have done long ago: the next step is to find out if there's any evidence Bailey was driving the train when it left Borleston. . . . Where's the telephone?"

"Behind you."

"Oh, yes. . . . I don't understand these inter-station phones, so I'll use the ordinary one. . . . God help us, hasn't that dolt Maycock made a note of the number anywhere?"

"In front of you."

"Oh, yes. . . . 51709." Humbleby lifted the receiver, dialled, and waited. "Hello, is that Borleston Junction?" he said presently. "I want to speak to the station-master. Police business. . . . Yes, all right, but be *quick*." And after a pause: "Station-master? This is Detective-Inspector Humbleby of the Metropolitan C.I.D. I want to know about a train which left Borleston for Clough and Bramborough at—at——"

"A quarter to midnight," Fen supplied.

"At a quarter to midnight. . . . Good heavens, yes, this last midnight that we've just had. . . . Yes, I know it's held up at Clough; so am I. . . . No, no, what I want is information about who was driving it when it left Borleston: eyewitness information. . . . *You did?* . . . You actually saw Bailey yourself? Was that immediately before the train left? . . . It was; well then, there's no chance of Bailey's having hopped out, and someone else taken over, after you saw him? . . . I see: the train was actually moving out when you saw him at the controls. Sure you're not mistaken? This is important. . . . Oh, there's a porter who can corroborate it, is there? . . . No, I don't want to talk to him now. . . . All right. . . . Yes. . . . Good-bye."

Humbleby rang off and turned back to Fen. "So that," he observed, "is that."

"So I gathered."

"And the next thing is, could Bailey have left the train between Borleston and here?"

"The train," said Fen, "didn't drive itself in, you know."

"Never mind that for the moment," said Humbleby irritably. "*Could* he?"

"No. He couldn't. Not without breaking his neck. We did a steady thirty-five to forty all the way, and we didn't stop or slow down once."

There was a silence. "Well, I give up," said Humbleby. "Unless this wretched man has vanished like a sort of soap-bubble——"

"It's occurred to you that he may be dead?"

"It's occurred to me that he may be dead and cut up into little pieces. But I still can't find any of the pieces. . . . Good Lord, Fen, it's like—it's like one of those Locked-Room Mvs teries you get in books: an Impossible Situation."

Fen yawned again. "Not impossible, no," he said. "Rather a simple device, really. . . ." Then more soberly: "But I'm afraid that what we have to deal with is something much more serious than a mere vanishing. In fact——"

The telephone rang, and after a moment's hesitation Humbleby answered it. The call was for him; and when, several minutes later, he put the receiver back on its hook, his face was grave.

"They've found a dead man," he said, "three miles along the line towards Borleston. He's got a knife in his back and has obviously been thrown out of a train. From their description of the face and clothes, it's quite certainly Goggett. And equally certainly, *that*"—he nodded towards the platform—"is the train he fell out of. . . . Well, my first and most important job is to interview the passengers. And anyone who was alone in a compartment will have a lot of explaining to do."

Most of the passengers had by now disembarked, and were standing about in various stages of bewilderment, annoyance and futile enquiry. At Humbleby's command, and along with the Guard, the porters and Mr. Maycock, they shuffled, feebly protesting, into the waiting-room. And there, with Fen as an interested onlooker, a Grand Inquisition was set in motion.

Its results were both baffling and remarkable. Apart from the motorman, there had been nine people on the train when it left Borleston and when it arrived at Clough; and each of them had two others to attest the fact that during the whole crucial period he (or she) had behaved as innocently as a new-born infant. With Fen there had been the elderly business man and the genteel girl; in another compartment there had likewise been three people, no one of them connected with either of the others by blood, acquaintance, or vocation; and even the Guard had witnesses to his harmlessness, since from Victoria onwards he had been accompanied in the van by two melancholy men in cloth caps, whose mode of travel was explained by their being in unremitting personal charge of several doped-looking whippets. None of these nine, until the first search for Bailey was set on foot, had seen or heard anything amiss. None of them (since the train was not a corridor train) had had any opportunity of moving out of sight of his or her two companions. None of them had slept. And unless some unknown, travelling in one of the many empty compartments, had disappeared in the same fashion as Bailey—a supposition which Humbleby was by no means prepared to entertain—it seemed evident that Goggett must have launched himself into eternity unaided.

It was at about this point in the proceedings that Humbleby's self-possession began to wear thin, and his questions to become merely repetitive; and Fen, perceiving this, slipped out alone on to the platform. When he returned, ten minutes later, he was carrying a battered suitcase; and regardless of Humbleby, who seemed to be making some sort of speech, he carried this impressively to the centre table and put it down there.

"In this suitcase," he announced pleasantly, as Humbleby's flow of words petered out, "we shall find, I think, the motorman's uniform belonging to the luckless Bailey." He undid the catches. "And in addition, no doubt . . . *Stop him, Humbleby!*"

The scuffle that followed was brief and inglorious. Its protagonist, tackled round the knees by Humbleby, fell, struck his head against the fender, and lay still, the blood welling from a cut above his left eye.

"Yes, that's the culprit," said Fen. "And it will take a better lawyer than there is alive to save *him* from a rope's end."

Later, as Humbleby drove him to his destination through the December night, he said: "Yes, it had to be Maycock. And Goggett and Bailey had, of course, to be one and the same person. But what about motive?"

Humbleby shrugged. "Obviously, the money in that case of Goggett's. There's a lot of it, you know. It's a pretty clear case of thieves falling out. We've known for a long time that Goggett had an accomplice, and it's now certain that that accomplice was Maycock. Whereabouts in his office did you find the suitcase?"

"Stuffed behind some lockers—not a very good hiding-place, I'm afraid. Well, well, it can't be said to have been a specially difficult problem. Since Bailey wasn't on the station, and hadn't left it, it was clear he'd never entered it. But *someone* had driven the train in—and who could it have been *but* Maycock? The two porters were accounted for—by you; so were the Guard and the passengers—by one another; and there just wasn't anyone else.

"And then, of course, the finding of Goggett's body clinched it. He hadn't been thrown out of either of the occupied compartments, or the Guard's van; he hadn't been thrown out of any of the *un*occupied compartments, for the simple reason that there was nobody to throw him. *Therefore* he was thrown out of the motorman's cabin. And since, as I've demonstrated, Maycock was unquestionably *in* the motorman's cabin, it was scarcely conceivable that Maycock had not done the throwing.

"Plainly, Maycock rode or drove into Borleston while he was supposed to be having his supper, and boarded the train—that is, the motorman's cabin—there. He kept hidden till the train was under way, and then took over from Goggett-Bailey while Goggett-Bailey changed into the civilian clothes he had with him. By the way, I take it that Maycock, to account for his presence, spun some fictional (as far as he knew) tale about the police being on Goggett-Bailey's track, and that the change was Goggett-Bailey's idea; I mean, that he had some notion of its assisting his escape at the end of the line."

Humbleby nodded. "That's it, approximately. I'll send you a copy of Maycock's confession as soon as I can get one made. It seems he wedged the safety handle which operates these trains, knifed Goggett-Bailey and chucked him out, and then drove the train into Clough and there simply disappeared, with the case, into his office. It must have given him a nasty turn to hear the station was surrounded."

"It did," said Fen. "If your people hadn't been there, it would have looked, of course, as if Bailey had just walked off into the night. But chance was against him all along. Your siege, and the grouping of the passengers, and the cloth-capped men in the van—they were all part of an accidental conspiracy—if you can talk of such a thing—to defeat him; all part of a sort of fortuitous conjuring trick." He yawned prodigiously, and gazed out of the car window. "Do you know, I believe it's the dawn. . . . Next time I want to arrive anywhere, I shall travel by bus."

HUMBLEBY AGONISTES

"IN MY JOB," said Detective-Inspector Humbleby, "a man expects to be shot at every now and again. It's an occupational risk, like pneumoconiosis in coal-mining, and when you're on duty you've obviously got to be prepared for it to crop up. But a social call on an old acquaintance is quite a different matter. Here am I on my Sabbatical. I drop in to see this man I've known ever since the 1914 war. And what happens? Before I have a chance to as much as open my mouth and ask him how he is, he snatches a damned great revolver out of his pocket and lets it off at me. Well, I was petrified. Anyone would be. I was so astonished I literally couldn't move."

"He doesn't seem to have hit you, though." From the depths of the armchair in his rooms at St. Christopher's, Gervase Fen, University Professor of English Language and Literature, regarded his guest with a clinical air. "I see no wound," he elaborated.

"There is no wound. Three times he fired," said Humbleby dramatically, "and three times he missed. Which, of course, makes it all the odder."

"Why 'of course'? I've always understood that revolvers——"

"I say 'of course' because Garstin-Walsh, whom I'm speaking of, is a retired Army man: a brevet-rank Colonel, to be precise. . . . Yes, I know what you're going to tell me. You're going to tell me that Army men seldom actually use revolvers, even though they may carry them; and that consequently it's naïve to expect them to be good marksmen. Agreed. But the trouble in this instance is that Garstin-Walsh has always made a hobby of shooting in general—he's the sort of man it's impossible to visualise outside the context of dogs and guns and an interest in dahlias—and of pistol-shooting in particular. That's why I'm so certain he missed me on purpose: at a yard's range even *I* could hardly go wrong. . . . But perhaps I'd better begin at the beginning."

Fen nodded gravely. "Perhaps you had."

"As you know," said Humbleby, "I was in Military Intelligence during the 1914 war; and it was while I was investigating an unimaginative piece of sabotage at an arms depot near Loos that I first met Garstin-Walsh, who at that time was a Captain in the Supply Corps. It'd be an exaggeration to say that we became close friends—and looking back on it, I can't quite see why we should have become friends at all, because our temperaments weren't at all alike, and we had very few interests in common. Still, for some obscure reason we did in fact get on well together; and I think that much of his attraction for me must have been due to his complete humourlessness—we were all a bit hysterical in those days, whether we knew it or not, and a man who never laughed was unexpectedly *restful*.

"We used to meet, then, as often as we could; and after the Armistice we kept up a sporadic correspondence and managed some sort of reunion once or twice every year. Then eighteen months ago Garstin-Walsh retired and went to live at a village called Uscombe, which is a few miles from Exeter; and since I was staying with my sister at Exmouth, and hadn't seen him for some considerable time, I decided, the day before yesterday, to drive over and pay him a surprise visit.

"I left Exmouth immediately after breakfast and got to Uscombe about ten-thirty. Uscombe's not as cut off from the rest of the world as some Devon villages, because it's only a quarter of a mile from the main London road; but in all other respects it's fairly typical—settled to some extent by middle-class 'foreigners,' I mean, with an unsuccessful preparatory boarding-school in a tumble-down manor-house, and a church tower scheduled dangerous; you know the sort of place. I hadn't been there before, so I stopped at one of the village shops to enquire for Garstin-Walsh's house. And the way they looked at me, as they gave me directions, was the first intimation I had that anything was wrong.

"The house proved to be a nice, trim, up-to-date little red-brick villa beyond the church, with lots of chrysanthemums in the garden and a carefully weeded front lawn; so that was all right. But then the trouble started. The painters were in, for one thing; an Exeter C.I.D. Inspector was hanging about the hall, for another; and an undeniably dead body was in process of being removed by a mortuary van. I need hardly tell you that if I'd known about all this I should have gone back to Exmouth and tried again some other day; but by the time the situation became clear I'd rung, and been let in by the housekeeper, and so couldn't very well escape without positive incivility.

"Garstin-Walsh was still upstairs dressing. But the Exeter man, Jourdain he was called, had heard me give my name to the housekeeper, and lost no time in introducing himself. 'You'll be curious,' he said dogmatically, 'about that body they've just taken away.' I denied this, but it was no good, he insisted on telling me about the affair just the same. And stripped of inessentials, the story I heard, while we waited in the hall for Garstin-Walsh to come down, was as follows:

"A year previously, the ramshackle cottage near Garstin-Walsh's house had been rented by one Saul Brebner, he whose remains were at present *en route* for the Exeter City Mortuary. A powerful, malignant, drunken, slovenly man of about fifty was Brebner, and the people of Uscombe had gone in fear of him almost from the day of his arrival. He was without family, lived alone in squalor, had money in spite of working not at all, and divided his time fairly evenly between poaching and *The Three Crowns*. The police kept an eye on him, of course, but he succeeded in steering clear of them. And the only person in the village who ever had a good word to say for him was, surprisingly enough, Garstin-Walsh.

"That there was a reason for this the village soon discovered: Brebner had been Garstin-Walsh's batman in the 1914 war, and it was realised that Garstin-Walsh's toleration of the creature derived from this. However, the toleration wasn't by any means mutual: Brebner made no secret of his loathing for Garstin-Walsh, and from time to time, when in liquor, was heard to hint that there were phases of the Colonel's career which would not bear investigation. The village, which quite liked Garstin-Walsh, discounted these innuendoes as the vapourings of malice, and even when Brebner became more specific, referring to misappropriation of supplies in France, refused to take him seriously. Indeed, on the night of the incident which wrote *finis* to Brebner's unlovely existence, he was so vituperative about Garstin-Walsh in the public bar of *The Three Crowns* that there was very nearly a riot, and when he left the pub at closing time—half past ten—he was dangerously enraged as well as, what was normal, dangerously drunk.

"Garstin-Walsh reached home that evening at about a quarter to eleven (I'm referring, you understand, to what to me, visiting him, was the previous evening). He'd spent the day acting as starter at the village sports, had dined at the Vicarage, and afterwards had worked with the Vicar at the parish accounts; and he got back to his house just in time to meet his solicitor on the doorstep, the said solicitor having driven there, on urgent business, from Exeter. Well, they went into the study, a large room on the ground floor, and got on with whatever it was they had to discuss. And according to the solicitor, a respectable old party named Weems, it was exactly five to eleven when the french windows burst open and Brebner, carrying a double-barrelled shotgun, lurched into the room.

"It was all over in a moment. Brebner levelled the gun at Garstin-Walsh and fired off one barrel. But he was pretty far gone, and the pellets spattered the room without touching their target. The second barrel remained. Steadying himself, Brebner aimed again. And Garstin-Walsh, grabbing up the pistol which he'd been using all day to start races, and which he'd reloaded immediately on his return, fired just in time to save his own life. It was good shooting, partly because the end of the room where Brebner stood was in semi-darkness, and partly because Garstin-Walsh, according to Weems' deposition, was fairly thoroughly unnerved. Brebner staggered, dropped the shotgun, and collapsed on the carpet with a bullet in his head.

"Well, the village constable was summoned; and since Brebner, though unconscious, was still just alive, a doctor was summoned too. The doctor refused to have Brebner moved, and Garstin-Walsh was forced to allow him to stay in the study, with a nurse to look after him, until next morning at nine o'clock he died there without recovering consciousness."

Humbleby sucked complacently at his cheroot. "That, then, was the story Jourdain told me while we waited for Garstin-Walsh to appear. A clear case of self-defence, and a very good riddance, and the only reason Jourdain was there was to have a look at the study where the thing had happened, for the purpose of making the usual routine report.

"He'd just finished his tale when Garstin-Walsh came downstairs. Garstin-Walsh has always been a stringy, bony sort of man, and even when I first knew him he looked old; so the years have really altered him very little, in comparison with the rest of us. At the moment he was a bit haggard and white, and I guessed he hadn't slept much; I got the impression, too, that all the time he was talking to us he was preoccupied, inwardly, with some sort of intellectual balancing trick: I mean that he had the precarious, *constricted* air you notice in people who are trying to think of two things at once. But he was very civil with us, brushing aside my suggestion that I should go away and come back at some more convenient time; and he took Jourdain and myself into the study as soon as the nurse, who'd been packing and tidying, quitted it.

"It was a pleasant room, its pleasantness a bit marred, at the moment, by surgical smells and paint smells (the painters hadn't finished with it till supper-time the previous day); and while Jourdain explained that he'd come to look at the shot-holes and so forth—rather needlessly, since he'd already said all that to the housekeeper, and she, presumably, had conveyed it to Garstin-Walsh—I had a look round. There was more shabbiness than I should have expected: Garstin-Walsh had—has—an unusually spick-and-span sort of mind, and there are considerable private means for him to spend as well as his pension, so that the threadbare carpet and the dented brass coal-scuttle, which you wouldn't notice these days in most people's houses, surprised me at first. But of course, there was, in view of Brebner's insinuations and independent income, one very plausible explanation of the shabbiness. And it'll show you how superficial my friendship with Garstin-Walsh was when I say that the possibility of blackmail neither shocked nor astonished me particularly, and that I wasn't conscious of there being any disloyalty involved in my having my suspicions about Garstin-Walsh's professional past.

"So there we all were: Garstin-Walsh fidgeting in a monkish kind of dressing-gown which he wore over his shirt and plus-fours instead of a coat, Jourdain gabbling away as only a County D.I. can gabble, and myself thinking disinterested thoughts about consignments of service dress which had gone astray, and never been recovered, during the first months of 1917. It's no use my pretending I was comfortable. I wasn't. On the other hand, my uneasiness had nothing whatever to do with blackmail or its pretexts, or with the problem of what, in this particular instance, I ought to do about them—since I intended, very firmly indeed, to do nothing about them whatever. No, it was more the sort of sensation you have when in crossing a road you hear a car coming at you and can't for the moment either see it or judge, from the sound of it, what direction it's coming from. I remember I was actually humming quietly, to keep my spirits up, as I strolled over to the french windows to have a look at the view.

"And that was when it happened.

"The village constable hadn't confiscated Garstin-Walsh's revolver—there was no reason, after all, why he should—and apparently Garstin-Walsh had taken it to bed with him. Anyway, he had it on him now, in a pocket of his dressing-gown, and I was just on the point of making some remark about the garden when he suddenly whipped the thing out, shouting incoherently, and fired it at me. I was simply flabbergasted, of course. I stood there helplessly trying to remember the details of Gross's suicidal method of disarming people with guns, and Jourdain stood there goggling, and one shot smashed a vase on a table beside me, and another smashed a pane of the french windows, and a third went heaven knows where, and then, when I thought my last hour had certainly come, Garstin-Walsh waved me away—still shouting, still incoherent—and backed out of the french windows and fled. Almost immediately Jourdain went after him—and to cut a long story short, caught up with him at the bottom of the garden, where he'd stopped and was standing like a man in a trance, staring at the revolver in his hand as if he couldn't imagine what it was or how he'd come by it. He surrendered it, and returned to the house with Jourdain, like a lamb; and he was more dazed and bewildered than I've ever seen anyone in my life. He knew what he'd done, all right, but he couldn't account for his motives in doing it. 'It—it was like last night,' he stammered.

'When I saw you standing by those windows I remembered Brebner, and the gun was in my pocket and——'

"Well, it wasn't attempted murder, because plainly there was no malice; and there's no such thing as attempted manslaughter. So we telephoned his doctor and got him to bed, still quite bemused—and in bed, for all I know, he is still. The doctor, of course, understood all about it: it was delayed shock, or post-traumatic automatism or some such thing, and the only surprising feature of the business was that I was still alive. I can tell you, I felt quite ashamed of myself for upsetting what otherwise would have been a perfect sample-phenomenon for the medical text-books. . . . Well, I went away, and today, as you know, travelled up here to Oxford, and——"

"Why?" Fen interrupted. "Why did you come to Oxford? To see me?"

"Well, yes."

"You're not satisfied, then?"

"I'm not," said Humbleby. "Everything about the affair fits, and seems quite innocent, excepting just one obstinate little fragment."

"And that is?"

"He unloaded the gun, you see. After he'd shot at me, and before Jourdain grabbed him, he unloaded the gun and threw the spent cartridge-cases away somewhere. When he handed the gun to Jourdain its chambers were empty. And why the devil, I ask myself, should he have done *that*?"

Outside the windows of the first-floor room in which they sat, a clock struck six. Dusk was falling; the gleam had gone from the gilt titles of the books ranged along the walls, and from the college dining-hall you could hear the clink and rattle of plates being laid for dinner. In the broad, high room, with its painted panels, its luxurious chairs, its huge flat-topped desk and its weird medley of pictures, Detective-Inspector Humbleby gestured expressively and fell silent—and for the time being Fen seemed disposed to let the silence stay. His ruddy, clean-shaven face was pensive; his long, lean body sprawled gracelessly, heels on the fender; his brown hair, ineffectually plastered down with water, stood up, as usual, in mutinous spikes at the crown of his head. For perhaps two minutes he remained staring, mute and motionless, into the amber depths of his glass. . . .

And then, suddenly, he chuckled.

"Rather nice, yes," he said. "Tell me, were the spent cartridges ever found?"

"No. At the time, of course, we didn't bother about them.

But Jourdain was hunting for them yesterday, and he couldn't find them anywhere."

Fen's amusement grew. "Nor will he ever, I imagine—unless your Colonel Garstin-Walsh is a hopeless blunderer."

"But how are they important? I don't see——"

"Don't you?" Fen lit a cigarette and reached for an ashtray. "I should imagine, myself, that they're important for the reason that one of them is a blank."

"A blank?" Humbleby's face was very much that.

And Fen roused himself, speaking more energetically. "You'll agree that Garstin-Walsh obviously *possessed* blanks; no man in his senses starts races at the village sports with live ammunition."

"Yes, I agree about that."

"And two of the shots he fired at you smashed things, so they were real enough. But what happened to the third?"

Humbleby was anything but stupid; after a moment's reflection he nodded abruptly. "If that third shot was a blank," he said, "then that would mean . . . No, wait. I see what you're getting at, but I can't quite work it out for the moment. So go on."

"We're assuming, remember, that Garstin-Walsh got rid of those cartridge-cases advisedly—that he wasn't, in fact, the maniac he seemed. Now, it's possible to conceive quite a number of solid reasons for his acting as he did; but so far as my deductions have gone, there's only one of them that covers all the facts. A blank cartridge is recognisably different from a live one. Let's take it, then, that the spent shells were thrown away in order to conceal the presence of a blank among them, in case either you or Jourdain should be curious enough to investigate the gun. What follows? Quite simply, the fact that Garstin-Walsh fired two live shots and a blank at you. And if he did that, it can only have been because Jourdain was just about to examine the study, and there was a bullet-hole in the wall which had to be accounted for somehow.

"Now, there was *no* bullet-hole in the wall prior to the Brebner shooting; if there had been, the painters would have found it and repaired it. So what would have happened if Garstin-Walsh hadn't staged his shooting act with you? Jourdain, finding a bullet-hole in the wall, would have reasoned thus:

"'This hole must be the result of the single shot Garstin-Walsh fired at Brebner last night.

"'It can't have been made subsequently, because Brebner and the nurse were in here all night.

"'Therefore when Garstin-Walsh fired at Brebner he missed.

"'But there is a bullet from Garstin-Walsh's revolver lodged in Brebner's skull.

"'Therefore Garston-Walsh must have shot Brebner earlier on, before he returned here and met Weems.

"'And that doesn't look much like self-defence; it looks like murder.'

"That Brebner was blackmailing Garstin-Walsh is obvious enough. It's obvious, too, that Garstin-Walsh decided he must put a stop to it. So as I see it, he must have shot Brebner after Brebner left *The Three Crowns*, have gone to the cottage to remove whatever evidence of misappropriation of Army supplies Brebner was using, and have then returned to his house. He'd shot Brebner in the skull, and so naturally assumed that he was dead, but——"

"Yes, that's the difficulty," Humbleby interposed. "The idea of a man with a bullet in his brain rushing about with a shot-gun intent on vengeance——"

"Oh come, Humbleby." Fen was mildly shocked. "It's not common, I grant you, but there are plenty of cases on record. John Wilkes Booth, who assassinated Lincoln, is one. Gross and Taylor and Sydney Smith quote others. Brain injuries don't kill at once, and in a certain proportion of cases they don't kill at all. They don't necessarily involve loss of consciousness or inability to act, either: there was that fourteen-year-old boy, you remember, who tripped and fell on an iron rod he was carrying; the rod went clean through his brain; but all that happened was that he pulled it out and went on home, and he didn't die until more than a week later, after an interlude during which he hadn't even felt particularly ill. . . .

"But Garstin-Walsh must have had a nasty turn when the man he'd left for dead burst in at his french windows. No wonder he was 'fairly thoroughly unnerved.' No wonder his shot went wild. But no wonder, also, that Brebner could hardly hold the shot-gun with which he intended to revenge himself; no wonder he collapsed just after Garstin-Walsh fired at him. . . .

"Garstin-Walsh must have rejoiced. He'd murdered a man, and now, by the queerest combination of accidents, the thing had been made to seem a perfect case of self-defence. The only snag lay in that superfluous, that tell-tale bullet-hole in the study wall. In the excitement following Brebner's collapse it wouldn't be noticed—the more so if a piece of furniture were unobtrusively shifted so as to conceal it. But there was no chance during the night of removing the bullet and plugging the hole; and there was very little chance that Jourdain would miss it when he examined the study next morning. So Garstin-Walsh, having heard from his housekeeper of Jourdain's presence and intentions, and seeing no opportunity, with such a crowd of people in the house, of slipping into the study and dealing with the hole before meeting Jourdain, loaded his revolver with two live cartridges and a blank; and then—you having placed yourself conveniently in position near the french windows and the bullet-hole—staged his nervous breakdown."

There was a long silence. Then Humbleby said: "Yes, I'm sure you're right. But it's all conjecture, of course."

"Oh, quite," said Fen cheerfully. "If my theory's false, there won't be any proof of it. And if it's true, there won't be any proof of it, either. So you can take your choice. The only possibility of checking it would be if the——"

He was interrupted by the shrilling of the telephone. "That might be for me," Humbleby told him. "I took the liberty of asking Jourdain to get in touch with me here if there was any news, so. . . ."

And in fact the call was for him. He listened long and spoke little. And presently, ringing off, he said:

"Yes, it was Jourdain. He's found those cartridge-cases."

"In a place where he'd looked previously?"

"No. And none of them is a blank. Which means——"

"Which means," said Fen as he picked up the whisky decanter and refilled their glasses, "that on this side of eternity there's at least one thing we shall *never* know."

THE DROWNING OF EDGAR FOLEY

In a room in Belchester Mortuary—a plain room with a faint smell of formalin, where dust-motes hung suspended in a single shaft of sunlight—the financier and the labourer lay on deal tables under greyish cotton sheets, side by side. The scene was of a sort to evoke facile moralising, all the more so since the labourer had left his wife moderately well off, whereas the financier had died penniless. But neither Gervase Fen—for whom, thanks to the repetitious insistence of the English poets, such moralising had long since lost its first freshness—nor Superintendent Best—who like most plain men felt that the democracy of death was too large and obvious and absolute a fact to require comment—was moved to remark, or even to reflect on, the commonplace irony of it. In any case, they were not, as yet, fully informed: at this stage the financier was not yet known to be a financier, was not yet docketed and filed as the undischarged bankrupt who had changed his identity, fled from London, and at last, in God knows what access of fear or despair, cut his own throat with the ragged blade of a pocket-knife in a lonely part of the moors. To the authorities he was still no better than an anonymous suicide; so that when Fen, after a brief scrutiny of the shrunken, waxy face, was able to announce that this was in fact the stranger with whom he had recently talked in the hotel bar at Belmouth, and whose touched-up photograph, issued by the police, he had seen in that morning's papers, Superintendent Best heaved a sigh of relief.

"That's something, sir, anyway," he said. "It gives us a starting-point, at least—and there's things in that conversation you had with him that'll narrow it down quite a lot. So if you wouldn't mind coming back to the station straight away, and making a formal statement . . ."

Fen nodded assent. "No other reaction so far? To the photograph, I mean?"

"Not yet. There's almost always a bit of a time-lag, you know."

"Ah," said Fen affirmatively; and his eyes strayed to the shrouded occupant of the further table. "Who's that?" he demanded.

"Chap called Edgar Foley. Drowning case. They picked him out of the water yesterday, and his widow's coming along this morning to have a look at him." Best consulted his watch. "And talking of that, I think it'd be a good thing if we were to clear out before they——"

But he was too late; and he was destined to reflect, later, that it was just as well he had been too late—for if Fen had never set eyes on the widow of Edgar Foley, the topic of Foley's death might well have lapsed, and in that case an unusually mean and contemptible crime would probably have gone unpunished. For the moment, however, Best was merely embarrassed, since the room possessed only one door, and with the arrival of the newcomers his retreat was cut off. He moved back against the wall, therefore, waiting; and with Fen at his side was witness to what followed.

A Sergeant, helmet under oxter, led the way; he stood aside, holding the door, until his two companions had entered. Inevitably, it was the smaller of the two, the man, who claimed attention first: for this was an imbecile in the technical sense of the word, an ament—flat-topped skull, decaying teeth, abnormal ears, tiny eyes, coarse skin; well below average height, but with long ape-like arms, muscularly well developed. The age—as so often with these tragic parodies of humanity—it was impossible to guess at; but you could see the terror mastering that feeble, inarticulate brain, and you could hear the whimpering as the deformed head moved from side to side. . . . Suddenly, with a sort of howl, the idiot turned and bolted from the room at a shambling run. And the woman who was with him said hesitantly to the Sergeant: "Shall I . . . ?"

"He'll be all right, ma'am, will he?"

" 'Im'll wait outside," she said. "Won't get run over nor nothing."

"Ah. Well, my orders were, he wasn't to be forced to do it if he didn't want. So long as he's safe . . ."

"Yes, he's safe," she said. "He won't go away from where I am."

And without so much as a glance at Fen or Best, she moved forward to where the body of her husband lay.

She was perhaps thirty-five, Fen saw: an uneducated country-woman with an impassive, slow-moving dignity of her own. Straight black hair was drawn back to a coil at the nape of her neck; her skin was very thick and smooth, ivory-complexioned; she wore no make-up of any kind. Her black coat and skirt were cheap and shabby, and her legs were bare; and because she was not dressed to attract, you overlooked, at first, the matronly shapeliness of her. She was calm, now, to the point almost of dullness; when the Sergeant drew back the sheet from the face of the man she had married, her expression never altered.

"That's 'im," she said emotionlessly. "That's Foley."

It was dispassionate and quite final. Replacing the sheet, the Sergeant ushered her out. And Fen, who had been unconsciously holding his breath, expelled it in a sigh.

"Rather a remarkable woman," he commented. "How did her husband come to be drowned? Accident?"

Best shook his head. "It was the idiot. The idiot pushed him in—according to *her*, that is: there wasn't any other witness, and the idiot can't talk at all, can't even understand what you're asking him, most of the time. . . ." Best crossed to the body of Foley, and uncovered the dead face; Fen joined him. "Not pretty, is he? Wasn't any too pretty when he was alive, either."

"M'm," said Fen. "It looks as if he must have been in the water a week or more."

For a moment Best was surprised; then abruptly he smiled.
"I was forgetting," he said, "that you knew about these things. . . . Six days, actually."

"And badly knocked about, too." Fen had pulled the sheet further down and was contemplating the body with some interest. "Rocks, I suppose: currents."

"Rocks," said Best. "And currents and rapids and weirs and deep pools."

"Rapids? Weirs?" Fen looked up. "The river, you mean? I was imagining he'd been drowned in the sea."

"No, no, sir. What happened—d'you know Yeopool?"

"I'm afraid not."

"Well, you probably wouldn't: it's only a tiny village, just down off the edge of the moors. Anyway, Yeopool's where Foley and his wife lived, and that's where he got pushed in. It's a treacherous bit of the river there, even for anyone who can swim—and he couldn't: so I don't imagine he lasted long. . . . *Afterwards*, he must have got tangled up under water somehow or other. It was fifteen miles downstream, at a village called Clapton, that they picked him up yesterday, and by that time he'd been so battered that he didn't have a shred of clothing left on him anywhere. . . . That's not uncommon, sir, as you'll know."

"In a fast-moving river," Fen agreed, "you could almost say it was the rule. Except of course for the——"

But at this point a Mortuary attendant looked in; and: "O.K., Frank," called Best. "All finished. Has that other lot gone?" Frank indicated that it had. "Then we'll go, too." Best pulled the sheet back into position. "Don't you waste your pity on Foley, though," he said to Fen as they left the room. "If you *should* feel like being sorry for him, just keep in mind what he was doing at the time the idiot shoved him in."

"Which was?"

"He'd hit his wife and knocked her on to the ground," said Best calmly, "and he was kicking her with his heavy boots. Not for the first time, either. . . . Yes. *He's* where he belongs. And if his widow isn't exactly inconsolable, you can hardly blame her, can you?"

In the police-car, on the way back to the police-station, Fen remained mute; it was only when they were actually pulling into the yard that he spoke again.

"This Foley business," he said: "are you handling it yourself?"

"No. The Chief's handling it."

"The Chief *Constable,* you mean?"

"That's it: Commander Bowen."

"But does he often do that sort of thing?"

Best parked the car tidily, switched off the engine, and leaned back. "No, thank God," he said with candour. "Point is, though, he himself *lives* at Yeopool. So when Mrs. Foley reported the accident—or the murder, call it what you like—to the village constable, the village constable went straight to the C.C.; and he, seeing it had to do with some of his own people—he rather fancies himself playing the Squire with 'em—he decided he'd deal with it personally. A good thing, too," Best added, "that it isn't anything more complicated than what it is. A year and a half in the Thames police, thirty years ago, isn't much training for serious C.I.D. work these days."

"That the only qualification he has, then?"

"The only *practical* qualification, yes. And he's probably forgotten most of that during the time he was in the Navy. He's all *right*, of course: too strict and rigid and pound-of-flesh and letter-of-the-law for my liking, but I suppose that's a fault on the right side; and I'll grant you he's read up all the text-books since he got his job with us—for what that's worth. . . . But they don't appoint his sort these days." Best reached for the door-handle. "They appoint proper full-time cops, and a darned good thing too."

With this view Fen was on the whole in agreement. But for the time being he only nodded abstractedly, and his abstraction appeared to be deepened, rather than otherwise, by the subsequent business of dictating a statement about his recent chance encounter with the suicidal financier; so that Best was not altogether surprised when presently, while they waited for the statement to be typed, he returned to the attack.

"Motive," he said without preamble. "Obviously Foley's brutality to his wife was enough in itself to make her wish him dead, but was there anything *more*?"

"There was life-insurance." Best shifted rather uneasily in his chair. "Not a fortune—not by any means—but a surprising lot for just a farm labourer. . . . Look here, sir, I quite see what you're getting at: it's obvious the wife *could* have done it, and put the blame on the idiot, and no one a bit the wiser. But there's no proof—can't be—and what with one thing and another——"

"You think it's best to let sleeping dogs lie." Fen lit a cigarette. "Only sooner or later, you know, they wake up of their own accord; and then there's liable to be trouble anyway. . . ,

Did they come on here from the Mortuary—the wife, I mean, and the idiot?"

"Yes. They're waiting here now for the C.C. to arrive." Best craned his neck to look out of the office window. "Which he hasn't done yet, because his car's not in the yard. He had an informal talk with them last night, after he'd been to Clapton to look at the body, and today he's going to have it all taken down in shorthand. . . . Hello, here he comes. We'll have to clear out of here now, I'm afraid—though why the devil he has to choose *my* office to hold his interviews in . . ."

"I want to stay," Fen interrupted. "I want to be present at this thing."

Best shrugged.

"Well, you can ask, can't you?" he said. "He'll have heard of you all right. But *I* shan't sponsor you, if you don't mind. Life's too short, and so's his temper, every now and again."

"I won't involve you in it," Fen promised. "What I'd better do, I think, is try to catch him as he comes in. . . . Oh, just one other thing."

"Yes?"

"What about the imbecile? Why was he *there*, that's to say?"

"Oh, that. . . . Well, the thing about it is, you see, that he dotes on Mrs. Foley—doggishly, I mean, nothing unpleasant—and he's always hung around her a good deal. He's the old-style Village Idiot, really—quite harmless, born in Yeopool, lived there all his life; but ever since he was a kid, Mrs. Foley's been the only person he's seemed to like or trust, so it's quite logical he should have attacked Foley, and pushed him into the river, when he saw Foley mauling her."

"Quite," Fen murmured. "Did she go to a doctor, afterwards, by any chance—or wasn't she hurt badly enough for that?"

Best raised his eyebrows. "Still sceptical, sir? Yes, she did see a doctor, that same evening, and he'll tell you she was horribly bruised, with actual marks of the boot-nails on her flesh in some places. Nothing phoney about that, in fact—quite enough, actually, if she *had* killed him, to justify a plea of self-defence."

"Manslaughter, more likely, I should have thought," said Fen. "And even a quite nominal sentence for manslaughter would prevent her from touching the insurance money."

Best's expression hardened. "You've got it in for her, sir, haven't you? You *want* her found guilty."

But Fen shook his head.

"Far from it," he answered. "There's one person I should

like to expose, if a certain guess of mine is right; but it's not the unfortunate Mrs. Foley." He rose. "And now I must go and look for your Chief."

Commander Bowen was a small, slim, cheerful man with a springy step, a brown face, and neat curly grey hair. As Best had predicted, he had heard of Fen, and seemed pleased enough to meet him. And although his assent to Fen's presence at the interview with Mrs. Foley was unenthusiastic, he did in fact give it. Accordingly, they were soon settled in Best's office, which Best himself had in the meantime grudgingly vacated; a shorthand writer was summoned to stand by; and presently Mrs. Foley and the imbecile, together with the Yeopool village constable, were ushered in and made as comfortable as the furniture, and their own several anxieties, permitted.

The woman was much as she had been when Fen had seen her earlier; though it seemed to him that on the present occasion her face was rather more flushed, and her breathing rather more rapid. She sat bolt upright in her chair, twisting a cotton handkerchief between her hands, with the idiot close beside her. And whereas she appeared more nervous now than she had been at the Mortuary, the half-wit, in contrast, was clearly more at ease. It was impossible, Fen found, to tell how much he understood of what was going on: little enough, probably. Only when the woman addressed him directly did he show any sort of intelligence, and then he would grow restless and excitable and uncertain, like a dog given an order which it does not understand. Bowen made no attempt to question him. He addressed himself solely to the woman, with an occasional aside to the village constable; and his manner, though brisk, was sympathetic and straightforward. For the record, even details which all of them knew were elicited. And so it was that for the first time Fen heard the story in a connected, coherent form.

Mary Foley was thirty-seven years old, she said; she had been married to Edgar Foley for nearly sixteen years, but they had had no children. They lived at Rose Cottage, a farm-labourer's cottage on the bank of the river just outside Yeopool, and Foley had worked for Mr. Thomas of Manor Farm, on whose land the cottage stood. Foley (she always spoke of him thus formally, never using his Christian name) had not been a good husband to her; he had beaten her on a number of occasions.

"Nor I couldn't stop 'un, neither," the village constable interposed indignantly at this point. "Us all knew 'twas goin' on—as you knew it yourself, sir—but 'er wouldn't never say nothin' against 'im, so what was us to do?"

"I'd taken 'im for better or for worse, 'adn't I?" she said lifelessly. " 'Twasn't no one else's business 'ow 'e treated me."

For a moment Bowen seemed to consider debating this; but he thought better of it, and resumed his questions. Last Monday, then——

Last Monday, she said, she had left the cottage at about six o'clock with a view to strolling along the river bank and meeting Foley on his way home. Orry (this was the idiot) had been at the cottage during the afternoon, and she had given him tea and a piece of cake. But she had supposed that by the time she set out Orry was back in the village, for he knew that Foley disliked him and was normally careful to keep his distance whenever the husband was at home. Mrs Foley had not walked far; about a hundred yards from the cottage she had halted and waited, and after some ten minutes Foley had joined her. He had been in an ill humour and had picked a quarrel with her, accusing her of idleness; and when she had attempted to defend herself he had knocked her down and kicked her. She was still not very clear about what had happened next; she had a dim recollection, she said, of Orry's shambling forward from the bushes and pushing her husband in the back, and that was all. In any case, the upshot of it was that by the time she had recovered her wits it was impossible to save him, even if she had been a swimmer, which she was not.

The idiot, who had watched her eagerly during the latter part of her story, at this point nodded vigorously, half rose from his chair, and made violent thrusting movements with his long arms. It was confirmation, of a sort. Bowen cleared his throat uncertainly.

"So that's about the lot," he said; and to Fen: "The river was dragged, of course, but the body must have got caught on an—ah—underwater snag of some kind, and it didn't reappear till yesterday. . . . Well, Mrs. Foley, I don't think there's anything more for you to worry about now. You'll have to give evidence at the inquest, of course, but that won't be at all a long business. As to Orry, we'll have to see what we can do about getting him into a—a Home." He turned back to Fen again, indulgently. "Is there anything you'd care to ask, Professor?"

"Just one thing," said Fen affably, "if you don't mind. It's this: after the recovery of Foley's body, what did you do with his boots?"

Bowen stiffened; and Fen, searching the man's eyes, saw in them the justification of what he had already guessed.

"His boots, sir?" said Bowen coldly. "Are you joking?"

"No," said Fen, unperturbed, "I'm not joking. What became of them?"

For a split second Bowen was obviously in the throes of some rapid tactical calculation; then: "The body was recovered stark naked, sir," he answered, all at once agreeable again: "As the Clapton constable, who—ah—landed it, will tell you. A week's immersion—rocks—the rapidity of the current——"

"Just so." Fen smiled, but it was not a pleasant smile. "So now, Commander, there's only one further question I need trouble you with. And it's quite a small point, really. . . ."

He leaned forward in his chair.

"What are you blackmailing Mrs. Foley *for*?" he enquired. "Money, or love?"

There are some episodes in Superintendent Best's professional career which he has no joy in recalling; and among these, the afternoon of that particular Monday takes pride of place. It is nothing if not disconcerting to be summoned from a tranquil cup of tea to hear a woman vehemently accuse your Chief of the nastiest variety of blackmail; and if such an accusation is patently the truth, and your own duty in the matter very far from plain, then your discomfort is liable to become extreme. What happened, in the event, was that both Bowen and his subordinates were stricken by a sort of mutual paralysis. The Chief Constable's blustering denials carried not an instant's conviction, as he himself plainly saw. But on the other hand, his men would scarcely have felt competent to take action against him even if the blackmail charge had rested on something more substantial than Mrs. Foley's unsupported word. Bowen had left, in the end, to go and see his solicitor, and to make—as he said—a telephone call to the Home Office; but that particular telephone call never went through. He had cooled down, and towards Best had become almost ingratiating, by the time he took himself off. But of his guilt there could be no shadow of doubt.

"All I could think of to do," said Best to Fen that same evening, in his office, "was to ring up the Home Office myself. And they're sending a deputation of bigwigs down here tomorrow to look into it all, so my responsibility's finished, thank God. . . . But, Lord, sir, you were taking a bit of risk, weren't you? If Mrs. Foley had been too frightened to back you up, you'd have been in *real* trouble, and no mistake."

Fen nodded. "I think it's probably one of the chanciest things I've ever done," he said. "But it wasn't so much the question of whether Mrs. Foley would back me up that was worrying me. She's obviously a morally decent sort of woman; I didn't think it was likely to be *money* Bowen was blackmailing her for; and so I was fairly sure that if she were given a chance of making a clean breast of the thing, she'd probably do it.

"No, the real danger was that Bowen simply hadn't *noticed* the evidence which proved Mrs. Foley guilty; or alternatively, that if he *had* noticed it, he was keeping quiet about it out of humanitarian feeling or local patriotism or something (there was the chance, too, that he'd been having an affair with Mrs. Foley, and was protecting her for that reason). To the first of these possibilities the objections were (*a*) that Bowen had been in the Thames police, (*b*) that he'd been in the Navy, and (*c*) that he'd recently read the standard text-books on Criminal Investigation. To the second, the objection was that—to use your words—Bowen was 'strict and rigid and pound-of-flesh and letter-of-the-law,' and therefore unlikely to let a criminal escape the consequences of his acts for sentimental reasons. Most dangerous of all, for me, was the possibility that he'd been having an affair with Mrs. Foley prior to Foley's death: in that case, *she* would in a sense have been blackmailing *him*.

No, I won't pretend there was anything waterproof about my ideas, in this instance; the balance of probability was in favour of them, and that was all. Even as it is, I take it that the evidence against him——"

"Won't be strong enough for prosecution," Best put in. "No, you're right about that, I'm afraid: after all, it's basically only her word against his. On the other hand, these deductions you made might help a bit."

"Not waterproof enough, as I said. He can always plead that he simply *overlooked* the particular bit of evidence that proved Mrs. Foley guilty—and you can't condemn a man for that. After all, Best, you overlooked it yourself."

"Damn me if I know what it is *yet*," said Best a shade grimly. "Come on, sir, don't be a tease: let's have it."

For answer, Fen ran his eye over the books ranged on Best's mantelpiece. Rising, he crossed the room and took one down.

"Listen to Gross," he commanded, searching through the pages. "Here it is: Hans Gross, *Criminal Investigation*, Third Edition, page 435, footnote. '*To say that footgear is the only thing a corpse does not lose easily through the action of water is inadequate;—the author has never been able to believe it is ever lost. Bodies often make horrible journeys, especially in swiftly flowing mountain streams, over boulders and trunks of trees, and thereby occasionally lose whole limbs. But if the feet are kept intact, and if the corpse has on boots or shoes, not mere sandals, these are never lost; the foot swells, the leather shrinks, and so the footgear "fits uncommonly tight."*'"

Fen replaced the volume on the shelf. "All of which rather makes hay of Mrs. Foley's story," he observed. "According to her, Foley was pushed into the river while in the act of kicking her with hobnailed boots; yet his body was eventually recovered without—to quote you again—'a stitch of clothing on it anywhere.' So either Mrs. Foley was lying or Gross is—and I know which of them *I'd* put my money on. What I think must have happened is that Foley assaulted his wife and then went into the cottage and took off his boots; whereupon Mrs. Foley seized a poker, or some such thing, and very justifiably knocked him unconscious with it, subsequently dragging him to the river-bank in his stockinged feet (possibly with the help of the faithful idiot, and possibly under the impression that he was already dead), and there shoving him in and leaving him to drown. However, she'll give us the details herself in due course, no doubt."

Best was sobered. "Yes, I certainly ought to have remembered my Gross," he said. "And I see now what you mean about the Thames police and the Navy and the text-books, in connection with Bowen: the boots business'd be the sort of detail he really *would* know, with that background."

"I was banking on that, yes," said Fen. "And when I saw the panic in his eyes—*his* eyes, not *hers*—at my mention of the boots, I knew my guess about the blackmail was right: knew that he'd realised her guilt as soon as the body was recovered, and was putting a price on his silence and protection. It was just chance, of course, that he happened to be personally in charge of the case. But once he *was* in charge of it, his position was pretty well impregnable: since even if any of his subordinates had wondered about the boots, they'd have assumed there was some perfectly good explanation which he knew of and they didn't—and in any case, they'd have thought more than twice about voicing suspicions against *that* particular quarter...."

Fen sighed. "Hence my interference. And now what are we left with?"

"Bowen will have to resign," Best told him. "That's the least that can happen. And there'll be a charge of manslaughter—murder, perhaps—against *her*."

"She'll get off lightly, though." Fen spoke with confidence which the event was to justify. "And when she comes out, I'll make a point of doing anything for her that I can. . . . I say, Best, do you think she'd have preferred the other thing—Bowen, I mean?"

"You heard the way she accused him, sir," Best pointed out. "If you ask me, she wasn't looking forward to their friendship one little bit. . . . No, sir, you can make your mind easy as regards *that* matter, I'm sure. I wouldn't be knowing if a certain fate's really worse, as they say, than actual *death*. But if I was a woman—well, sir, as between Bowen and a couple of years in Holloway, I know which I'd choose."

"LACRIMAE RERUM"

"You chatter about 'the perfect crime,'" said Wakefield irritably, "but you seem incapable of realising that it isn't a topic one can *argue* about at all. One can only pontificate, which is irrational and useless."

"Have some more port," said Haldane.

"Well, yes, I will. . . . The perfect murder, for instance, isn't known to be a murder at all; it looks like natural death, and no suggestion of foul play ever enters anyone's mind. Only the *imperfect* murders are *known* to be murders. And consequently, to argue about 'the perfect murder' is to argue about something which you cannot, by definition, prove to exist."

"Your logic," said Fen, "isn't exactly impeccable."

Wakefield gazed at him stonily. "What's wrong with my logic?" he demanded.

"Its major premise is wrong. You've gone astray in defining the perfect murder."

"I have n—— How have I gone astray?"

"The sort of thing you suggest—the apparently natural death—has one disadvantage from the murderer's point of view."

"And that is?" Wakefield leaned forward across the table. "That is?"

"At the risk of boring you all, I could illustrate it." Fen glanced at his host and his fellow guests, who nodded a vinously emphatic approval; only Wakefield, who hated losing the conversational initiative, showed any sign of restiveness. "What I have in mind is a murder which was committed several years before the war—the first criminal case, as it happens, with which I ever had anything to do."

"Quite a distinction for it," Wakefield muttered uncivilly.

"No doubt. And it was certainly the most daring and ingenious crime I've ever encountered."

"They all are," said Wakefield.

"It succeeded, did it?" Haldane interposed rather hurriedly. "That's to say, the criminal wasn't discovered or punished?"

"Discovered," said Fen, "but not punished."

"You mean there was no case against him?"

"There was a cast-iron case; conclusive proof, followed by a circumstantial confession. But the police couldn't act on it."

"Oh, well," said Wakefield disgustedly, "if all you mean is that he escaped to some country he couldn't be extradited from——"

Fen shook his head. "That isn't at all what I mean. The murderer is at the present moment living quite openly almost next door to New Scotland Yard."

There was a general stir of interest.

"I don't see how that's possible," Wakefield said sourly.

"And you never will," Haldane told him, "if you don't stop talking and give us a chance to hear about it. . . . Go on, Gervase."

"The murder I mean," said Fen, "is the murder of Alan Pasmore, in 1935."

"Pasmore the composer?" someone asked.

"Yes."

"I remember it caused quite a commotion at the time," said Haldane thoughtfully. "And then it all seemed suddenly to fade out, and one heard no more about it."

Fen chuckled. "The authorities were over-precipitate," he explained, "and naturally they were anxious that their shortcomings shouldn't be advertised. Hence the conspiracy of silence. . . .

"Pasmore and his wife were living at Amersham, in Bucks. He was forty-seven at the time of his death, and at the height of his reputation; though since then he's sunk almost completely into oblivion, and nowadays his stuff's hardly ever performed.

"His wife, Angela, was a good deal younger—twenty-six, to be exact. Attractive, intelligent, competent. As well as seeing to it that his house was kept like a new pin, she acted as his secretary. There was plenty of money—his, not hers. No children. Three servants. Superficially it seemed quite a successful marriage, as marriages go.

"On the afternoon of October 2nd, 1935, two visitors came to tea.

"One was Sir Charles Frazer, the conductor, who lived only a few miles away. The other was a wholly unimportant young man called Beasley, who worked at an insurance office in the City. Both of them, it appears, were to some extent infatuated with Angela Pasmore. Sir Charles was there by invitation; Beasley just 'dropped in.' And neither of them was pleased to find the other there, since at tea-time, if she were at home at all, you could be sure of having Angela to yourself. Her husband always worked from two to six in the afternoon and had his tea alone in the study upstairs.

"At four o'clock, then, tea was served in the downstairs drawing-room to Angela, to Sir Charles, and to Beasley. Five minutes later the afternoon mail arrived. It was taken from the postman at the front door by Soames, the manservant, who carried it straight to the drawing-room and gave it to Angela. It consisted of a card for Soames, several letters and cards for Angela, and a single type-written envelope for Pasmore. This last Angela immediately opened. She glanced through the letter inside and then handed it, with a slight grimace, to Sir Charles."

"And why," Wakefield inquired, "did she do that?"

"The letter," Fen continued unperturbed, "was from another conductor—Paul Brice, to be specific. He was in Edinburgh (where, as it was afterwards proved, this letter had been posted on the previous afternoon), and there, at the Usher Hall in two days' time, he was scheduled to conduct the Hallé Orchestra in a concert whose programme included Pasmore's symphonic poem *Merlin*. *Merlin* was at this date quite a new work. It had had only one performance so far, under Sir Charles Frazer at the Queen's Hall. And since the score was tolerably complicated, Brice wanted advice from the composer on a good many points of interpretation.

"That was what his letter was about. I've seen it, and it consisted of a long list of things like: '*At 3 after C, can I relax tempo in the bar and a half before the B entry?*' and: '*At 5 before Q, string accompaniment and clarinet solo are both marked p, but clarinet doesn't come through; pp accompaniment would blur harmonic texture; can clarinet play mf?*' and: '*At 7 after Y, do you want the più mosso as in the exposition?*' There were, I think, at least two dozen such queries. Conductors aren't normally so conscientious, but Brice and Pasmore were lifelong friends, and Brice took Pasmore's music rather more seriously than its actual merits warranted.

"You will understand now"—and Fen eyed Wakefield with a certain severity—"why Angela should show this letter to Sir Charles. Having conducted the first and only performance of the work in question, he might be expected to be interested. He read the letter attentively, commenting, uncharitably one gathers, on Brice's artistic perceptivity. Then he gave it back to Angela.

"She in turn handed it to Soames, who was still hovering in the background, and told him to take it up to her husband with his tea, which by immutable custom was served to him at four-fifteen. This he did, testifying subsequently that at four-fifteen Pasmore was alive, uninjured and in every way normal.

"At four-twenty Angela excused herself to her two visitors and left the drawing-room—in order, she asserted later, to 'powder her nose.' Beasley and Sir Charles remained together, making mistrustful small talk, until at half-past four she returned. She then stayed with them up to a quarter to five, when—as she'd previously warned them—she was engaged to drive her cook, Mrs. May, to the Chesham Cottage Hospital to visit her son, who had recently smashed himself to bits in a motor-cycle accident. Beasley and Sir Charles weren't much pleased at being superseded by this work of mercy, but there was nothing they could do about it, so, with Angela, they left the drawing-room and went out into the hall. Here she asked them to wait while she went up to her bedroom, whose door was clearly visible at the head of the stairs. And I'd better emphasise at this point, to save futile racking of brains, that both men saw her go straight into this room, and that both were prepared to swear she couldn't have entered any other room upstairs, let alone the study, without their knowing."

"There being, of course"—Haldane picked up his glass and stared pensively at it before drinking—"no means of communication between the bedroom and the study."

"None whatever; care was taken to establish that. Moreover, Angela wasn't, according to Sir Charles and Beasley, in the bedroom for more than a minute at most. Emerging from it, she ran straight downstairs, went to the clothes closet in the hall, disappeared into it for a few seconds, departed to the kitchen to fetch Mrs. May, returned with her immediately, took a coat from the clothes closet and put it on, and finally shepherded Mrs. May and Sir Charles and Beasley to the front door. Outside, she said good-bye to the two men and got into the car with Mrs. May. And from then on she was with Mrs. May continuously, in the car or at the hospital, until at least twenty minutes after her husband's body was found.

"All of which boils down to this: that if Pasmore was killed by his wife, she could only have done it between four-twenty and four-thirty, when she was away from the drawing-room.

"It was Soames who found the body, when at six o'clock—again in accordance with immutable custom—he took whisky and water up to the study for Pasmore's pre-prandial drink. There proved, on investigation, to be nothing in the immediate circumstances of the crime that could help the police. Pasmore had been stabbed in the back while sitting at his desk, and had died instantaneously. The weapon was an eighteenth-century Venetian stiletto which hung normally over the study mantelpiece. There had been very little bleeding. The room had not been disturbed, and nothing, so far as could be discovered, was missing. There were no fingerprints on the weapon, and none in the room except such as were to be expected: the servants', Angela's, the dead man's. The police doctor arrived on the scene too late to be able to state the time of death with any certainty: 'probably between four and five' was the most he could say. A cake had been eaten and a cup of tea drunk, Pasmore's prints being on the cup; and he had been killed, according to the post-mortem findings, between five and fifteen minutes after consuming these things. But since there was no evidence as to when he had consumed them—whether immediately after being brought the tea-tray, or later—that didn't help either.

"In short, the police had uncommonly little to work on; all the same, within three days Angela was under arrest.

"Only a very brief investigation had been needed to reveal the fact that the marriage was not as successful as on the surface it appeared; that, not to be longwinded about it, Pasmore's *ménage* was on the rocks. For some reason which I never clearly understood, Pasmore and Angela had recently quarrelled—a violent, fundamental quarrel of the sort that can never really be made up. And the first result of that was that Pasmore took steps to make a new will leaving the whole of his considerable fortune away from her (this, of course, was before the Inheritance Act came into force in 1938). His solicitors, thanks to some error, sent a draft of the new will to his home for his approval, and Angela saw it. So she had, obviously, a very substantial motive for killing him before the will could be signed and become operative. There was opportunity too—those ten minutes during which she had been absent from the drawing-room. Questioned about whether she'd entered her husband's study during that time, she denied doing so. And that was fatal, since it happened that both Soames and a maid-servant had seen her do so. . . . Mind you, all the evidence against her was circumstantial; there wasn't, nor apparently could there be, any conclusive proof of guilt. But circumstantial evidence is quite commonly hanging evidence, and the police were perfectly justified in making the arrest. In due course a charge was preferred by the Director of Public Prosecutions, and Angela, reserving her defence, was committed for trial at the Assizes.

"She pleaded 'Not Guilty,' admitting, in the witness-box, that she had entered Pasmore's study, but stating that she left him alive and well—'writing a letter; I don't think he'd started his tea'—after a couple of minutes' casual conversation about household matters. The Prosecution's case being on the thin side, the Defence had reasonable hopes of an acquittal; and but for Angela's own behaviour in the witness-box, they would have been fairly confident of it. Unfortunately, however, she blustered and contradicted herself and told transparent lies and in general made a very poor impression. What would have happened if the trial had run normally at the end, one doesn't know. And the question's academic, since it didn't run normally at the end. At almost the last possible moment, when the judge was on the point of starting his summing-up, the Defence quite unexpectedly applied to admit new evidence which conclusively established the prisoner's innocence. The judge allowed the evidence to be given, and as a result of it summed up in the prisoner's favour; the jury brought in a verdict of Not Guilty; and Angela Pasmore was acquitted of her husband's murder.

"You'll have guessed that the 'new evidence' had to do with Brice's letter. What actually happened, during the final day of the trial, was this:

"Angela remembered something which, she said, had been completely driven out of her mind by her husband's death, by the investigation, and by her own arrest—namely, the existence of a reply by Pasmore to that letter from Brice which had arrived by the afternoon post. It was Pasmore's habit to put letters which he wanted mailed on the dressing-table in her bedroom (the servants, by the way, corroborated this). And on going up to her bedroom, just prior to leaving the house with Mrs. May, she had found this reply there, had put it in an envelope and addressed it, and had taken it downstairs in her pocket, transferring it at once to the pocket of her outdoor coat, which was hanging in the clothes closet in the hall. Thereafter (I continue to quote her own account of the matter) she not only forgot to post it—as one does occasionally forget to post letters, important ones particularly—but also forgot, in the eventual confusion and distress, that the thing had ever existed. And presumably it was still in the pocket of her coat.

"All of this Angela communicated to her Counsel. And he, naturally, wasn't slow to see the importance of it. *If* Brice's letter had not reached Pasmore till four-fifteen, as it probably hadn't; *if* he had written a reply to it; *if* that reply had taken him more than fifteen minutes to write, as it probably had—then Angela could not have murdered him, since the only opportunity she had had was between four-twenty and four-thirty. Someone was sent off post-haste to Amersham. The letter was found. Handwriting experts were unanimous in agreeing that Pasmore had written it—that no part of it was forged. Tests established the fact that the absolute minimum time required to write it must have been twenty minutes. As to its contents that was a seriatim answer to Brice's queries, such as Pasmore could only have produced with the details of those queries in front of him. The arrival of Brice's letter by the afternoon mail was sworn to, beyond the possibility of contradiction, by the postman, by Soames, by Beasley and by Sir Charles. And Brice was emphatic that by no conceivable means could Pasmore have become acquainted with the questions about *Merlin* prior to the arrival of the letter. You'll see what all this evidence added up to: Pasmore couldn't have been killed before twenty-five to five at the earliest; and therefore it was not Angela who killed him."

Finishing his port, Fen lit a cigarette and leaned back more comfortably in his chair.

"As for myself," he went on after a moment's consideration, "I had no personal contact with the affair until after the trial was over. I read about it more or less attentively in the papers, and that was all. But about a week after Angela's acquittal I was dining with the Chief Constable of Buckinghamshire, and he, knowing I had a lay interest in criminology, showed me the dossier of the case. Most of it was just a repetition and expansion of what I already knew. There was also, however, a complete typewritten copy of Pasmore's letter to Brice. And something in the last paragraph of that letter sruck me as being ever so slightly odd. . . .

"The bulk of the thing, as I've told you, was simply a point-by-point reply, impersonal and businesslike in tone, to Brice's queries. The final paragraph, though, ran like this:

"*'Forgive me if I don't write more. I'm in the middle of scoring* Ariadne (*with a concert on my next-door neighbour's wireless*—lacrimae rerum!—*to help me along*) *and am anxious, as you know, to get it done as quickly as possible. Good luck to the performance—I am sorry I can't be there. Yours*——' and so forth.

"Well, the police had checked this business of the concert at the time Pasmore's letter was produced in Court: and Pasmore's neighbour's radio had, in fact, been on between three-thirty and four-forty-five. So far, so good. But '*lacrimae rerum*'—somehow that particular tag was wrong in that particular context. One's neighbour's radio is often tiresome, no doubt. But one doesn't use, as a comment on it, a phrase intended to express the profound, essential melancholy of all human activities—and more, of existence itself; the nuisance is too trivial and localised. And it occurred to me, as a consequence of this disparity, that '*lacrimae rerum*' might carry some specialised meaning for Brice and Pasmore—might in effect be a sort of private joke. Luckily, Brice was conducting at Oxford three or four days later, and I was able to make contact with him and to ask him about it. And my notion turned out to be right. Brice and Pasmore had been at school together, and had been close friends there, united in a passionately earnest devotion to music—a devotion whose naïvety occasionally bordered on the ludicrous. And on one occasion, when they had been listening together to Tchaikowsky's Sixth Symphony, Pasmore had remarked, in solemn, awestruck tones: '*Lacrimae rerum*, Paul; it sums up the whole tragedy of humankind.' Brice had been much amused by this pretentious gloss on the music, and thereafter '*Lacrimae rerum*' had been often used between them as a means of referring to that particular work.

"So naturally I went away and hunted through back numbers of the *Radio Times* until I found the programme of the concert which had been broadcast on the afternoon of Pasmore's murder. It consisted of two works, the Walton Symphony followed by the Tchaikowsky Sixth; and there was no difficulty in calculating that the Tchaikowsky must have begun at about a quarter past four and gone on until the end of the concert at a quarter to five. All quite straightforward, you see; no discrepancy with the suggestion that Pasmore's reply to Brice had been written more or less immediately after receiving Brice's letter at four-fifteen.

"There I might have left it, but for the chance that I was lecturing in Amersham a week or so later, and having an hour or so to spare, decided to go and interview Pasmore's neighbour—he of the radio. He turned out to be a pleasant little man—something to do with the Home Office, I fancy—and naturally enough he still remembered the events of the crucial afternoon quite clearly. He'd had that concert on all right, from beginning to end, but beyond that there didn't seem to be anything of value he could tell me. And I was on the point of leaving, in a welter of civilities, before he quite unexpectedly let the cat out of the bag.

"'Of course, the police questioned me about it,' he said, 'and even though that wasn't till several weeks afterwards, I had no difficulty in recalling the concert—partly, no doubt, because of the change in the advertised programme.'

"I must have looked as though I'd seen a ghost. 'Change?' I echoed.

"'Why, yes. For some mysterious reason of their own, they played the Tchaikowsky first and the Walton second.'

"And they had. I checked with the B.B.C., and it was true. Owing to some kind of mismanagement, the orchestral parts of the Walton hadn't been in the studio at the start of the concert, and the Tchaikowsky had had to be played while they were searched for. Therefore, the Tchaikowsky—'*lacrimae rerum*'—had *finished* at four o'clock; and therefore, if the reference in the final paragraph meant anything at all, Pasmore's letter to Brice had been completed by four o'clock."

Fen chuckled suddenly. "And given that, it didn't really require much thinking to deduce how Angela's alibi had been contrived. The police, as I discovered, had worked it all out for themselves—but not, unfortunately, until after the acquittal."

Fen paused, and Haldane shook his head. "I'm afraid that for my own part——"

"Oh, come. . . . Brice's letter had been posted in Edinburgh on the previous afternoon. It arrived at Amersham, of course, by the *morning* post on the day of the murder. Angela opened it—I've mentioned, I think, that she acted as Pasmore's secretary—and saw in it her opportunity. She destroyed the envelope in which it arrived, made a note of Brice's queries, typed a fresh envelope, inserted the letter, stamped it, and *posted it again*. She could thus be fairly sure of its arriving a second time, in the presence of the invited and infatuated Sir Charles, by the afternoon post. And in the meantime she went to her husband and said something like this:

"'Brice rang up from Edinburgh while you were out. He's written you a letter about *Merlin*, but it struck him that it might possibly not arrive soon enough for your reply to reach him in time for the final rehearsal. I've made a note of his queries, and if you write off to him some time this afternoon, that should be all right.'

"Pasmore would believe this—why shouldn't he?—and the reply to Brice would be written. And all that Angela had to do after that was to destroy the notes she'd made of Brice's queries and the envelope, typed by herself and with a local postmark on it, in which Brice's letter arrived at the house for the second time. Between four-twenty and four-thirty, of course, she entered Pasmore's study and killed him."

There was a brief, astonished silence; then: "Brilliant!" Haldane exclaimed. "Really brilliant. . . . Only"—his enthusiasm waned slightly—"there are a lot of things which *could* have gone wrong. Pasmore might just have omitted to write the reply; or it might not have been long enough—though I suppose that in view of the number of queries he had to answer it was bound to be fairly long; or it might have contained some very definite reference to the hour of day at which it was being written. Or Sir Charles mightn't have turned up; or the letter—life being what it is—mightn't have arrived by the afternoon post; or——"

"Yes, yes, I know all that," said Fen. "But you must realise that all those possible accidents and possible flaws in the scheme have one thing in common: if they were going to happen at all, they would happen *before the murder*. So if anything had gone wrong, Pasmore would quite simply not have been killed—not on that day, and in that particular way. Angela, I can assure you, is a cautious woman as well as a clever one."

"*Is*," said someone sombrely; and again there was silence.

"I suppose she missed the point of '*Lacrimae rerum*,'" said Haldane at last. "Interpreted it, that's to say, as just a general comment on neighbours' radios. . . . She'd read the letter, of course, before killing Pasmore."

Fen nodded. "Certainly she would. It's to be presumed that Pasmore put it in her bedroom about four o'clock, and that she read it there, at twenty past four, before going to the study and killing him. . . . I don't know why I say 'presumed.' By Angela's own admission, that's what in fact happened. I wrote to her, you see, and by return of post she sent me congratulations on my perspicuity and a circumstantial account of the crime. It's a queer document—unique, of course: no trace of vanity or megalomania, and yet it makes me shiver every time I look at it."

"She got Pasmore's money, then?"

"Oh, yes. And has lived very comfortably on it ever since."

"But look here," said Wakefield with sudden energy, "you can't possibly maintain that she arranged for Pasmore's letter to be her alibi and then *forgot* about it."

"Of course she didn't forget. She only pretended to—that was the whole point of her scheme. We're back where we started, you see; this is where the business of the 'perfect crime' comes in. Your murder which looks like natural death —well, it's satisfactory up to a point; but the murderer can never be *quite* sure that one day, perhaps years after, some accident may not reveal the truth and send him to the gallows. His only road to absolute immunity from punishment is to be tried and acquitted, for it's a basic principle of English Common Law that *nemo debet bis vexari*—that no one may be tried a second time for the same offence. Angela *wanted* to be tried, in order that she might be acquitted and live afterwards in perpetual immunity. Hence Pasmore's letter was 'forgotten' until the right moment for its use arrived. Angela took a great deal of risk, of course. But it worked out very nicely for her in the end."

"Well, I consider it's abominable," said Haldane with disgust. "When one thinks that nothing—*nothing*—can be done to punish the woman . . ."

"There are those"—Fen spoke very mildly—"who would maintain that such injustices are invariably rectified at a higher court."

"Ah." Wakefield sat up abruptly. "And why do they maintain that? They maintain it because they believe the Universe to be subject to Laws, and they believe that because the phenomenal flux, without the concept of Order, is psychologically intolerable. Aldous Huxley——"

"Have some more port," said Haldane.

WITHIN THE GATES

IT WAS IMMEDIATELY outside the entrance to an office building, within a stone's throw, almost, of New Scotland Yard, that the thing happened.

The Whitehall area is sacred—if that is the right word—to Government. Trade leads a hole-and-corner existence there, and a house given over to non-ministerial purposes is enough of a rarity in the district to attract fleeting attention from the idle passer-by. Thus it was that Gervase Fen, ambling with rather less than his usual vigour from St. Thomas's Hospital, where he had been visiting a friend, towards St. James's Park, through which he proposed strolling prior to dinner at the Athenaeum, paused to examine the brass plates and sign-boards flanking this particular doorway; and in so doing found himself shoulder to shoulder with a man who had just half a minute to live.

At this time—eight o'clock in the evening—the street was almost empty, a near-vacuum shut away from the Embankment traffic on one side and the Whitehall traffic on the other. A street-lamp gleamed on the brass and the white-lettered wood: trade journals mostly, Fen noted—*Copper Mining, Vegetation,* the *Bulb Growers' Quarterly, Hedging and Ditching.* A little beyond the doorway, an elderly woman had halted to rummage in her shopping-bag; and immediately outside it, a neatly dressed man with a military bearing, who had been preceding Fen along the pavement, glanced up at the street-lamp, drew from a pocket three sheets of typewritten foolscap clipped together with a brass fastener, came to a stop, and began reading. Fen was beside him for no more than a moment, and had no cause to notice him particularly; leaving him still scanning his typescript, he walked on past the woman with the shopping-bag and so up to the end of the street. Behind him, he heard a car moving away from the pavement—presumably it was the black sedan which he had seen parked at the entrance to the street. But there was no way in which he could have anticipated the tragedy that followed.

The note of the car's engine altered; one of its doors clicked open and there were rapid footsteps on the pavement. Then, horribly, the woman with the shopping-bag screamed—and Fen, swinging round, saw the soldierly-looking man grapple with the stranger who had emerged from the waiting sedan. It was all over long before Fen could reach them. The assailant struck viciously at his victim's unprotected head, snatched the typescript from his hand as he fell, and scrambled back into the car, which slewed away from the curb with a squeal of tyres, and in another instant was gone. Pausing only to note its number and direction, Fen ran on and bent over the huddled body at which the woman was staring in dazed, helpless incomprehension. But the skull was crushed; there was nothing, Fen saw, that he or anyone else could do. He stood over the body, allowing no one to touch it, until the police arrived.

And at eleven o'clock next morning: "Very satisfactory," said Detective-Inspector Humbleby of the Metropolitan C.I.D. "Very satisfactory indeed. Between you, you and that Ayres woman are going to hang Mr. Leonard Mocatelli higher than Haman. And a good riddance, too."

"The man must be quite mad." As was allowable in an old and trusted friend of the Inspector's, Fen spoke somewhat petulantly. "Mad, I mean, to commit murder under the noses of two witnesses. What *did* he expect?"

"Ah, but he hadn't got a record, you see." Humbleby lit a cheroot with a new-fangled pocket-lighter which smelled of ether. "*He* didn't think Scotland Yard had ever heard of him, and it must have given him a nasty turn when we hauled him out of bed in the middle of the night, and brought him along here. He was the only member of the group whose viciousness was likely to extend to murder, and that being so——"

"Wait, wait," Fen interposed fretfully. "I don't understand any of this. Who *is* Mocatelli? Whom did he kill, and why? And what is the 'group' you mentioned?"

At this, Humbleby's satisfaction diminished visibly; he sighed. "It's not," he said, "that I'm *personally* unwilling to give you the facts. But there's a certain rather delicate matter involved, and . . ." His voice trailed away. "Well, there you are."

"Discretion," said Fen with great complacency, "is my middle name."

"I dare say. But very few people *use* their middle names. . . . Calm, now: because I think I shall tell you about it in spite of everything. It's possible you can help. And God knows," said Humbleby seriously, "this is a case where we can do with some help."

He had been standing by the window. Now, with an air of decision, he turned and planted himself firmly in the swivel-chair behind the desk. His office, to which they had returned immediately after the identification parade, was high up, overlooking the river, in a corner of New Scotland Yard: a small overcrowded room with a large number of (illegal) gas and electric stoves over which you tripped every time you attempted to stir. Filing-cabinets lined the walls; queerly assorted books were piled in tottering heaps in the corners; and the decorations ranged from a portrait of Metternich to a photograph of an unattractive pet Sealyham which had passed to its reward, at an advanced age, in the year 1919. Scotland Yard is as strictly run as any other office, and more strictly than most. But Humbleby's position there was a peculiar one

—in that for reasons which seemed good to him he had always refused to be promoted to Chief-Inspector—and so to a considerable extent he was allowed to legislate for himself in the matter of his surroundings. To that eyrie had come many who had allowed its untidy domesticity, and the tidy domesticity of its occupant, to make them over-confident. And not one of a long succession of Assistant Commissioners, on first introduction to it, had been short-sighted or stupid enough to do anything more than smile.

Sprawled in the one armchair, Fen waited. And presently Humbleby—having outlined on the blotter, to his own immense satisfaction, a fat bishop—said:

"We start, then, with this more than ordinarily cagey, more than ordinarily well-organised *gang*. It's two years now since we first became aware of its existence; and although we've got a complete, or almost complete, list of the members' names, together with a certain amount of good court-room evidence, we've been avoiding making arrests—for the usual reason that there's been nothing very damning so far against the man we know to be in charge, and we've been hoping that sooner or later his agents, if left to themselves, will incriminate *him*. In that respect we're not, even after last evening, very much better off than we were at the outset; and I think it's quite likely that in view of Mocatelli's arrest, which but for the murder we shouldn't have contemplated, the head man will pack it up and we'll never catch him. However, that remains to be seen."

"Any speciality?" Fen asked.

"No. They've been very versatile: blackmail, smuggling, smash-and-grab, arson—all the fun of the fair. From our point of view it hasn't been any fun, though, and that for more reasons than one. So there was a good deal of rejoicing the other evening when one of the gang, a man named Stokes, got drunk, picked up one of these crazy children who start painting their faces and wearing high-heeled shoes at the age of fourteen, and attempted a criminal assault in an alley within five yards of a constable on his beat.

"We didn't rejoice at the actual *event*, of course: that was as nasty and depressing as these things always are. But it did enable us to arrest the man and to search his rooms. There, in due course, we came on a letter addressed to him and typewritten in code; and it wasn't exactly difficult to deduce that this letter had something to do with the operations of the gang.

"As you know, we've got a biggish Cipher Department here on the premises; and you're aware, too, that complex ciphers—such as this one obviously was—are dealt with by quite elaborate team-work, helped out by machines. That's as it should be, of course—but at the same time it tends to be rather a slow business: method, as opposed to intuition, always *is* slow. On the off-chance, then, of getting results more rapidly, I gave a copy of the cryptogram to Colonel Browley, and——"

"Browley?" Fen interrupted. "You mean the man who ran the Cipher Department of M.I.5 during the war?"

"That's him. He retired in 1946 and went to live in Putney, where he's been spending most of his time on botany and scientific gardening and stuff like that. But we still used him as a consultant expert from time to time, because there's no doubt that he had a real flair for codes, and could sometimes solve them by a sort of inspired guess-work."

Fen nodded. "Putney," he said. "Direct Tube-line to Westminster—and that was about where I picked him up."

"Oh yes: it was Browley who was murdered, unhappily. And having got that far, you'll easily see why."

"You mean that he'd succeeded in decoding this letter; and that the letter was so important to the gang that they had to silence him and steal his report."

"Exactly. . . . I can't say"—here Humbleby wriggled uncomfortably—"I can't say that any of us *liked* Browley very much. He was one of those men who somehow contrive to be fussy and careless at one and the same time—an exhausting combination—and latterly his mind had been going to seed rather: he was getting on for seventy, you see, though admittedly he didn't look it. . . . Well anyway, to get back to the point, Browley rang me up yesterday afternoon about this letter. I was out, as it happened; so he just mentioned his success and told the constable who answered the phone that he'd be coming here with his report during the evening—by which time I myself would be back. I'd warned him, you see, that the report was to be delivered to me and to me only."

There was a brief silence; then:

"Oh," said Fen, in a particular tone of voice.

"So that when the constable offered to have it collected from Putney, Browley said that he had to come in to Town in any case, on some private errand or other . . . with the result you witnessed. From what we knew of this gang, Mocatelli was by far the likeliest man to have done the job. So we picked him up, and you and the Ayres woman have now identified him as the murderer, and that's that."

"The sedan," said Fen, "was *waiting* for Browley—not following him. It was *known* that he was coming."

And reluctantly Humbleby inclined his head. "Oh yes," he

said, "there's a leak all right. There's a leak somewhere in this Department. That's half the reason why Mocatelli and his merry men have been getting away with it so easily—though since I first suspected a leak, some weeks ago, I've been keeping the more important information about the gang unobtrusively to myself; I imagine that if I hadn't done that, we'd hardly have found Mocatelli at home when we went to call on him last night. . . . Well, there it is: not a nice situation. Rare, thank God—miraculously so, when you compare our salaries with what a well-heeled crook can afford to offer—but very bad when it *does* happen." He glanced at his watch. "I'm seeing the Assistant Commissioner about it in five minutes' time. If you'd like to wait till I get finished, we can have lunch together."

Fen assented. "And you've no notion," he added, "about what was in the stolen report? You didn't find any rough notes, for instance, in Browley's house?"

"None. His training had made him careful about *that* sort of thing, at least, and he'd certainly have destroyed anything at all revealing before leaving home to come here. . . . There's this, of course." Humbleby fished in a dossier and produced a crumpled scrap of paper. "It was evidently torn off the bottom of one of the pages of his report when the thing was snatched out of his hand."

Fen raised his eyebrows. "The blow came first, you know, and the snatching not till——" He checked himself. "No, wait, I'm being stupid. Head injury: cadaveric spasm."

"That's it. I had the devil of a job getting this fragment away from him, poor soul. . . . But it doesn't help at all."

Fen examined the line or two of typewriting on the paper. Literally transcribed, it ran: '. . . *so that x in the treatment of this var eetyof cryptogam care mut be taken to* . . .' "Not," Fen observed, "one of the world's more expert typists, was he?"

"No. All his reports were like that. And he could never resist the temptation to incorporate sermons, on the basic principles of deciphering, in everything he sent us. If only he'd stuck to the point, that bit of paper might have been useful. As it is——" Humbleby broke off at a knock on the door. "Come in!" he called, and a youthful, pink-cheeked Sergeant appeared. "Yes, Robden? What is it?"

"It's about the contents of Colonel Browley's pockets, sir."

"Oh yes, it was you who turned them out, wasn't it. . . . All the stuff will have to go to his lawyer, as there aren't any relatives. I'll give you the address. And do *please* remember, this time, to get a detailed receipt."

"I say, Humbleby"—Fen spoke pensively—"may I ask the Sergeant to do an errand for me? I've just developed the first symptoms of an idea—though it probably won't come to anything."

"Well, provided it isn't anything too elaborate or lengthy——"

"No, just a phone-call." Fen was scribbling some words on the back of an old envelope, which presently he handed to Robden. "And from an *outside* phone, please, Sergeant. I don't want there to be any possibility of your being overheard."

The Sergeant glanced at the envelope and then at Humbleby, who nodded; whereupon, collecting the address which Humbleby had jotted down for him, he took himself off. "No questions for the moment," said Humbleby, rising, "because it's time I visited the A.C. But I shall expect an explanation when I get back."

Fen smiled. "You shall have one."

"And also I shall expect a conference about this business we've been speaking of. Over beer. It's been well said that salt, once it has lost its savour——"

"Do stop talking, Humbleby, and go."

"Wait here, then, and try not to meddle with things. I shan't be long.'

In fact he was not absent for much more than a quarter of an hour; and his return coincided with Robden's.

"No, sir," said the Sergeant cryptically. "Nothing of that sort. He *had* sent in one or two, but they'd always been rejected, and he was so angry about that that the Editor was positive he'd never try again. There was nothing commissioned, in any case."

And Fen sighed. "You're much too unsuspicious for a policeman, Robden," he said mildly. "And much too unsuspicious for a crook. And for the two things combined, quite hopelessly gullible."

His tone altered. "It apparently never occurred to you that I sent you to an outside phone in order to have time to ring the Editor of *Vegetation* before you did. And the story he told me—and which he assured me he would tell you also when you telephoned—was rather different from what *you've* just said."

Robden had gone white, so that dark rings appeared round his normally candid brown eyes. He looked, and was, very young. But Fen, as he gazed out across the river at the expanses of South London, was thinking of old women in little shops who might one day go in intolerable fear because their protection against the thug and the delinquent had become a mockery and a sham; of pimps and bawds who might flourish at the cost of a few pounds slipped weekly into the right hands; of night-watchmen burned alive without hope of reprisal in well-insured warehouses, and of little girls violated by degenerates whose services were valuable to their bosses and whose immunity was therefore worth paying for. Robden's youth and folly, weighed in the scale against these possibilities, were no better than a pinch of sand, and so Fen hardened his heart, saying:

"It's possible, of course, that the Editor of *Vegetation* did in fact tell you a story different from the story he told me. But since he agreed to have witnesses listening to what he said—very friendly of him, that, in view of the fact that he didn't know me from Adam—that's not a point we need argue about for the moment."

"*Vegetation?*" Humbleby echoed dreamily. He had already nudged his leg against a bell-push in the knee-hole of his desk, and now, as Robden backed abruptly towards the door, a revolver appeared, as if by some kind of noiseless magic, in his right hand; so that all at once Robden was rigid and motionless. "*Vegetation?*" Humbleby repeated.

"Just so," said Fen. "Here is a botanist with a private errand in Town. He is found standing outside the offices of *Vegetation* with an article on cryptogams in his hand."

"Crypto*grams*."

"No. Crypto*gams*. A class of plants without stamens or pistils. So it seemed worth while getting in touch with the Editor of *Vegetation* and finding out if he was expecting such an article from Browley. And he was.

"This article is what the murderous Mocatelli stole; and very disappointed he must have been when he found out what he'd got. But since, as we know, Browley definitely had the report on the gang's code-letter with him, what in the world became of *that*? Mocatelli simply grabbed the wrong typescript and ran—he didn't do any rifling of Browley's pockets. Nor did anyone else, subsequently, because I myself stood guard over the body and refused to allow it to be touched. Which leaves the police. *Someone* was a traitor—that much was already certain. So that when the Sergeant who turned out Browley's pockets failed to mention the code-report which must certainly have been there, I set a trap for him and he fell into it head first."

Out of a dry mouth Robden said:

"Plenty of people had to do with Browley's body before I did."

"No doubt. But you're the only person so far who's lied about the *Vegetation* article. And since you would come under immediate suspicion if the truth about that article were known, it's not difficult to see just why you lied."

Behind Robden the door opened quiely, and at a nod from Humbleby the two constables advanced to grip their whilom colleague's arms. For an instant he seemed to contemplate resistance; but then all the valour went out of him, and he shrivelled like a dead leaf in a flame.

"He'll get a stiff sentence, I'm afraid," said Humbleby when the party had gone. "Much stiffer than he really deserves. That's always the way when one of *us* goes off the rails, and you can see why." He brooded; then: "Cryptogams," he muttered sourly. "*Cryptogams*. . . ."

"Like formication," said Fen. "Which, although you might not believe it, has no connection whatever with——"

"Quite so." Humbleby was firm. "Exactly so. And now let us get something to eat."

ABHORRÈD SHEARS

DETECTIVE-INSPECTOR HUMBLEBY, of New Scotland Yard, sipped his coffee, glanced at his watch, and sighed. In part, the sigh expressed contentment with the lunch he had just eaten; but it was also perceptibly tinged with the exasperation of a man faced with some tedious but inescapable duty, such as weeding a lawn or composing a letter of thanks. Humbleby, his moon-face aggrieved beneath his neatly-dressed greying hair, sipped his coffee and sighed. And Gervase Fen, whose guest he was at the United University Club, was moved by this plaintive noise to enquire what was wrong.

"It's the Bolsover case," said Humbleby dolefully. "A person named Bolsover has been murdered, and I can't make out how it was done."

Fen was interested. "Do you, on the other hand, know who did it?"

"No, I don't know that, either." Humbleby's gloom grew. "There are three possibilities, and suspicion's divided between them in that horrid ounce-for-ounce fashion which one associates with detective fiction. . . . May I smoke in here?"

"You mayn't, I'm afraid. We'll go downstairs in a minute. In the meantime, have some more cheese and tell me about Bolsover. Has he been in the papers?"

"A paragraph or two this morning, but nothing detailed. The thing only happened last night. One of his heirs killed him by putting a dose of atropine in his beer."

"Enterprising," said Fen with misplaced approval. "How did it happen?"

"I'll start at the beginning." This fatuous assurance was so far below Humbleby's normal conversational level that Fen surveyed him in some alarm; clearly he was finding the Bolsover case more than usually oppressive. "In the beginning there's Bolsover," he proceeded scripturally. "And Bolsover is —was, I mean—a Birmingham business man. Soap-flakes and other such—um—detergents. Fairly wealthy, as such people go. But he married—in the opinion of his wife—above him. She was a bossy sort of woman, it seems, who kept him well under her thumb and refused to have any truck with his few relatives, on the grounds that they were her natural inferiors. But about a month ago she died—I think of pneumonia—and for the first time since his early marriage, Bolsover, at fifty, found himself able to live his life as he pleased. This novel situation went to his head rather. He was apparently one of those men to whom family ties are hugely important, and as soon as his wife was safely under ground he set about making contact with such of his near relations as still survived. There weren't many of them. Not to be tedious about it, there were only three, and none of them, it turned out, had ever met any of the others, let alone met Bolsover himself. To Bolsover this seemed a very shocking and unnatural situation; he decided that he must remedy it without delay, and his first step was to make a will leaving his entire fortune divided equally between these three relatives."

"He had no children of his own?"

"None. . . . Having taken this ill-considered action, then, with regard to the will, Bolsover idiotically wrote to each of the beneficiaries to inform them of their agreeable prospects and to suggest a family reunion. There were difficulties about holding this in his own home in Birmingham, so eventually it was arranged that Bolsover should visit London and there combine family piety with a—a binge. He travelled up yesterday by the morning train, settled in at the Mosque Hotel, and after dinner —one of his guests wasn't able to get away in time for the meal itself—the family reunion did in fact take place.

"Now, Bolsover's three heirs, whom I spent half last night questioning, are as follows. First, there's George Laurie, his sister's husband's brother, a withered, vacant, failed-looking man who works in an eyewash factory at Westminster."

"You're not referring——"

"No, I'm not. Now, most eyewashes contain atropine, and the sort manufactured by Laurie's firm isn't any exception. Access, you see," explained Humbleby kindly. "Laurie is colourless, fiftyish, a bachelor and a backer of horses. At the present moment he owes his bookie close on two hundred pounds."

"Motive," said Fen intelligently.

"They all have that, you'll find. They all have access, too. . . . The second of the three is Gillian Bolsover, the murdered man's niece. A frippet." And Humbleby looked furtively about him, apparently in doubt as to the propriety of using such a word in his present urbane surroundings. "Age twenty-seven, pretty, unmarried, and employed as dispenser to a Wimpole-Street doctor. The third suspect, Bolsover's nephew and Gillian's cousin, is a youth called Fred Bolsover, who works as a kind of lab.-boy at a wholesale chemist's near Watford. Very earnest and science-minded, is young Fred: the sort," said Humbleby with all the savagery of a cornered humanist, "that reads books in his spare time about how motor-cycles work, with a widow's peak and dotty-looking eyes behind his glasses and a brash, cocky way with him. I hope it was he who did it, but I don't see how it can have been—I don't see how it can have been any of them."

"Do get on," said Fen restively. "The man isn't even dead yet."

"He'll be dead in a minute, don't you fret. Well, at eight-thirty last evening these three turned up at the Mosque Hotel, and there were introductions and politenesses and—— By the way, do you know the Mosque Hotel?"

"Never heard of it."

"It's one of those great rambling places with dozens of dreary little semi-private lounges all over the ground floor, and it was to one of these that Bolsover took his relations for a drink. By the time they arrived, Bolsover himself was fairly exalted, having already had a few—but in case you're thinking Bolsover might have been poisoned before the party began, I can assure you we've been into all that, and it's quite out of the question.

"Figure to yourself, then"—here Fen dutifully adopted an introspective, imagining look—"a dull, dusty room in the bowels of this awful hotel, too high for its furniture, too narrow for its height, and too gloomy for anything; with moulded cornices, inadequate lighting, and a blacked-out window, unopened in years, giving on a well. At the right of the empty fireplace," said Humbleby dramatically, "sits young Fred Bolsover, at a table of his own. At the table to the left of the fireplace sit the other three—Gillian (nearest the fireplace, and facing out into the room), Bolsover (opposite Gillian) and Laurie (away from the fireplace, between Bolsover and Gillian)."

Fen shifted restlessly in his chair. "Do these positions matter?" he demanded. "Do I have to remember them?"

"As far as I can see," said Humbleby annoyingly, "they don't matter in the slightest. I was just filling in the picture, that's all. . . . Gillian is drinking gin and lime (she's the sort of girl who does), Bolsover has a pint pewter tankard of bitter, Laurie has Guinness, and Fred, odious young prig, has refused alcohol and is rotting his guts with grapefruit squash. There's only one other person in the room, but she's important—a spinster named Lucy Gamble, who's on her own, drinking coffee, and who being temperamentally inquisitive sees, hears and remembers everything that goes on during the whole of the relevant period. She's thoroughly reliable, in my opinion, and her evidence agrees with the evidence of the Bolsover heirs in every possible respect. She's got no connection with any of them, either, so we really can be *sure* what happened—which isn't often the way.

"Well, the Bolsover party talked of this and that, and Gillian showed her legs, and teetotal Fred was jocosely persuaded to try a sip of his uncle's beer, and Laurie did imitations——"

"*Imitations?*"

"Yes. He rather fancies himself at imitations. Did one for me, at half past two this morning. Churchill." Humbleby shook his head. "Not good. It seems to have amused Bolsover, though—as you'll have gathered, he was rather a simple-minded man, and in any case, he was half tight. They'd not been together much more than half an hour before it began to appear that he was completely tight, and whichever two of them were innocent don't seem to have had the wit to realise that an unfinished pint of bitter couldn't possibly, of itself, have produced the sudden deterioration they witnessed. In actual fact, of course, Bolsover's apparent drunkenness was the atropine working. Eventually he fell into a coma which they mistook for sleep; and though at that stage a stomach-pump would probably have saved him, they let him stay slumped in his chair while they went on talking and drinking among themselves for an hour or more. Then Gillian said it was time for her to leave; and on their attempting to rouse Bolsover, they found he was dead.

"About midnight, the Divisional Superintendent rang up the Yard, and that was how I became involved in the affair. By the time I arrived, most of the spade-work was done—the story elicited in outline, poison diagnosed, and the remnants of Bolsover's beer impounded. From the look of the body, I was able to suggest atropine straight away to the night staff of our analytical laboratory, and it didn't take them more than half an hour to test the beer for it and find it there in quantity. In liquid form, they said—and obviously if you shook a powder into a man's drink, he'd be only too likely to notice it before it was all dissolved.

"Well, liquid has to have a container of some sort; you can't carry it about loose in your pocket, or in the palm of your hand. And that looked like a promising line, because, by a combination of circumstances which I needn't trouble you with in detail, no one in that room—not even Lucy Gamble—had any chance to dispose of such a container, elsewhere than *in* the room, up to the time they were all searched. But could we find anything? We most certainly could not. I had a theory about cigarette-lighters or scent-bottles, but there weren't any cigarette-lighters or scent-bottles. There wasn't, in fact, *anything* on these people capable of containing liquid atropine, and I can assure you that between us we scrutinised their clothes and their belongings pretty thoroughly.

"Having failed there, we went on to search the room—and to be brief about it, I'm ready to swear that there wasn't a single thing in it, of any description, which could possibly have held atropine; we made quite certain, too, that nothing had been thrown out of the one window, or in some fashion palmed off on the waiter who served the drinks."

"Glasses?" Fen enquired. "Couldn't an extra glass have been brought in, emptied of its poison, and then removed by the waiter under the natural impression that it belonged to the hotel?"

But Humbleby shook his head. "I thought of that—and there isn't a chance of it. The waiter was able to account for every glass he carried back or forth that evening—and like Lucy Gamble, he's a reliable, and innocent, witness. By the way, we did, early on in the proceedings, think we'd made a find. One of the first places we searched was the grate. It was full of rubbish—pipe-dottle, cigarette-stubs and cigarette-packets mostly—and obviously it hadn't been cleared out for weeks. And among that rubbish we found a lot of splinters of thin glass, which we happily and quite prematurely concluded were the remains of a phial. Well, they weren't; we fitted them together, and they were the remains of a broken watch-glass. None of the suspects' watch-glasses were broken, none of their watches had been used to carry atropine—and so that was that: probably the broken glass had been in the grate for days.

"The next thing, obviously, was to discover which of our three suspects had opportunity to drop atropine into Bolsover's tankard. And for our sins, we found that they'd all had opportunity. Taking them one by one:

"Gillian could have poisoned the beer at almost any stage in the evening: when Bolsover wasn't actually drinking, his tankard stood on the table next to her glass. So at some moment when attention was distracted in another direction, *she* could have done it.

"The same consideration applies to Laurie—except that he was sitting further away from the tankard than Gillian was. On the other hand, his half-witted imitations apparently involved his getting up and striding about and waving his hands—on several occasions waving them immediately above Bolsover's beer.

"Young Fred had one chance, and one only, the moment when the beer was handed across for him to taste. But of course, everyone was watching him closely—they were waiting to see what his reaction would be—and moreover, Laurie, Gillian and Lucy Gamble are all agreed that his left hand was stuck firmly in his coat pocket from before he received the tankard till after he handed it back, while with his *right* hand, naturally, he was *holding* the thing. And that, I'm afraid, lets him out—the others are unanimous that he wasn't anywhere near the tankard on any other occasion. It seems that he took only the tiniest sip, so if the atropine was already in the beer it wouldn't have harmed him. No lead there."

Fen considered. "He couldn't," he suggested, "have been holding the poison in his mouth? And have spat it into the tankard while pretending to drink?"

"No, he couldn't. Not only was he *speaking*, immediately before he put the tankard to his lips; he was speaking with a pipe in his mouth—and it's quite impossible to do that and keep liquid under your tongue at the same time. He's out of it, I'm sorry to say.

"And that's really all. Three suspects, all of them with motive—the will—all of them with access to atropine (and if either Gillian or Fred did the murder, she or he obviously chose atropine because that was the *only* poison to which Laurie had access), and all of them with more or less of opportunity. No container discoverable on them, or in the room; no means by which they could possibly have rid themselves of such a container—unless you count swallowing it, which would have been so dangerous that it's out of the question. No collusion—I'm as sure of that as one can be of anything. . . . So how in heaven's name was it done?"

"Three questions," said Fen pensively. "Or rather, three statements, which you can confirm or deny. The watch-glass you found was a lady's watch-glass—that's to say a small one."

"Yes, it was. But——"

"Also, it was *round*—not oval or octagonal or rectangular or any other of the possible shapes."

"Yes. And finally?"

"Finally, the pipe Fred Bolsover was smoking was a brand-new one."

Humbleby nodded. "It was. But I still don't see——"

"Oh, come. . . . You told me that just before he received his uncle's tankard, Fred Bolsover was talking with a pipe in his mouth. All right; but you don't *drink* with a pipe in your mouth. So the question is, what did he do with it when he removed it? He didn't hold it in his left hand—that was in his pocket. He *may* have put it down somewhere—you'll have to enquire about that. But my bet is that he held both tankard and pipe in his right hand while he tasted the beer. You can go into any pub, any time, and see how it's done. The bowl of the pipe nestles between thumb and forefinger; the stem projects to the left; the four fingers grip the handle of the tankard. And thus the mouthpiece of the pipe, a very good natural dropper, overhangs the edge of the tankard, and by dipping it, as you tilt the tankard. . . .

"Yes. Take a new pipe—it must be new, otherwise the muck inside it will discolour the colourless atropine and betray its presence in the beer—and make sure that it's a pipe the diameter of whose bowl decreases gradually from top to bottom. Buy a round watch-glass to fit the bowl about halfway down. Seal it in position with a drop or two of liquid rubber. Remove the pipe's mouthpiece. Pour in atropine to fill the stem and the part of the bowl under the watch-glass. Keeping the pipe bowl-downwards, replace the mouthpiece and fill the bowl, above the watch-glass, with partly-burned tobacco for camouflage. Carry the pipe bowl-downwards in a waistcoat pocket. When you've used it, in the completely natural-seeming way

I've described, to poison the beer (and if you can't contrive, as a teetotaller ripe for conversion, to get Uncle to offer you a taste of his beer, you're hopeless), poke about in the bowl with one of those metal things pipe-smokers use, thereby smashing the thin glass inside. Knock out glass and tobacco into the fireplace, refill the pipe and smoke it, wait confidently for the police. You will not, of course, have on your person anything that could possibly hold liquid atropine (being a lab.-boy with a scientific bent, you're aware that analysis can and will distinguish between the liquid and powdered forms), and if either Gillian or Laurie is carrying such a container, so much the worse for them."

"Odious young devil." Humbleby stood up. "You're obviously right, but to clinch it, I'll go back now and let our laboratory have that pipe. If it's been used to hold atropine, there'll still be traces left."

Fen nodded. "Ring me up here, will you?" he said, "and let me know."

It was little more than three-quarters of an hour later when the call came through.

"Quite right," said Humbleby from New Scotland Yard. "No doubt about it at all. He's under arrest already."

"How old is he, by the way?"

"Unfortunately only seventeen."

"You mean they won't hang him. A pity. By the time he's forty, he'll be let out and able to do it again. Such are the victories of enlightenment. But don't, for heaven's sake, tell him it was I who suggested the method to you. Twenty years hence he'll be so altered I shan't be able to recognise him—and even in my dotage I hope still to be drinking beer."

THE LITTLE ROOM

"AND THAT DOOR THERE," said Fen: "where does that lead to?"

They had toured the whole house from cellar to attic and were now back in the large, draughty entrance-hall. Startled, Mrs. Danvers peered about her. "Which, the which," she said incoherently.

"That one." Fen pointed. "Of course, if it's private——"

"Not at all." Mrs. Danvers rallied and became brisk again.

"I quite imagined I'd shown it you already. But really, there are so *many* rooms. . . ." Changing course abruptly, like a small yacht in a high wind, she marched back in the direction indicated. "So *very* many," she added on a note of artificial complacency, "that I feel sure that your—your——"

"My boys," Fen prompted her, following.

"That your boys would fit in excellently." And Mrs. Danvers gave a little nod, for emphasis, as she unbolted the door in question and threw it open. "*Yes*," she said brightly, in the tone of one who has as yet no notion what words are to follow. "*Yes*. . . . Well, here it is, then. You could use it for—for—well, for a store-room, perhaps."

"Ah," said Fen. But he could distinguish very little, he found, of what was being shown him. "Is there a light, by any chance?"

"Of course." She switched it on, revealing a musty square box of an apartment with a boarded floor and all the windows bricked up; there was no furniture in it of any kind. "By fixing shelves," said Mrs. Danvers, "it would be possible——"

"Just so." Fen was already backing away. "Very nice indeed."

"Or you might even turn it into a little museum." A Black Museum, Fen supposed: he sat on the Committee of a Society for the regeneration of delinquent youth, and it was their search for a new Probationary Home which had brought him to this ill-planned mansion. "Ah," he said again, unimaginatively; but Mrs. Danvers, who was still talking, swamped it. She was a trim elderly woman, well laced in, with greying hair and rather hard features, and she had a good command of that most devastating of a salesman's weapons, uninterrupted speech.

"It was my uncle," she was saying now, "who had the windows sealed—against burglars, you understand—at the time when he was thinking of putting his very *valuable* collection of porcelain in here, rather than have it scattered all over the house. In actual fact he never *did*, put it in here, I mean, because the income-tax people made a quite outrageous *claim* against him, for years back, and he had to sell most of the collection so as to be able to pay, at least he always said he couldn't avoid selling it, though I really think it must have been partly *pique*, because Betty, that was his daughter, inherited *investments*, really quite *substantial* investments, when he died, and so there you are, but most schools *do* have a museum, I believe, butterflies and bits of rock and things, and since that's what it was originally *intended* for . . ."

"I'll keep the suggestion in mind," Fen interposed firmly. "And now I'd better be going, I think. My Committee's due to meet again in a few days' time, and the Secretary will write to you." He started edging towards the front door. "You've been very kind indeed, most kind."

"And you *will* remember to tell them that it's a *new* house, won't you?" With a skilful flanking movement, Mrs. Danvers got ahead of him, thereby temporarily cutting off his retreat. "I mean, so many of these *huge* places are *old* and *falling to bits* that the mere *size* of it may give a *wrong impression*, but this was built only just before the war, the 1939 war that is, and although I've had to keep so many of the rooms shut up it really is in *very good condition*, no one but the family has lived in it, it's never been *let* even, and as to small children and animals, so destructive don't you think, they just *haven't been allowed inside*, not ever, so you see it really has been *looked after*."

Mumbling assent, Fen made a break for it and gained the doorstep. "Very kind," he said. "Put you to a lot of trouble, I'm afraid. . . . Other houses being looked at. . . . Can't be sure what my Committee will decide. . . . Let you know as soon as possible." Emitting other such reassurances and farewells, he fled.

The house wouldn't do, of course, he reflected as he turned into the road through the ornate lodge-gates: it was grotesquely inconvenient for almost any purpose. There was one aspect of it which had aroused his curiosity, however, and he remained pensive, weighing and rejecting alternative hypotheses, as he strolled into the little town. . . . Presently, coming to the Market Square, he halted uncertainly. He had intended to catch the 6.13 bus back to Oxford, and so be in time for dinner in Hall; and it would be inconvenient, from the point of view of eating, if he missed that bus. On the other hand, he was by nature voraciously inquisitive, and the oddity he had observed, though apparently trivial in itself, would remain, he knew, to perplex and irritate him so long as he made no attempt to investigate it. In the end, curiosity triumphed. Retracing his steps, he made his way back to a public-house which he had noticed quite close to the house he had been inspecting.

Its landlord proved affable; and on learning Fen's mission in the neighbourhood, became voluntarily informative. " 'Ti'n't the sort of place *I'd* want to buy," he confided, breathing heavily with the effort of keeping his massive form adequately supplied with oxygen. "All right for a school, I dessay, but that's all. What old Ridgeon wanted to build it so big for, I really don't——"

"Ridgeon?"

"Ah. Old chap as collected china and stuff. You'd think he'd had a family of twenty-seven, what with the size of the place, but there was only the one daughter. But ' 'Iggs,' 'e used to say to me, 'I just can't abide these little rat-traps of houses. A gentleman,' 'e'd say, ' 'as to 'ave space to move about.' Well, sir, I ask you, what a line to take, with the servant situation being what it is. It wa'n't so bad *then*, mind. 'E started off all right, with three or four. But then there was the war, and by the time that was 'alf over 'e'd only got one left, and 'alf the rooms 'ad 'ad to be shut up. Foolishness, I call it. Arrogance. And that one maid, even she left when 'e died, a couple o' years ago, and the niece, Mrs. Danvers, 'oo'd come to 'ouse-keep for 'im, 'ad to do everything 'erself, and there was more rooms shut up, and it's small wonder she's trying to get shot of it."

"What about the daughter, though?"

"Ah, Betty 'elped, o' course. Only she wasn't really the practical sort, and then when it came to the tragedy——"

Fen stiffened slightly. "The tragedy?"

"Didn't you never 'ear of that? But I dessay you wouldn't, being a stranger 'ere. Real shocking, it was." And here the landlord addressed himself to the bar's only other occupant, a quiet, well-dressed, middle-aged man who was drinking a double whisky in a corner. "None of us 'll forget that in a 'urry, Doctor, shall we?"

"It was atrocious." The doctor spoke in a low voice, but with unexpected vehemence. "And when you think that there are still a lot of damned vociferous fools who go around saying children oughtn't to be taught about sex. . . ." He checked himself, shrugging and smiling; finished his drink and ordered another. "But you'd better not get me on to that subject."

"What happened?" Fen asked.

The doctor studied him, and appeared to decide, by some process of intuition, that the question was prompted by some better motive than mere sensation-seeking.

"There was this girl, you see," he said. "This girl Betty—Ridgeon's daughter, Mrs. Danvers's cousin. A nice girl. Very pale ginger hair, and brown eyes with it. But nervous—highly strung. About a year after her father died she met a chap called Venables, Maurice Venables, and fell for him in a really big way."

"Fair daft about 'im," confirmed the landlord. "Fair daft about 'im, she was."

The doctor grimaced. "To tell you the truth," he said, "I rather liked Betty myself. But after she met Venables, there just wasn't a chance for anyone else. He was a good chap, too, I've got to hand it to him. . . .

"Well, they got engaged, and the wedding was all set for a day last June. And then, on the actual morning of her wedding-day, Betty disappeared."

Fen's eyebrows lifted; and if the doctor had been less engrossed in his story, he might have seen an odd look, almost like satisfaction, flicker across the stranger's face. "Disappeared?" Fen echoed.

"Vanished. Went. Some time in the very early morning, they thought. She took some cash with her, but they never traced where she went during the fortnight that followed."

"But what reason——"

"Well, she was frightened, it seems—frightened about the physical side of the marriage. Mrs. Danvers knew that, and there were one or two girl-friends who confirmed it. She wasn't cold, mind you, not that sort at all; just scared." The doctor's brow darkened. "Why they don't *teach* these girls something about it. . . . However. Oh, and by the way, I'm sure it wasn't Venables's fault. He's a nice gentle chap. No, it's just that the girl was both ignorant *and* highly-strung, and the combination turned out fatal. In spite of being so much in love with him, she funked it at the last moment. Poor kid. . . ."

He brooded while Fen ordered fresh drinks for himself and for the landlord. Then, resuming:

"Anyway, for a whole fortnight she vanished," he said. "And then, one night, she came back. No one *saw* her, and she didn't go to the house. Instead, she seems to have slept in an old barn just outside the town, Abingdon way. But you can imagine what she was feeling. She must have felt she could never face Venables again—though, Lord knows, he'd have forgiven her all right. With him gone, everything was gone. So she got hold of an old kitchen knife somewhere—they never found out where—and cut her throat with it, and that was how they found her."

There was a brief silence, broken only by the landlord's asthmatic wheezing. Then, dismissively, the doctor said:

"They'd searched for her, of course. It was quite a to-do, I can tell you. Everything ready—cake, reception, parson and all the trimmings—and then Mrs. Danvers had to ring up Venables and the police and meet them at the gate and tell them what had happened, and you can imagine how everyone felt. Though that was nothing to what they felt when the body was found. . . ."

"Who," Fen demanded abruptly, "was to have given her away?"

The doctor looked at him in surprise. "Why d'you ask? It was an old friend of her father's, actually, because the only *relative* she had living was Mrs. Danvers."

"And was he staying at the house?"

The doctor's puzzlement visibly grew; but it was the landlord who answered.

"No, sir," said the landlord. " 'E was staying 'ere. . . . Mrs. Danvers," he added with some gratification, "said 'e'd be more comfortable 'ere than with them, so there was only Mrs. Danvers in the 'ouse when young Betty did 'er bunk."

"That was what I was getting at, yes," said Fen. "Interesting. Has the house ever been let?"

The landlord shook his head. "Not to my knowledge, sir, never. But why——"

"And just one other thing." Fen's smile robbed the interruption of all offence. "Mrs. Danvers can't stand small children and dogs, I believe."

"That's so, sir. D'you remember the time you went there with your Alsatian, Doctor, and 'aving to leave 'im tied up outside? In'uman, I call it, but there's no accounting for some people. O' course, when old Ridgeon was alive, and before 'e sold 'is collection, it'd have been silly to 'ave dogs and kids rushing about knocking valuable pieces over and smashing 'em. I dessay if old Ridgeon 'ad put all 'is vases and so forth in that room 'e 'ad got ready for 'em, it'd 'ave been all right then. But 'e never did—and anyway, 'e di'n't like children nor animals, nor Mrs. Danvers don't, neither."

With this stately procession of negatives Fen seemed very content. "In that case," he said, "if you could just tell me whether Mrs. Danvers has a car, and something about her shopping habits. . . ." And presently he was able to finish his beer and depart, well primed.

There was a silence in the bar after he had left. Then the doctor said:

"Impressive sort of bloke, in an odd way. Formidable, somehow. I wonder what he thought he was getting at?"

The landlord grunted. "For-mid-ab-le, yes," he agreed, pronouncing the word with the precaution which its length required. "Not the sort o' chap you'd like to 'ave for an enemy, really. As to what 'e was after, *I* don't know. 'E di'n't look like police, not to me anyway. A bit cracked, per'aps." Then, dismissing the topic: "Well, Doctor, 'ow about another of the same? Does you a bit of good, this weather, doe'n't it—whatever anyone may say."

But neither of them saw the object of these varied compliments when he returned next morning—for Fen's second visit was not one which he wished to have generally known. For all his faults, he is not a particularly expert housebreaker; but on this occasion no great expertise was required, since Mrs. Danvers had gone to the shops leaving several ground-floor windows open; and so he was able to do his work, and get away after it, without leaving any traces behind him. He had with him only a thin-bladed knife, some sheets of paper, and some envelopes. But on arriving back safely in Oxford he supplemented these with various purchases at a chemist's; and once home, he went straight to that room which, to the disgust and apprehension of his family, he uses as a makeshift laboratory, and locked himself in. For some little time he was happily occupied with filter paper, hydrogen peroxide, and a solution of benzidine sulphate in glacial acetic acid. Then he went to the telephone. . . .

By a stroke of luck, it was Detective-Inspector Humbleby who was eventually sent down from Scotland Yard to handle the case.

"Oh yes, it's *blood* all right," said Humbleby. "And what's more, it's human blood. And what's even better, it's the same group and sub-groups as Betty Ridgeon's (good thing she was a blood-donor, by the way: that's saved us an exhumation). So the assumption is that she did in fact cut her throat in that little room, and not in the barn where she was found."

"You got plenty of it, did you," said Fen, "out of those crevices between the floor-boards?"

"More than enough, even after you'd been at it. The wretched girl must have bled pints. . . . We managed to salvage some from the barn, too—cat's blood, most of it, part of Mrs. Danvers's ingenious scene-setting. Apparently it never occurred to anyone to test it, at the time. So far so good, then: Betty killed herself——"

"Or *was* killed."

But Humbleby shook his head. "No proof of that. There were all the proper suicidal signs, apparently, the little tentative cuts before the final one and so forth. . . . Oh yes, I grant you Mrs. Danvers had *motive* enough. Betty was intestate: if she died *after* her marriage, the estate she'd inherited from her father would go to Venables, and if she died *before*, it'd go to Mrs. Danvers—as in fact it did. But we can't hope to prosecute for murder. In my view, the likeliest way for it to have happened is this: Mrs. Danvers, in mere panic at the thought of losing the chance of old Ridgeon's money for good, shuts Betty up on the wedding morning, and invents this very plausible tale about the girl being scared and running away. Then——"

"But look here," Fen interrupted fretfully, "what the devil can the Danvers woman have imagined she was going to *do* with the girl, after she'd locked her up? She'd either have to let her out eventually, and take the consequences, or else silence her for good. So that, surely, is reason enough in itself for supposing——"

"It isn't, you know." Humbleby was unexpectedly brusque. "In my view, Mrs. Danvers simply acted without thinking. What I will admit as likely is that she deliberately gave the girl a sharp kitchen knife to eat her food with; and that the girl, unhinged by her imprisonment and by whatever psychological warfare, on the subject of Venables and the marriage, Mrs. Danvers chose to subject her to, eventually used the knife on herself: it was only her fingerprints that were found on it, you know. . . . *Afterwards*, Mrs. Danvers must have taken the body and the knife by night to that barn, in her car, and dumped it there with the cat's blood."

"Fingerprints," Fen grumbled. "As if they proved anything. . But if what you say is right, it was *morally* murder."

"Oh, quite. Only unfortunately our law doesn't punish people for moral murders."

"Well then, at least there's the imprisonment—assault, battery, unlawful restraint or whatever you call it."

"My dear Gervase, we've no *proof* of that whatever. The *only* thing we can prove is that Betty Ridgeon died in that little room, and not in the barn. And you know what sort of a charge that leaves us with, to punish that abominable woman? Concealing a body in order to prevent an inquest. Seven days, if the magistrates are harsh. That's a nice, fat, satisfying revenge for poor Betty, isn't it?"

Fen contemplated him gloomily. "The father," he ventured, "Ridgeon, I mean——"

"Died naturally. The post-mortem was done yesterday, immediately after the exhumation, and the Home Office isn't a bit pleased at our having dug him up and not found anything, even though we warned them it was a gamble. . . . Mrs. Danvers isn't saying anything, by the way—anything at all, I mean.

She refuses to make a statement or answer questions until she's charged."

For a long while after that both men were silent, angry at the law's impotence. Then Humbleby said:

"The only thing I *don't* see is what put you on to it in the first place, before you knew anything about Betty."

"Oh, that. . . . I should like to think that it would help," said Fen, "but I'm afraid it won't. Here was this room, you see, with the windows blocked up, so that there was no question of burglars from outside getting through it into the rest of the house. And the house had never been let, and there had never been any small children or dogs in it, to be excluded from the room in case of damage they might do. . . .

"So can *you* think of any reason—other than imprisonment, I mean—why there should have been a bolt on the *outside*, the hall side, of that door?"

EXPRESS DELIVERY

THE LIGHTNING WINKED over Westminster, and office workers queueing for buses in Whitehall looked up apprehensively at the lowering grey of the late afternoon sky. The day had dawned hot, so that most were without their coats and many without umbrellas, and the odds were against their reaching their homes before the rain began to fall. Distantly, above the rumble of rush-hour traffic, the thunder spoke. And in a room high up in a corner of New Scotland Yard, Detective-Inspector Humbleby walked to a window, looking out and down.

"Here they come," he said. "And whether they're guilty or innocent the Lord alone knows." His eye followed the two diminutive, foreshortened figures until they disappeared with their uniformed escort into the doorway below. "*If* they're guilty, then their nerve must be colossal. But presumably nerve is one of the things experienced big-game hunters do acquire, so . . ." He completed the sentence with a shrug.

"They're both that?" Gervase Fen, Professor of English Language and Literature in the University of Oxford, spoke out of a cloud of cigarette smoke. "The wife as well as the husband?"

"Oh yes, certainly—though I understand that the woman

isn't quite as good a shot as the man. . . ." Rummaging, Humbleby had unearthed an old copy of the *Tatler*. "This," he added as he handed it across, "will give you an idea of what they *look* like."

They looked slightly like giraffes, Fen concluded as he studied the photograph in question; and you would have taken them for brother and sister rather than for husband and wife. The woman was older than he had expected—forty at least. Her lean and apparently sunburned countenance wore a hard unspontaneous smile showing large buck teeth, and her short hair had been permanently waved by no niggardly hand. Her long nose was almost duplicated by her husband's, and the eyes of both of them were disagreeably small. It was he, however, who contrived to look the younger and the more human of the two; a large pipe projected manfully from his lips, and he was in the act of lighting it with a frown of preoccupation and a vesta match. The caption stated that also present (at a charity garden party) were Mr. and Mrs. Philip Bowyer, recently returned from a big-game expedition in Tanganyika; and "*Mrs. Bowyer*," the *Tatler* hastened to explain, fearful of being thought to include mere *polloi* in its Society pages, "*is the second daughter of Sir Egerton and the late Lady Joan Wilmot, of Wilmot Hall in Derbyshire*."

Fen was still digesting this information when a telephone rang on the desk, and Humbleby picked it up.

"Yes," he said. "Yes, I saw them come in. Keep them downstairs for a few minutes, will you? I'll let you know when I'm ready for them." He replaced the instrument with a grimace. "Cowardice," he observed. "Procrastination. But I thought that perhaps you wouldn't mind hearing about it, and telling me what you think."

Fen nodded. "By all means. Your story's been rather scrappy so far, and I'm still not really clear about what happened."

Lightning flickered again in the narrow room, and this time the thunder was close after it; the storm was coming in fast from the south-west, and at its coming the wind had risen, spattering a handful of rain-drops against the panes. Humbleby put his hand up to the sash, shut the window, returned to his desk. The heat had dishevelled his accustomed neatness, and he wiped sweat from his forehead as he slumped into the revolving chair.

"Here's this girl, then," he said. "Eve Crandall. Twenty-four, brunette, as pretty and graceful as you expect a mannequin to be, sharing a tiny flat in Nottingham Place with another girl. She has a rich old uncle, Maurice Crandall, who's made her his heiress. She has a big-game-hunting cousin, Philip Bowyer, who's at present downstairs with his wife Hilary. And she has a studious cousin, James Crandall, who teaches at an elementary school in Twelford."

"James Crandall?" Fen was frowning. "In my undergraduate days, there was a James Crandall contemporary with me at Magdalen. A gawky, conscientious, desperately dull sort of man with thick-lensed glasses and a stammer. He was one of those unfortunate people who are obviously doomed to come to nothing however hard they try, so that an elementary school, twenty years later——"

"Yes, he could be the same one. I can vouch for the gawkiness and the glasses, though as to the rest," said Humbleby a shade grimly, "I just wouldn't know—not at first hand, anyway. . . .

"Still, that's by the way. The real *point* about all this set-up of uncle and cousins is this: that if Eve predeceases Maurice, the estate will be shared on Maurice's death by Philip Bowyer and James Crandall; and that if both Eve *and* James Crandall predecease Maurice, the estate will go to Philip Bowyer intact. In other words, and not to be too delicate about it, schoolmaster James has a motive for killing Eve, and big-game-hunter Bowyer (together with his wife) has a motive for killing both Eve *and* James. Clear so far?

"Now, Uncle Maurice has carcinoma of the lungs. He may live two months or two weeks or only two days, but in any event he's dying, and like most of us he has no particular relish for dying among strangers in a nursing-home. So he asks Philip and Hilary Bowyer, the most well-to-do of his relatives, to take him in at their house near Henley."

"A rather sanguine request," Fen commented, "in view of the fact that he hadn't willed them his money."

"Oh, he'd left them something; the bulk of his fortune was to go to Eve, but he'd left the Bowyers *something*—and he was quite capable of cancelling that arrangement if they refused to have him in their house. The Bowyers aren't, it turns out, as well off as they look—not well enough off, in any case, to sniff at the chance of an odd thousand or two: no doubt big-game hunting is an expensive hobby. Anyway, they agreed to have him.

"They agreed to have him, and on the day he was due to arrive, rather more than a week ago, Eve travelled to Henley to see him settled in. That was to be expected; what was not to be expected was that James Crandall should forsake his little boys and turn up too. Turn up, however, he did—in the hope, maybe, of wheedling a rather larger bequest out of Maurice than the five hundred pounds he was destined for as things stood—and by the early afternoon they were all, excepting Maurice who was presumably still *en route* in an ambulance from the nursing-home, on the spot.

"The Bowyers' house stands on high ground overlooking the town and the river, about a mile out. It's biggish—ten-bedroom calibre—and like a lot of biggish houses these days it's going to seed for lack of an adequate staff. But Philip and Hilary are the sort of people who prefer pretension to comfort, so there they stay—and it may be that they're attracted by the fact that there's quite a lot of land attached, with things to shoot on it: though rabbits, I take it, must be something of a come-down after lions. There's just one servant, a wretched overworked little woman who makes one feel that there's something to be said, after all, for the independent, take-it-or-leave-it type that's cropped up since the war. And it was this Mrs. Jordan who opened the door to Eve Crandall when at about three o'clock she arrived in a taxi from the station.

"By the time she got there, Hilary had left for the town to do some shopping, James had gone for a stroll, and Philip—since the ambulance wasn't expected until tea-time at the earliest—was on the point of walking down to meet his wife and help her with her packages. So apart from the servant, Eve spent her first hour on the premises alone, and after she'd unpacked she wandered round the garden and eventually settled down in a deck-chair under a beech-tree, facing a coppice of beeches about three hundred yards away beyond the garden fence. She sat very still in the chair with her eyes closed, and anyone watching her must certainly have thought her asleep. But for some unexplained reason she was nervous, and her sideways jerk, when she heard the shot, was about as instantaneous as it's possible for such a reflex to be. The bullet, from an express rifle, tore a track in her scalp and grazed her skull; another fraction of an inch and it would certainly have killed her. As it was, she was knocked unconscious, according to the doctors, the moment it touched her, and so failed to hear the second shot which immediately followed.

"Both shots, however, were heard by Mrs. Jordan and by the postman on his way up the drive, and these two witnesses converged in front of the house thirty seconds later to find Eve lying in a huddle beside the deck-chair and Hilary, white and shaken, emerging from the coppice opposite. Two minutes later Philip arrived. His wife had hurried home ahead of him, leaving him to collect and carry her parcels. And the situation was this, that James Crandall, shot through the head by Hilary, was lying in the coppice clutching the express rifle which had been fired at Eve.

"Well, the local police took over, and in due course I was called in to work with them, and we got statements from everyone concerned." From a salmon-pink cardboard folder Humbleby extracted a sheaf of typescript. "Here, for instance, is Hilary's, what's relevant of it:

"'*I left my husband in the village because he had things to buy and I did not want to stay with him in case I should not be home in time to meet the ambulance. I came home across the fields, which is the shortest way, and entered the house by the back door. At this time I did not see Eve, since she was in the front garden. I was on my way up to my room to take off my hat when I saw through the open door of the gun-room that a Mannlicher express rifle was missing, and my suspicions were aroused because I knew that my husband did not have the gun, and no one else should have touched it. I thought of my cousin James Crandall, who had been asking questions about the guns. I put a small automatic pistol in my pocket and went out to look for him. I took the pistol because I was afraid James might intend some harm to Eve, whose death would benefit him. I had not liked his manner and was frightened of what he might do. I went round to the front garden where Eve was asleep in the deck-chair, and I thought I saw someone moving in the coppice. As quickly as possible I returned to the back garden and from there crossed into the field where the coppice is, entering the coppice from the side away from the garden. In the coppice I saw James with the Mannlicher pointed at Eve. I pointed my pistol at him and was about to speak when he fired and Eve fell. Immediately I fired at him. It was self-defence, I consider, because he would have killed me because I had seen him shoot Eve, but I did not intend to kill him. I am a fairly good shot with a rifle, but not with an automatic, which is a different kind of shooting.*'"

Humbleby pushed the papers aside. "So much for that. Philip Bowyer heard the two shots, but by his own account he arrived too late to see anything. And that, really, is all there is to it. James Crandall's prints were on the Mannlicher all right, and the position of his body was perfectly consistent with his having fired at Eve. On the other hand, the Bowyers undoubtedly had a very strong motive for wishing both James and Eve dead, and it's easy to see how the thing *could* have been arranged. Thus: first they shoot off the rifle and hit Eve (I say 'they' because of course there's no proof whatever that

Philip didn't catch up with his wife, in spite of their having left the village separately); next, James having previously been lured to the spot on any pretext you like to think of, they kill him with the automatic before he has time to as much as open his mouth; then Hilary rushes out of the coppice, leaving Philip behind to arrange the scene and put James's fingerprints on the rifle; and finally, two minutes later, Philip appears with the astonished air of one who's just arrived from the village with the weekly groceries. . . . That, I repeat, is how it *could* have been done. But *was* it done like that? Or is Hilary's story the simple truth?"

If these questions were other than rhetorical, Fen gave no sign of recognising the fact. "As a matter of interest," he said, "how will Hilary's story stand up in court?"

"Rather well, I should imagine. After all, James Crandall did have a very good motive for killing Eve, and as long as a jury can be induced to believe that he tried to do so, Hilary will never be censured for shooting him. Yes, she'll get away with it all right. But I'm still not quite satisfied."

"And Eve," said Fen. "What became of her?"

"She was taken to hospital and is still there; but she's pretty well recovered by now. I got her statement about what happened up to the moment the rifle bullet knocked her out, this morning. . . ." Humbleby paused hopefully. "Well?" he said. "Any ideas?"

But for once Fen could only shake his head. The rain, falling heavily now, drummed against the window, and it had grown so dark that Humbleby leaned forward and switched on the desk-lamp. Lightning filled the room, and Humbleby had counted aloud up to four before the thunder came.

"The storm's going away," he said absently. "Well, well, I suppose there's nothing for it except——"

And then he checked himself, for Fen was staring at him with the eyes of a man half blinded by unaccustomed sunlight. "And what the devil," said Humbleby, startled, "are you——"

He got no further. "The girl's statement," said Fen abruptly. "Is there a copy of it I could look at?"

"*Eve's* statement, you mean." Humbleby sought for it in the folder and passed it across the desk. "Yes, here it is. But why——"

"Here's what I wanted." Fen had turned at once to the final page. "Listen to this. '*I remember moving to one side as I heard the shot; then straight away everything went black.*'"

"Well? What about it?"

Fen tapped the papers with a long forefinger. "Do you consider this girl's story trustworthy?"

"Yes, I most certainly do. Why shouldn't it be? *She* didn't kill James Crandall, if that's what you're getting at. Quite apart from the fact that she had no motive, it'd have been a physical impossibility."

"All right, all right. But the point is, she's not likely to have *imagined* any of this?"

"No. She's not the sort."

"Excellent. And now, two questions—no, sorry, three. First, is it certain that there weren't more than two shots fired?"

"Absolutely. Philip and Hilary and the postman and Mrs. Jordan are all agreed about that."

"Good. And, secondly, is it certain that the rifle bullet knocked Eve out the moment it touched her?"

"Good Lord, yes. It'd be like a superhuman blow with a tiny hammer. There are cases on record——"

"Bless you, Humbleby, how didactic you're getting. . . . And now here's my final question: is it certain that Hilary's shot killed James Crandall instantaneously?"

"My dear chap, his brain was *pulped*. Of course it's certain."

Fen relaxed with a little sigh. "Then providing Eve's a good witness," he murmured, "there's a fair chance of getting Philip and Hilary Bowyer hanged. Their motive for wanting Eve and James dead is so overwhelming that they'll be at a disadvantage from the start, and that one little scrap of evidence ought to tip the scales against them."

Humbleby groaned. "God give me patience," he said meekly. "*What* little scrap of evidence? You mean that in fact they did arrange it all the way I suggested?"

"Just that. I've no doubt they'd been contemplating something of the sort for some time past, but of course the scheme they eventually adopted, depending as it did on Eve's settling in the deck-chair, must have been improvisation. One of them —I presume Hilary—must have fetched the guns from the house while the other got hold of James; and they could take James to the coppice on the pretext of showing him—well, perhaps rabbit-snares: that would account for their bringing a rifle, and James doesn't sound to me the sort of person who'd know enough about guns to realise the incongruity of a Mannlicher express model in the context of rabbits. On the other hand——"

"These are happy speculations," said Humbleby with restraint. "But I have the idea that a moment ago you mentioned evidence. If it wouldn't put you to too much trouble——"

"Evidence!" said Fen affably. "Yes, I was almost forgetting that. The evidence of the storm—or to be more accurate, of the storm and yourself in combination. Like so many people, you counted out the interval between the lightning flash and the thunder. Why? Because light travels faster than sound, and by gauging the interval you can gauge how far away the storm is. But there are other things, as well as light, which travel faster than sound; and one of them, as you well know, is a bullet fired from an express rifle.

"On a hot day, sound travels at about 1,150 feet per second; but on any sort of day, over a distance of three hundred yards, a bullet from a Mannlicher rifle travels nearly three times as fast, at an average speed of about 3,000 feet per second. Therefore the shot Eve heard was not the rifle-shot at all—she *couldn't* have heard that, since the bullet grazed her, and knocked her out, before the report of the rifle could reach her ears. But she did hear *a* shot—and since there were admittedly only two shots fired, the report she heard must have been the report of the automatic which killed James. In other words, the report of the automatic *preceded* the report of the rifle; which means that James was dead before the rifle was fired; which means, in turn, that it certainly wasn't he who fired it."

"Well, I'm damned," said Humbleby. "What it amounts to, then, is that the Bowyers fired their two shots in the wrong order. If Eve had been killed, as they intended, that wouldn't have mattered. But as it is——" He reached for the telephone.

"Will you be able," Fen asked, "to get a verdict of Guilty on that evidence?"

"I think so, yes. With any luck we shall hang them." Humbleby put the receiver to his ear. "Charge Room, please. . . . But it's a pity they should have had all that trouble for nothing."

"For nothing?"

"Yes. Mrs. Jordan took the telephone message, but there was no one about to pass it on to. It was from the nursing-home, of course. . . . You see, Maurice Crandall died—leaving all his money to Eve, whose will was decidedly *not* in the Bowyers' favour—while they were actually carrying him out to the ambulance: that is, a comfortable two hours before the shooting started. Poor dears—(yes, Betts, you can send them up now)—they never had a chance."

A POT OF PAINT

THE HOUSE ITSELF WAS unremarkable—a small, trim brick villa built at a moderate cost some time between the wars. What was noticeable about it was its relative isolation: you expected a row of near-replicas on either side, but there were only fields, a coppice and a disused barn. "It couldn't hardly have happened, else," said Inspector Bledloe uninspiredly. "Not in broad daylight, anyhow." He pushed the gate open, and with Fen at his heels entered the tidy front garden. "This," he added laboriously, pointing, "is the scene of the occurrence."

Fen examined the spot with the attentiveness which seemed to be required of him. There was a fence; there were bushes; there was a sundial in a circle of paving; there were the impedimenta with which the luckless housekeeper had been occupied when he was struck down—brushes, turpentine, and a messy tin, not large, of waterproof paint. But the assault and presumed robbery of two hours before had left no traces on the hard earth, not even blood. It was the flat of the spade that had knocked Church out, Fen supposed, and not the edge: lucky for him.

"You can see he didn't have a chance to get much of his painting done." Bledloe indicated the fence, on which the undried area was certainly diminutive, and the almost brim-full paint-tin; he nudged the tin illustratively with the toe of his boot, and a fragmentary green ellipse became visible on the paving-stone where it had rested. "So the way I work it out is this. We know it was twenty past three when he fetched the paint from the scullery——"

"That's the evidence of the housekeeper, is it?"

"The evidence of the housekeeper *and* her lady-friend she was gossiping with. Which means—judging from the amount of painting he got done—that he must have been attacked round about half past. He wasn't actually *found*, of course, till after four."

Fen nodded. "Yes, I'd been meaning to ask you about that. Was it the housekeeper who found him?"

"No. It was a family party out for a walk." Bledloe grimaced. "Five of them, including kids, so you needn't waste your energy suspecting *them*. One of the kids saw his shoe sticking out from behind a bush, that's the way it was. And then, as to the nephew——"

"Nephew?" said Fen rather testily. "This is the first time you've mentioned any nephew. *Church's* nephew, you mean?"

"Yes. Didn't I tell you about him? Merrick, his name is—George Merrick. He came here soon after lunch to visit Church, and——"

"And left when?"

"Ah. That's one of the things I'm not sure of. You see, the housekeeper and her lady-friend, they were out in the back garden till a quarter past three, so *they* didn't hear him go. The only thing was, they naturally assumed he'd left because of Church fetching that paint from the scullery at twenty past, just after they'd come back in to make a cup of tea."

"Yes, I see. The two women didn't hear Church talking to anyone, then?"

"No. They heard the front door open and shut when he came out here with his paint, and that was all."

"Is there any reason for suspecting Merrick?"

Bledloe hesitated. "Not what you'd call a *reason*," he said cautiously. "But just the same, I wouldn't put it past him: he's the sort of relative a man's better without, if you ask me—a waster, and worse. But if it *was* him, Church is going to be badly upset about it. He's the son of a sister of Church's who died years ago, and I've heard that when she was dying she asked Church to look after him after she was gone. Which he's done, and not got much thanks for it, either. . . . Well. If there's nothing more you want to look at here, we'll go and find out if he's fit to talk yet."

Fen assented. "And it'll be helpful," he observed as they went on up the path towards the front door, "to know if he really has been robbed."

"Not much doubt about that." Bledloe spoke with a certain gloomy relish. "Most weekends he brings diamonds and so forth back here from his shop in London, so as to look them over. . . . Risky, of course, but he's pretty careful with them—carries them on him during the daytime, and the house is locked up nice and tight at nights. That front door, now—that's got three bolts on it, *and* a chain, *and* two Yale locks, and he won't even have those catches on the locks that hold them open, because he says they get fixed like that and forgotten. . . . Well, you see what I mean: he does take precautions."

This information Fen was able to confirm when the door in question was opened to them by the constable on duty. Behind the constable, in a state of considerable agitation, was a thin, worn-looking elderly woman—Mrs. Ryan, the housekeeper; and at the foot of the staircase lurked a stoutish lady, also elderly but with an air of settled misanthropy, who was presumably Mrs. Ryan's so far unlabelled visitor. The hall in which they stood appeared at a first inspection to be commonplace enough, but Fen none the less prowled conscientiously about it while Bledloe conferred with the constable, and this thoroughness was presently rewarded by an interesting, though admittedly negative, discovery. Interrupting the constable, who had at last succeeded, with great prolixity, in conveying the news that Church was better and that the doctor had authorised a brief interview, Fen picked up a newspaper which was lying on the table beside the front door, handed it to Bledloe, and said:

"Tell me if you see anything unusual about that."

The interruption took Bledloe sufficiently unawares to make him obey Fen's request before enquiring its motive. "No, I don't," he answered, examining the paper somewhat bemusedly. "Except that it's several days old, there's nothing unusual about it that I can make out. Why?"

Fen turned to Mrs. Ryan. "Was Mr. Church keeping this paper for any particular reason?" he asked.

"Oh no, sir." Mrs. Ryan shook her head vigorously. "It was me as left it there, when I was laying the fires this morning."

"I see. And it was just this one paper you left? No others?"

"No, sir. Just the one. But——"

"Thank you," said Fen; and glanced round him. "The house is very beautifully looked after, Mrs. Ryan."

"It 'as to be," Mrs. Ryan replied with some candour. "Very 'ouse-proud, the master is. More like a woman, as far as that goes."

"With a man fussy like that," said the stoutish lady with sudden malevolence, making her sole recorded independent contribution to the matter, "I'm sorry for his wife, and I don't care who hears me say it." Upon which doubtfully relevant pronouncement, Bledloe, who by now was eyeing Fen with considerable mistrust, decided that the time had come to make a move upstairs.

They found the injured man propped up against pillows with his head in a bandage. He was perhaps fifty—small, slender, large-eyed and at the moment unnaturally pale. "He's had a lucky escape," said the doctor, in the slightly petulant tones of one to whom an interesting fatality has been denied. "Very lucky indeed. No concussion and no amnesia. But you're not to tire him out, mind. Ten minutes—no more. I'll wait downstairs." He took himself off.

Though Church was obviously still suffering a good deal of pain, he was game enough, and quite lucid. His story did not, however, incriminate his nephew George Merrick, who had left, he said, at about ten or a quarter past three. Questioned as to the reason for the visit, Church freely admitted that Merrick had been trying to borrow money. "Not for the first time, either," he added wryly. "George suffered from the delusion that jewellers are necessarily rich, because of the value of their stock. As if *that* had anything to do with it! Anyway, this time I couldn't afford to help him. For his mother's sake I'd have liked to, but it was out of the question. I offered him a smaller amount than what he was asking for, but that didn't suit his lordship, and so off he went. Then after he'd left I fetched my paint and trotted out to the garden to get on with painting the fence, and I hadn't done more than a couple of inches before——"

"One moment, Mr. Church," Fen interposed; at which Bledloe, balked of his climax, momentarily glowered at him. "You say you fetched your paint. But was the other stuff—brushes and so forth—already out there?"

Church was surprised. "Yes," he said. "I took it out there immediately after lunch, and would have fetched the paint at the same time if George's arrival hadn't interrupted me. But I don't quite see——"

"And you have in fact been robbed?"

"Certainly I have." Church frowned. "Do you mean to say you didn't—— No, sorry: I'm being stupid. Of course you couldn't possibly know. Anyway, I *was* robbed. At the time I was hit I had a bag of diamonds worth, oh, close on two thousand in my waistcoat pocket. And they aren't there now."

Bledloe cleared his throat. "But the point is, sir, did you see who hit you?"

"For a split second, yes. I heard him moving behind me, and I swung round just in time to get a glimpse of him."

"It wasn't your nephew, then?"

"George?" Church snorted contemptuously. "Good God, no! I don't hold much stock in George's morals, but he hasn't got the guts to go round knocking people out. No, this man——"

There followed an indeterminate description which patently conveyed as little to Bledloe as it did to Fen. "And that's all you can tell us, sir?" said Bledloe, disappointed.

"I'm afraid so. It's vague, I know, but you must remember that I didn't have a chance to get a proper look."

"Tell me, Mr. Church"—Fen had crossed the room and was gazing rather vacantly out of the window—"are you going to claim insurance on the stolen jewels?"

Church stared at him. "Look here," he said after a moment's pause, "who the devil are *you*? I don't remember that I've ever——"

"A colleague, sir," said Bledloe smoothly. "And if you wouldn't mind answering his question . . ."

"Well, damn it, of course I'm going to claim. I can't afford to drop a small fortune like that." Church's expression hardened. "If you're implying that I hid the diamonds, and then knocked myself out, so as to——"

"No," said Fen with emphasis. "The one discrepancy in the evidence won't fit *that* explanation, at all. But there's another explanation it certainly will fit, so I think you'd better tell us the truth. Being attacked and robbed is (up to a point) your own business, and if only that had been involved, I'd have kept quiet. But claiming insurance money and at the same time lying in such a way as to hinder recovery of the jewels is another matter. We know it was Merrick who attacked you—attacked you in the virtual certainty that you'd do what you have done—namely, cover up for him for his mother's sake and so give him time to leave the country. And these things being thus——"

"Oh, so I'm lying, am I?" Church regarded Fen with curiosity, but not with any special perturbation. "And just what makes you imagine that?"

"I'll tell you," said Fen. And did.

There was a silence when he had finished; then Church nodded abruptly. "Well, I've done what I could," he said. "And you're quite right, of course. George didn't go at ten past three—in spite of the fact that I'd told him I couldn't help him. He followed me into the garden, still arguing, and then when my back was turned——" Church shrugged. "Well, you know the rest."

Later, over beer in the parlour of *The Three Tuns*, Bledloe sighed dismissively and said: "So that's settled. But I still don't understand how you could be *sure*."

Fen grunted. "*Someone* must have opened the front door for Church when he went out to paint his fence," he explained: "and since he didn't mention that important fact, the someone was fairly obviously Merrick. The two women heard the door *being* opened, remember—so it wasn't open already. Church couldn't have opened it himself for the reason, you understand, that he was carrying that pot of paint. And he didn't put the pot of paint down in order to open the door, because the old newspaper—the obvious and only place for a house-proud man to deposit the messy paint-tin—wasn't marked at all."

"But look here, he only needed *one* hand to carry the paint. So why couldn't he have opened the door with the other?"

Fen chuckled and drank deep. "When there were *two* knobs to turn—and neither could be fixed? Well, I suppose he just *might* have used his teeth or his toes, but really, Bledloe . . ."

THE QUICK BROWN FOX

THE PORT HAD BEEN round several times, and Wakefield's temperamental dogmatism was by now somewhat inflamed by it.

"Just the same," he said, irrupting on a discussion whose origin and purpose no one could clearly remember, "detective stories *are* anti-social, and no amount of sophistries can disguise the fact. It's quite impossible to suppose that criminals don't collect useful information from them, fantastic and far-fetched though they usually are. No one, I think"—here he glared belligerently at his fellow-guests—"will attempt to contest *that*. And furthermore——"

"*I* contest it," said Gervase Fen; and Wakefield groaned dismally. "For all the use criminals make of them, the members of the Detection Club might as well be a chorus of voices crying in the wilderness. Look at the papers and observe what, in spite of detective fiction, criminals actually do. They buy arsenic at the chemist's, signing their own names in the Poisons Book, and then put stupendous quantities of it in their victims' tea. They leave their fingerprints on every possible object in the corpse's vicinity. They invariably forget that burnt paper, if it isn't reduced to dust, can be reconstituted and read. They spend, with reckless abandon, stolen bank-notes whose serial numbers they must know are in the possession of the police. . . .

"No, on the whole I don't think criminals get much help from detective stories. And if by any chance they *are* addicts, that fact by itself is almost certain to scupper them, since their training in imaginary crime—which as a rule is extremely complicated—tends to make them over-elaborate in the contriving of their own actual misdeeds; and that, of course, means that they're easy game. . . . For instance, there was the Munsey case."

"It has always been my opinion," said Wakefield to the ceiling, "that after-dinner conversation should be general rather than anecdotal. Moreover——"

"I'd known all the family slightly," Fen went on, unperturbed, "over quite a long period of years; but I suppose that it was George Munsey, the head of the house, whom I knew best. Chance threw us together in Milan in 1928, when I was lecturing at the University there and he was engaged in some prolonged financial transaction to do with motor-cars. And although his household, which I met later, proved to be a pleasant one, I never got to know any of its members well enough to be able to regard them as individuals—as other, I mean, than the natural appendages of George. George himself was a little, round, chuckling man who'd made money on the Stock Exchange; but I've always felt that he must have made it more or less accidentally, because he had none of that appalling narrowness which you normally get in people who are engaged in breeding money from money. On the contrary, in fact: George was a man with hobbies—collecting ghost stories; running a toy theatre which he made and wrote the plays for, himself; bird-watching; illuminated manuscripts; and heaven knows what not else—and that fact made him livelier and more intelligent and more human even than the average non-business-man—a novelist, for instance—whose interests are necessarily fairly wide. He was thirty-seven when I first encountered him; so that in 1947, when the events I'm speaking of occurred, he was getting on for sixty—though his cherubic looks belied that, and his baldness was the only sign of ageing in him that I could see.

"I'd travelled up from Oxford to London to deal with some odd scraps of business and to get myself a new portable typewriter (eventually it was a second-hand one I bought, in Holborn). On the following morning I had to attend a Ministry of Education conference, and I was proposing to stay overnight at the Athenaeum. At lunch-time, however, I happened on George Munsey in the Authors' Club bar, and when he heard how I was placed he suggested I should stay with him instead; it was several years since we'd met, and he said the family would never forgive him if he allowed me to go back to Oxford without paying them a visit. I warned him I'd have to do some work while I was in the house—there was a long memorandum to be typed out for presentation at the M. of E. conference—but he was quite agreeable to that; and so at about half past two in the afternoon I duly appeared on his doorstep, typewriter and all.

"The Munseys' house was in St. John's Wood: a tall, narrow, grey-stone place with a long, narrow, rather sooty strip of garden behind it. They don't live there now; with a single exception, I've no idea of the whereabouts of any of them these days, and there are good reasons why I shouldn't enquire. But in 1947 they were old-established residents who'd survived two wars and were well-known and popular in the neighbourhood. And I rang their bell with the vaguely guilty, vaguely nostalgic feeling one has about people from whom, for no adequate reasons, one has allowed oneself to drift apart.

"I rang their bell; and the door was opened to me by Judith, the younger daughter.

"George Munsey's two daughters were both good-looking; but if I'd had to choose between them, I think I should have chosen Judith rather than Eleanor. Eleanor had the more dizzying figure of the two, but that, of course, is only a *relative* judgment: Judith's figure, though without the heroic mouth-drying splendour of her sister's, was still capable of making the average girl look as if she'd been hammered out of a milk-churn, and in addition to that her *features* were more beautiful than Eleanor's. I'm sorry to be talking about nothing but externals; the trouble is that I didn't then, and don't know, really know much about the two girls' characters—other, I mean, than such obvious facts as that Judith was noisy while Eleanor was quiet, and that Judith was energetic while Eleanor was lazy. There were three years between them—Judith, at twenty-two, being the younger; Judith was fair while Eleanor was dark; and Eleanor dressed better than Judith. None of which is very vivid, I'm afraid—but then, healthy, attractive young women *aren't* very vivid, except in the flesh.

"'Aha!' said Judith from the doorway. 'The Great Man-hunter in person, how nice to see you again, I didn't have so much *embonpoint* when you were here last do you think it's improved me, oh look let me take your things, I'm sorry everyone's making that God-awful row but they're playing Racing Demon, how long are you going to stay, come on in.'

"So I went on in.

"I ought to explain, at this point, that the Munseys were a well-to-do family, since Mrs. Munsey and Judith and Eleanor had all inherited substantially from Mrs. Munsey's father, who had owned flour-mills. They kept no servants, however, preferring, on the whole, to lead a mildly Bohemian existence, looking after themselves. For some reason, they had never quite grasped the practical advantages, in a household, of the principle known to economists as Division of Labour, and when anything had to be done they tended all of them to try and do it simultaneously, frequently with disastrous results. But the atmosphere of their house was very friendly, and the shouts of irate laughter from the drawing-room were so characteristic of it that for a moment time was telescoped, and it seemed a matter of hours rather than of years since I'd been there last.

"'Me,' said Judith, 'I'm Doing Something In The Kitchen and you'd better not ask what it is because you'll probably have to eat it later on, and now just dump your bags, and that other thing oh it's a typewriter isn't it, *here* and come and meet everyone, we're stuck with Aunt Ellen these days did you know, I really can't *bear* the woman'—this with a sudden access of genuine feeling which rather startled me—'but the others don't seem to mind her so it's hopeless to try and turn her out, if she'd only accept *money* instead of battening on us *here* I shouldn't mind so much, but look at her now, she's upstairs slaving away at a lot of rubbishy embroidery which she can't do for nuts in the hope that someone'll pay her a few shillings for it, and God knows I'd be willing to finance her myself if only she'd go *away*, you remember her don't you?'

"I did remember her. George Munsey's sister Ellen was one of those desperately willing, desperately inefficient middle-aged women whom one associates with the Women's Voluntary Services and an atmosphere of utter confusion: short-sighted eyes, wispy greying hair, and a walk like a cripple in a hurry. Her poverty, which was genuine enough, could, as Judith remarked, have been remedied easily out of the family resources if only she had not been obstinate about receiving direct help; as it was, she lodged with them free of charge, a situation which all of them except Judith endured very patiently; and Judith's dislike of her hadn't, I think, any rational basis, but was more in the nature of a violent temperamental aversion such as does sometimes crop up between dissimilar personalities. Aunt Ellen didn't reciprocate it, by the way: if anything, she was rather fonder of Judith than of the others.

"I didn't, of course, take all of this in straight away; most of it emerged during conversation over the cards—and it was to the cards that Judith conducted me as soon as I'd deposited my things. There were four of them playing: George Munsey, his wife Dorothy, his eldest daughter Eleanor, and a young man who was a stranger to me, but who I gathered was occupying the second spare-bedroom. He had the sort of looks which people describe as 'over-handsome'; his thick, curly, jet-black hair was heavily oiled; he chewed gum; and he was manifestly vain—though the vanity was too naïve to give serious offence, and it was relieved on occasion by a queer, earnest, dog-like, rather touching humility. Physically he was splendid. 'This is Philip,' said Judith, introducing him. 'In full, Philip Odell. His speciality'—here a glint of malice appeared in Judith's eye—'his speciality is changing horses, or perhaps I should say mares, in mid-stream.'

"'Judith,' said Mrs. Munsey reproachfully. 'The image is hardly—hardly——' But reproof tailed away into benevolence. Dorothy Munsey, vague, stately and benign, who had acquired something of a reputation as a poetess in the earlier twenties and lost it again, conclusively, in the later, was temperamentally incapable of rebuking anyone, and it was a wonder her daughters had grown up as unspoiled as they were. 'What Judith *means*, Professor Fen——'

"'Is that I,' said Odell, 'have not been behaving like the perfect gentleman.' His hearty tones didn't quite conceal his uneasiness, I thought. 'The fact is, sir,' he went on, that for a time I was engaged to Judith. But of course, she couldn't stand me'—he showed very white teeth in a not altogether convincing laugh—'not for long, anyway. So that when Eleanor decided *she* could stand me, I got engaged to Eleanor. And there, as they say, the matter rests.'

"'He felt,' Eleanor put in, 'that it ought to be kept in the family. And since apart from Aunt Ellen I was the only other unattached female to be had——'

"'Now, darling, you know very well I adore——' Odell checked himself abruptly. 'Hell,' he said. 'Why wasn't I brought up properly?' He grimaced. 'It's the gigolo in me,' he added ruefully, 'that makes me want to gush in public. *I'm* sorry.'

"And somehow I liked him for that.

"I learned later that he was the owner of a chain of milk bars in the West End; and although clearly he was passionately interested in them, he took the Munseys' gentle mockery on the subject in really very good part. I also gathered, indirectly, that in spite of what he'd said it was he rather than Judith who had been primarily responsible for the breaking-off of the first engagement. However, neither he nor Judith nor Eleanor seemed much discomfited by the exchange, and until the next day I wasn't in the least aware of anything's being amiss in the house at all.

"In the meantime, we played cards.

"I myself ought to have been working; but I have a fondness for Racing Demon, so when Judith had gone back to the kitchen I joined the game, and the five of us played uninterruptedly for the next two hours—George Munsey with gusts of helpless laughter at his own inefficacy, Eleanor lazily, Odell with great seriousness, and Mrs. Munsey with her usual stately vagueness; so that it was always surprising when, as generally happened, Mrs. Munsey came out on top. At half past four, on the Munseys' departing in a body to make tea, I retrieved my new typewriter and settled down in the library to work. And there I stayed—recruited by food and drink which the family brought in to me at irregular intervals—until nearly midnight. I hadn't any occasion to leave the library, so I've no idea what the others did with themselves; and I don't remember that anything more eventful happened to me, during the remainder of the day, than having to put a new ribbon into my machine. By the time I'd finished my job they'd all gone to bed, and I wasn't at all sorry to follow them.

"But next morning, Odell being not yet up and the others unitedly engaged in cooking breakfast, Judith took me aside and confided to me certain matters which I must confess disturbed me a good deal."

Fen leaned back, staring rather blankly at the roses in the centre of the dinner-table. "We went down the garden," he said, "so as to keep out of people's way. There was a ramshackle tool-shed, I remember, and a few spiky cabbages, and dust on all the grass; and we could hear the clatter of plates from the kitchen. Judith, in slacks and a sweater, was unusually subdued: her conversation had some full stops in it for once. And the reason soon appeared.

" 'I—I don't know whether I ought to be telling you this,' she said. 'But it's so like a Providence, you actually being here. . . . Look, you're not officially connected with the police, are you?'

" 'No.'

" 'I mean, anything I told you, you wouldn't have to pass it on to them?'

" 'No, of course not,' I said uneasily. 'But——'

" 'It's about Philip, you see. Philip Odell. I've sometimes wondered if that's his real—— Well, but never mind that. The point is, you see, that last night something *happened*.'

" 'What sort of thing?'

"'It—I say, you *will* keep this to yourself, won't you? It's something rather horrible, you see, and I—— Oh damn, I'm havering—— Well, anyway, here goes.'

"And then it all came pouring out. Summarised—for conciseness' and Wakefield's sake—what it amounted to was this:

"Judith had heard me come up to bed at midnight, and having finished her book, and being still sleepless, had set off, as soon as the closing of the bedroom door signalled me out of the way (since in spite of her talk she was quite a modest child, and apparently had very little on), to fetch a magazine from the hall. Arriving at the head of the stairs, however, she had looked down and seen Odell slip quietly out of the drawing-room—where they'd left him chewing gum and playing dice with himself—and into the library; from which shortly fterwards she heard the rattle of my typewriter, which I'd left down there. In the normal way she wouldn't have thought much about this, but Odell's manner had struck her as distinctly furtive, and she was curious to know what he was up to. She hid in the hall cloaks closet, therefore, until after about ten minutes Odell emerged, still stealthily, and crept up to his room. Then she went into the library to see if she could find any indication of what he'd been doing there. Well, she did in fact find something, and in due course showed it to me, and——"

Fen broke off rather abruptly; and when after a moment he resumed, it was to say:

"You know that when you're using thin typing-paper you generally put a backing-sheet behind the sheet you're actually typing on?"

Haldane nodded. "Yes, I know."

"That's what Odell had done. And he'd left the backing-sheet in the waste-paper basket. And you could read what he'd typed by the indentations on it. And what he'd typed was not in the least pleasant "

Fen paused to refill his glass. "As I recall it," he continued after drinking, "the message ran like this: '*You remember what happened at Manchester on December 4th, 1945? So do I. But a thousand pounds might persuade me, I think, to forget about it. I'll write again and tell you where to leave the money. It will be the worse for you if you try to find out who I am.*'"

Haldane nodded again. "Blackmail," he murmured thoughtfully.

"Quite so. Odell was the sort of person who might well be unscrupulous enough to try that particular game; and the Munseys—Aunt Ellen apart—were a good rich mine for that kind of mining: I don't mean in the sense of their having dubious pasts, of course, but rather in the sense that each one of them was well off *independently of the others*. It all seemed plain enough—and yet somehow it was a bit *too* plain; and I got the impression that even Judith, distressed as she was, had inexplicit doubts about it. Besides, there was an odd thing about the message on that tell-tale backing-sheet, and that was its heading."

"Its *heading*?"

"Yes. At the top of it there were four additional words typed: '*The—quick—brown—fox*.'"

There was an instant's bemused silence. Someone said: "What on earth...?"

"Yes. A little mystifying, I agree. But anyway, there it was —and there too, more importantly, was the impress of the blackmail note. And if in fact, despite Judith's and my misty doubts, Odell *was* blackmailing someone in the house, then the situation required very delicate handling indeed. Judith wanted my advice, naturally enough" ("Tcha," said Wakefield) "as to what she ought to do. But I never had a chance to give it her, because it was at that point in our conversation that we heard Eleanor's scream. Eleanor had gone to call her *fiancé* down to his breakfast, and had found him murdered in his bed.

"Well, the police came, and the Ministry awaited me vainly, and as soon as the routine of the investigation was over, Superintendent Yolland took me into consultation. I was glad to get away from the family, I can tell you. Odell's death had plainly strengthened the hypothesis that he was blackmailing one of them—that he had slipped the blackmail note under a certain door on his way to bed, I mean, and that the occupant of that room had guessed the blackmailer's identity and decided to kill rather than pay; and I was finding it difficult to look any of the Munseys in the eye. Eleanor was in a state of hysterics; George Munsey was as fathomlessly miserable as only a normally jovial man can be; his wife's usual vagueness had grown monstrously, so that she scarcely seemed to be present in the spirit at all; and Aunt Ellen's well-meant efforts to be helpful were really, in the circumstances, quite exceptionally trying. Judith stayed outwardly more or less normal; but although she said nothing further to me about the subject of our conversation in the garden, I could see that in spite of her apparent self-possession she was horribly afraid.

"Yolland proved to be a Devonshire man transplanted to London: slow, thorough and by no means unintelligent. But the facts he had to offer weren't at all enlightening. Odell had been killed, while sound asleep, by a single blow on the forehead. The weapon was a heavy brass poker from the drawing-room, and no great strength would have been needed to wield it effectively. Death had occurred between five and six a.m. and had been instantaneous. There were no fingerprints, and no helpful traces of any kind.

"Naturally, I felt bound to tell the Superintendent what Judith had told me; and by way of response, he produced for my inspection two sheets of typing-paper which he'd found hidden away in one of Odell's drawers. The first one I looked at bore, in faint and spidery typescript, the blackmail message I've already quoted—but *not* the odd superscription. The second sheet was identical with the first in every possible respect, *except* that it was addressed, like the backing-sheet Judith had found, to The Quick Brown Fox. And that being so——"

"That being so," Wakefield interrupted, "you didn't, I trust, have to do any very strenuous thinking in order to solve the mystery."

Wakefield had been unnaturally silent during Fen's narrative. And it now became immediately clear to everyone at the table that this silence had been due to some massive feat of cerebration on whose results he was proposing to lecture them. "You think the solution obvious?" said Fen mildly.

"I think it child's play," said Wakefield with much complacency. "With what, after all, does one associate the words 'the quick brown fox'? One associates them, of course, with the sentence 'The quick brown fox jumps over the lazy dog,' which has the peculiarity of containing all the letters of the alphabet. To cut a long story short, Odell wasn't *writing* a blackmail note: he was *copying* one, *in order to find if it had been typed on that particular typewriter*.

"In other words, Odell was not a blackmailer: he was a blackmailer's victim.

"He started to type out the Quick Brown Fox sentence, as a means of comparison, and then decided it would be simpler just to copy the complete message. And the original, together with his copy, was naturally enough found in his drawer. I take it that he wasn't the man to accede meekly to blackmail, and that he'd made up his mind to find out who was threatening him; at which the blackmailer took fright and brained him while he slept. . . . Any objections so far?"

But there were no objections—not even from Fen

"As to who the blackmailer was," Wakefield went on, "That's easy, too. And for this reason:

"As I understand it, both messages *were* in fact typed on Professor Fen's machine." Fen assented. "Just so. Well then, between the time Professor Fen entered the house and the time Odell made his copy, what opportunity was there for anyone to use his typewriter? One, and one only—the period during which Professor Fen was playing Racing Demon in the drawing-room.

"And—well, we know there were only two people who weren't uninterruptedly engaged in that game: to wit, Judith, who was in the kitchen, and Aunt Ellen, who was upstairs. Judith we can eliminate on the simple grounds that if she'd been the blackmailer she'd scarcely have told Professor Fen what she did tell him. And that leaves Aunt Ellen. . . . Did you ever find out anything about Odell and Manchester and that date?"

"Yes," said Fen. "Odell—and that wasn't his real name—had deserted from the Army on that date and in that place. And Aunt Ellen, who'd been in the A.T.S., had had to do, at one time, with the dossiers relating to deserters. In one of those dossiers she'd seen a photograph of Odell, and consequently she recognised him the first time he entered the house."

"She didn't attempt to deny having recognised him?"

"Oh no. She couldn't very well deny it, because—having discreetly checked back to make sure she hadn't made a mistake—she'd confided the facts to Judith after Odell became engaged to Eleanor; and Judith had advised her to do and say nothing, on the grounds that Odell had a first-rate fighting record, and that his desertion, at the end of the war, was therefore a technical rather than a moral offence."

There was a hush while they assimilated this. Then: "Well, well. . . . It really does seem," said someone unkindly, "as if Wakefield has made the grade for once."

"The problem was elementary," said Wakefield smugly—forgetting, in the utterance of this rash echo, the awful dooms which the gods have decreed for those whose self-confidence is premature. "I'm not asserting that on the case I've outlined you could convict Aunt Ellen of the *murder*—even though it's pretty certain she did it. But she was arrested, I take it, for the blackmail?"

"Oh dear, no. You see, Wakefield," said Fen with aggravating tolerance, "your answer to the problem, though immensely cogent and logical, has one grave defect: it doesn't happen to be the right answer."

Wakefield was much offended. "If it *isn't* the right answer," he returned sourly, "that's only because you've not given me all the relevant facts."

"Oh, but I have. You remember my telling you about changing the ribbon in my typewriter?"

"Yes."

"And you remember my saying that one of the blackmail messages was in 'a faint and spidery typescript'?"

"So it would be, if it was typed in the afternoon, before you changed the ribbon."

"But you remember also, no doubt, my saying that apart from the words 'the quick brown fox', the second sheet was identical with the first *in every possible respect*?"

For once Wakefield was bereft of speech; he subsided, breathing heavily through his nose.

"Therefore," said Fen, "*both* messages were in faint, spidery typescript. Therefore they were *both* typed while I was playing Racing Demon. And therefore Judith's story about Odell and the typewriter and the blackmail was a deliberate pack of lies from beginning to end."

Haldane was groping for comprehension. "You mean the two messages were *planted* in Odell's drawer?"

"Certainly. At the time of the murder."

"So that in fact Odell never either sent *or* received a blackmail note at all?"

"Of course not. Neither he, nor anyone else."

"But the business about his being a deserter. . . ."

"That was genuine enough," said Fen. "But its only function in the affair was to provide Judith with raw material for her frame-up. The frame-up might well have come off, too, but for the chance of my changing the typewriter-ribbon. But for that, there'd have been no proof, other than Aunt Ellen's word, that the blackmail attempt hadn't in fact occurred. If Judith had had the sense to type the second copy of the message, the 'quick brown fox' one, after I'd gone to bed. . . . However, she didn't."

Fen twisted his glass between his fingers; drained it, and reached for the cigarette-box. "And I liked her," he murmured, as he struck a match. "That was the trouble. Until I knew the truth, I liked her very much. I liked all of them. But——"

"But you told the police about changing the ribbon."

Fen nodded briefly.

"Yes, I told them; you see, I'd liked Odell, too. . . .

"Under examination, Judith broke down and confessed to the murder. She was frightened—I mentioned that, didn't I? She'd bitten off very much more than she could chew. And since if she'd pleaded Not Guilty at her trial it would have come down to her word against mine, I was heartily relieved when she caved in. Her acting had certainly deceived *me*; and in a court-room tussle between us she might easily have got the best of it. A plea of Guilty to a murder charge is very rare, of course, but it had the great advantage, in Judith's case, of obscuring the cold-blooded attempt to incriminate Aunt Ellen, and so making a recommendation to mercy possible. So that in the end she wasn't in fact executed; the death sentence was commuted to imprisonment for life."

"And her motive for the murder?" Haldane asked.

"Jealousy. She hated Odell for jilting her in favour of her sister; and if she hadn't planted the messages in Odell's room, and spun me her fairy-tales in a sophisticated, double-bluff attempt to incriminate Aunt Ellen, she might have got away with the killing.

"But the trouble was, she was a reader of detective stories; and what she dreamed up—in the hope that everyone would make the deductions Wakefield has just been making, and probe no further—was in consequence a detective-story device. . . . I hope no one will imagine I'm mocking at detective-story devices. In point of fact, I dote on them. But so long as criminals take them for a model, the police are going to have a very easy time; because, like the wretched Judith, your genuinely murderous addict will dig his cunning and complicated pits for the investigators, only, in the upshot, to fall head first into one of them himself."

BLACK FOR A FUNERAL

AT TEN O'CLOCK ON the evening of July 24th, 1951, Police-Constable Albert Tyler set out on his bicycle from the little police-station in the village of Low Norton. He would be back from his night-beat, and reporting to his Sergeant, at twelve-thirty prompt—for both of them took a pride in punctuality. In the meantime, he had much ground to cover. Cycling steadily past the cottage where his wife was already retiring to bed, past the *Norton Arms*—whose only guest at the moment, he had heard, was an Oxford Professor seeking peace and quiet in order to finish a book—and beyond that past the diminutive church and the old almshouses, P.C. Tyler struck out on the road eastwards and was presently swallowed up by the night.

Thus began the curious affair of the disappearing car, the black neck-tie, and the abortive burglary.

Incidents on P.C. Tyler's extensive but not populous rural beat had hitherto belonged infallibly to one or other of three categories: (*a*) lost wayfarers; (*b*) poachers; and (*c*) burning ricks. Sergeant Beeton was consequently a good deal startled when at a minute to midnight Tyler rang him up to report murder. "Chap bashed on the head with a stone," gabbled Tyler, whose misfortune it was to always sound much more agitated than he actually felt. "Middle-aged. Reddish hair. Raincoat and black tie. It's at 'The Moorings'—you know. Might be that chap Derringer, who rented the place, but I've never seen him close to, so I can't be sure. He's lying in the road, just outside the gate. . . . Dead? Lord, yes: he's dead all right."

Our police forces err, if anything, on the side of economy: despite the extent of the district under his charge, Beeton had never been granted the use of a car. As a result of this, it was more than half an hour before, winded from cycling at top speed up a succession of hills, he arrived at the scene of the crime; and it was an hour more before the doctor came.

"Yes, it is Derringer," said Beeton, as he contemplated the huddled form in the shadow of the gate-post. "Poor devil. . . ." He stooped lower. "But it's queer about the clothes, Bert, isn't it? He can't have been to a *funeral*, can he?"

For the one really puzzling thing about the body was that along with the brown sports suit it wore a neat, plain black tie.

"Nor," said Sergeant Beeton somewhat pedantically, in the police-station next afternoon, "is that the only strange feature of the affair. . . . But look here, sir"—he recollected himself suddenly—"it's not right I should be bothering you about it, and——"

"No bother at all." Gervase Fen, Professor of English Language and Literature in the University of Oxford, regarded the Sergeant out of mild blue eyes. "All I'm afraid of is that I may be wasting your time. But Humbleby did tell me to look you up while I was here, so you must forgive me if I'm a nuisance. . . . You worked with Humbleby for a time, didn't you?"

"I did indeed, sir. But I found C.I.D. stuff wasn't my line, so I got a transfer back into the Uniform Branch and they sent me here. Suits me a long sight better, really. . . . As to you keeping me from my work, all I'm doing now is just marking time till the County C.I.D. man gets here. It'd be nice to be able to hand him the murderer all nicely tied up and ticketed, but the fact is, I'm downright dizzy with it all. *Nothing* makes sense."

The police-station in which they sat resembled, in all outward essentials, a small private villa. As well as being a police-station, it was Beeton's home. And its personnel consisted of Beeton and Tyler exclusively—for in spite of the overcrowding of our islands, there are still many country areas where the houses are few and far between, areas where the police-constable's beat is a dozen times the length of a city beat, where ten or fifteen square miles support as few as a couple of hundred souls, and where the tiny branch railway-lines are for ever in peril of being pronounced redundant and closed down. Such areas—of which Low Norton was one—do not require anything very elaborate in the way of policing and their police headquarters can afford to be homely as well as diminutive. It is true that Beeton, being an earnest man, not to say conscientious, had striven to give his office an official look; but in this he had not been completely successful. Thus, there were a few portentous books on the mantelpiece—*Police Regulations*, Kenny's *Criminal Law*, Stone's *Justices' Manual*; but their impressiveness was marred by a piece of knitting which had been put down on top of them. And there was a safe containing heaven knows what explosive secrets, which also contained, however, several bottles of stout and a broken toy aeroplane, belonging to Beeton's small son, which Beeton had promised several weeks ago to repair and which had been swept hurriedly out of sight, and hence forgotten, on the occasion of an unexpected visit from the Chief Constable. All this was comfortable and pleasing. And Fen, settled in a wicker chair which creaked every time he shifted his weight, looked on it with an approving eye.

Outside the open window, the village drowsed under a hot sun. Beeton's coat was unfastened; and from the room adjoining, where Constable Tyler (whose gruesome experience had left him in a state of very ill-suppressed emotion) was supposed to be writing a report, came the sound of liquid being poured from a bottle into a glass. This roused Beeton, and he resorted to the safe on behalf of his visitor and himself. And having seen to that small matter: "Yes," he said, "it's a funny business altogether. I don't know if it'd be of any interest to you to . . ."

"It would," Fen assured him. "Where crimes are concerned, I'm the one and only original Elephant's Child."

"Ele—— Ah, I get you. 'Satiable curiosity." Beeton grinned. "Well then, where do you want me to begin?"

"The first thing is, who *was* Derringer? I mean, what did he do?"

"He wrote adventure stories for boys." Beeton leaned back with an air of luxury, his heavy bulk overflowing the swivel-chair; he was the archetypal countryman, slow but intuitive, blank of eye yet with a vein of simple cunning such as all those who trap or shoot animals tend in time to acquire. "Adventure stories," he reiterated, "for boys—though they, I take it, wouldn't be about the sort of adventures he was partial to himself."

"Oh," said Fen. "Oh."

And Beeton nodded slyly.

"Yes, he was a funny bloke: mad about the women, and not too scrupulous as to whether they were married or not. But in spite of that, you couldn't help liking him—same way you can like a cat, provided you keep your pet goldfish out of its reach."

And Fen remembered Beeton's own wife, whom he had glimpsed on arrival: brunette and by no means unattractive. "Someone," he pointed out, "doesn't seem to have been quite so tolerant."

"Ah. You're right there, sir. It's the husbands of women there's been scandal about that we'll have to be keeping an eye on. . . . But now look; here's what happened:

"Derringer hadn't been renting 'The Moorings' long: not more than six months, anyway. And he was planning on starting for America some time today, with the idea of living there permanently. Well, now: last evening—according to Mrs. Jerrold, Bert Tyler's ma-in-law that is, who was Derringer's housekeeper—Derringer was due to go to a posh dinner in London. There was some sort of a quarrel about it, and at the last moment he decided not to go to the dinner. But he *did* go to *London*, by the late afternoon train. How he spent his time there, we haven't found out yet. But he came back on the train that gets to Windover Halt at 11.10, and at that time he was wearing a *green* tie; the porter who took his ticket is ready to swear to that. So the conclusion you're forced to, really, is that for some unknown reason the murderer took the green tie off, and put the black one on, after he'd done the murder. . . . Perhaps," said Beeton without much conviction, "as a sort of gruesome joke: black for a funeral, you know."

Fen nodded. "Go on."

"Derringer gets back from London at 11.10, then. And he stays at Windover Halt for twenty minutes or more, talking to the porter, who he's pally with. All right. But now here's the second queer thing. Bert Tyler found the body at five to twelve; and the trouble about that is that Windover Halt's much too far from 'The Moorings' for Derringer to have walked the distance, or even cycled it, in twenty minutes or so. He was on foot when he left the Halt—the porter's sure of that. So what it *must* mean is that somewhere on the way he was picked up by a car. . . . Only trouble is, we can't find the car."

"Can't *find* it?" Fen echoed rather blankly.

Beeton reached for a map. "See here, sir. Here's 'The Moorings'. Well now, there's only two roads away from it a car could possibly take. One direction, all the road does is just peter out at the edge of an old quarry. And in the other direction—quite apart from the fact that any car'd have had to pass Bert, and no car did—there's *this*." Beeton's stubby forefinger hovered again above the map. "Level-crossing," he explained. "It's the sort that's only opened to road traffic on demand; and there are good locks on the gates, so you can't get them open on your own. . . . Anyway, the gate-keeper's willing to take his oath that not a single car or motor-bike (apart from the doctor's) went through all last night, after a quarter to midnight. Nor none's been through today, either."

"What about before a quarter to midnight?"

"Ah. That's a bit different. Old Willis—that's the gate-keeper—he left the crossing open between 11.15 and 11.45, while he was away from his cottage. Shouldn't have done, strictly speaking, but there's no trains go through between 11.5 —that's the one Derringer came home on—and 1.30 in the morning."

"M'm. I see. To sum up, then: a car travelling from Windover Halt to 'The Moorings' would have had to go via that level-crossing. It could have got *through* all right, up to 11.45. But it wouldn't have had time to get *back*."

"That's it, sir, exactly. And I know what you're going to say now—that the car must still be somewhere in that area between the level-crossing and the old quarry beyond 'The Moorings'. Only it isn't. We've searched everywhere—woods, sandpits, barns, sheds, and of course the quarry itself. And there's not a trace of it."

Fen examined the map again; then: "I *think*," he said slowly, "that I can probably tell you what became of the car. But before I do that, let's hear the rest of it."

"Well, sir, there's only one other thing—which doesn't make sense any more than the black tie or the disappearance of the car—and that's the burglary at 'The Moorings'. Window smashed, and someone had definitely climbed in through it. Bert Tyler discovered that when he entered the house—using the door-key from Derringer's pocket, of course—to phone me after finding the body. But the thing is, that as far as we can make out, there was nothing at all taken."

With that, they both fell silent. A hay-cart rumbled past outside, and a fly sang on the pane. Though the sun was now westering, it seemed hotter than ever—and with a muttered apology, Fen rose, while Beeton swallowed the last of his stout, and set the door ajar. "If there is any through-draught," he said, "we'd better have it." And Beeton nodded. "A few questions, then, if you can bear them." Beeton nodded again. "First, if Derringer had walked home from Windover Halt, starting at 11.10 when his train got in, what time would he have arrived?"

"Well, he was quite a fast walker. Around midnight, I'd say. But——"

"Secondly, where was the doctor between 11.30 and 12.30? The doctor who examined the body, I mean."

Beeton smiled. "I was wondering if you'd think of that. It's no go, though. He was at a confinement—definitely."

"Thirdly, then, just how reliable is the evidence of the porter at Windover Halt and the evidence of the gate-keeper at the level-crossing?"

"Well, sir, as far as the porter's concerned, his evidence is *confirmed*—confirmed by two chaps who were going home late and actually saw Derringer leaving the Halt on foot, at 11.30. As to old Willis, I admit we've only got his word for it. But he's not daft, not by any manner of means, and I'm willing to take my oath he's telling the truth."

"Then here's my last question: what time was Tyler due to report back here at the end of his beat?"

"12.30, sir. And starting from 'The Moorings' at 12.0, he'd have had to pedal pretty hard to——" Beeton broke off. His eyes widened. "Good Lord, sir! You can't be thinking that *Bert*——"

"Look," said Fen. "If you haven't found a car, then there just wasn't a car. Which means that Derringer, on foot, must have reached home about 12.20. Which in turn means that Tyler's telephone call to you was a simple lie."

"But why, sir? *Why?*"

"Because Derringer was delayed, that's why. The murder had to take place last night, because Derringer was to have left for America today. On the other hand, if Tyler hung about waiting for him, he'd have to explain to you why he was so late back from his beat—and although there were plenty of excuses he *could* have made, he didn't want there to be anything out-of-the-way about his doings on a night when a murder had been committed. Well, he knew you'd need a good half-hour to get to 'The Moorings'. So he took a risk, announcing the murder as a *fait accompli* before the victim had even arrived. . . . 'Black tie', he told you; which at once suggests evening dress. *Tyler* thought that Derringer had gone to London for a posh dinner—he didn't know that that plan had been altered. So when, having killed Derringer, he found that his victim *wasn't* wearing a black tie, he was obliged to do something about it, in order that your suspicions shouldn't be aroused by a discrepancy between his statement on the telephone and the clothing you saw when you reached the scene."

"Then the burglary——"

"Wasn't a burglary at all. In order to telephone you from 'The Moorings', Tyler was obliged to break into the house since Derringer hadn't yet turned up with the keys. . . . Is Tyler married?"

"Yes. To a pretty, flighty girl, a good bit younger than him; so—— My God, what's that?"

A pistol-shot had sounded in the next room; and now the smell of cordite was in their nostrils. Cursing, Beeton leaped to his feet

"Blasted door half open," he said incoherently. "If I'd had any idea where this was leading——" Then he turned savagely to Fen. "For God's sake, man, why couldn't you keep your voice down? Why——" He checked himself. As comprehension came, his anger faded as quickly as it had arisen. "Oh, I see. Yes. You——"

"I get on well with policemen," said Fen. "That's all. And if it can be avoided, I don't like seeing their good name dragged through the mud; for the reason, you understand, that the good name is genuine and deserved. So what could be more natural than that a constable, who sometimes has to handle guns, should be involved in an accident?"

He got up and moved towards the door. "Come on, Beeton," he said. "Let's make sure that it *was* an accident."

THE NAME ON THE WINDOW

BOXING DAY; snow and ice; road-surface like glass under a cold fog. In the North Oxford home of the University Professor of English Language and Literature, at three minutes past seven in the evening, the front door bell rang.

The current festive season had taken heavy toll of Fen's vitalitv and patience; it had culminated, that afternoon, in a quite exceptionally tiring children's party, amid whose ruins he was now recouping his energies with whisky; and on hearing the bell he jumped inevitably to the conclusion that one of the infants he had bundled out of the door half an hour previously had left behind it some such prized inessential as a false nose or a bachelor's button, and was returning to claim this. In the event, however, and despite his premonitory groans, this assumption proved to be incorrect: his doorstep was occupied, he found, not by a dyspeptic, over-heated child with an unintelligible query, but by a neatly-dressed greying man with a red tip to his nose and woebegone eyes.

"I can't get back," said this apparition. "I really can't get back to London tonight. The roads are impassable and such trains as there are are running hours late. Could you possibly let me have a bed?"

The tones were familiar; and by peering more attentively at the face, Fen discovered that that was familiar too. "My dear Humbleby," he said cordially, "do come in. Of course you can have a bed. What are you doing in this part of the world, anyway?"

"Ghost-hunting." Detective-Inspector Humbleby, of New Scotland Yard, divested himself of his coat and hat and hung them on a hook inside the door. "Seasonable but not convenient." He stamped his feet violently, thereby producing, to judge from his expression, sensations of pain rather than of warmth; and stared about him. "*Children*," he said with sudden gloom. "I dare say that one of the Oxford hotels——"

"The children have left," Fen explained, "and will not be coming back."

"Ah. Well, in that case——" And Humbleby followed Fen into the drawing-room, where a huge fire was burning and a slightly lop-sided Christmas tree, stripped of its treasures, wore tinsel and miniature witch-balls and a superincumbent fairy with a raffish air. "My word, this is better. Is there a drink, perhaps? I could do with some advice, too."

Fen was already pouring whisky. "Sit down and be comfortable," he said. "As a matter of interest, do you believe in ghosts?"

"The evidence for *poltergeists*," Humbleby answered warily as he stretched out his hands to the blaze, "seems very convincing to me. . . . The Wesleys, you know, and Harry Price and so forth. Other sorts of ghosts I'm not so sure about—though I must say I *hope* they exist, if only for the purpose of taking that silly grin off the faces of the newspapers." He picked up a battered tin locomotive from beside him on the sofa. "I say, Gervase, I was under the impression that your own children were all too old for——"

"Orphans," said Fen, jabbing at the siphon. "I've been entertaining orphans from a nearby Home. . . . But as regards this particular ghost you were speaking of——"

"Oh, I don't believe in *that*." Humbleby shook his head decisively. "There's an obscure sort of nastiness about the place it's supposed to haunt—like a very sickly cake gone stale—and a man *was* killed there once, by a girl he was trying to persuade to certain practices she didn't relish at all; but the haunting part of it is just silly gossip for the benefit of visitors." Humbleby accepted the glass which Fen held out to him and brooded over it for a moment before drinking. ". . . Damned Chief-Inspector," he muttered aggrievedly, "dragging me away from my Christmas lunch because——"

"Really, Humbleby"—Fen was severe—"you're very inconsequent this evening. Where is this place you're speaking of?"

"Rydalls."

"Rydalls?"

"Rydalls," said Humbleby. "The residence," he elucidated laboriously, "of Sir Charles Moberley, the architect. It's about fifteen miles from here, Abingdon way."

"Yes, I remember it now. Restoration."

"I dare say. Old, in any case. And there are big grounds, with an eighteenth-century pavilion about a quarter of a mile away from the house, in a park. That's where it happened—the murder, I mean."

"The murder of the man who tried to induce the girl——"

"No, no. I mean, yes. *That* murder took place in the pavilion, certainly. But then, so did the other one—the one the day before yesterday, that's to say."

Fen stared. "Sir Charles Moberley has been murdered?"

"No, no, no. Not *him*. Another architect, another knight—

Sir Lucas Welsh. There's been quite a large house-party going on at Rydalls, with Sir Lucas Welsh and his daughter Jane among the guests, and it was on Christmas Eve, you see, that Sir Lucas decided he wanted to investigate the ghost."

"This is all clear enough to you, no doubt, but——"

"Do *listen*. . . . It seems that Sir Lucas is—was—credulous about ghosts, so on Christmas Eve he arranged to keep vigil alone in the pavilion and——"

"And was murdered, and you don't know who did it."

"Oh yes, I do. Sir Lucas didn't die at once, you see: he had time to write up his murderer's name in the grime of the window-pane, and the gentleman concerned, a young German named Otto Mörike, is now safely under arrest. But what I can't decide is how Mörike got in and out of the pavilion."

"A locked-room mystery."

"In the wider sense, just that. The pavilion wasn't actually locked, but——"

Fen collected his glass from the mantelpiece, where he had put it on rising to answer the door-bell. "Begin," he suggested, "at the beginning."

"Very well." Settling back in the sofa, Humbleby sipped his whisky gratefully. "Here, then, is this Christmas house-party at Rydalls. Host, Sir Charles Moberley, the eminent architect. . . . Have you ever come across him?"

Fen shook his head.

"A big man, going grey: in some ways rather boisterous and silly, like a rugger-playing medical student in a state of arrested development. Unmarried; private means—quite a lot of them, to judge from the sort of hospitality he dispenses; did the Wandsworth power-station and Beckford Abbey, among other things; athlete; a simple mind, and generous, I should judge, in that jealous sort of way which resents generosity in anyone else. Probably tricky, in some respects—he's not the kind of person *I* could ever feel completely at ease with.

"A celebrity, however: unquestionably that. And Sir Lucas Welsh, whom among others he invited to this house-party, was equally a celebrity, in the same line of business. Never having seen Sir Lucas alive, I can't say much about his character, but——"

"I think," Fen interrupted, "that I may have met him once, at the time when he was designing the fourth quadrangle for my college. A small dark person, wasn't he?"

"Yes, that's right."

"And with a tendency to be nervy and obstinate."

"The obstinacy there's evidence for, certainly. And I gather he was also a good deal of a faddist—Yogi, I mean, and the Baconian hypothesis, and a lot of other intellectual—um—detritus of the same dull, obvious kind: that's where the ghost-vigil comes in. Jane, his daughter and heiress (and Sir Lucas was if anything even better off than Sir Charles) is a pretty little thing of eighteen of whom all you can really say is that she's a pretty little thing of eighteen. Then there's Mörike, the man I've arrested: thin, thirtyish, a Luftwaffe pilot during the war, and at present an architecture-student working over here under one of these exchange schemes the Universities are always getting up—which accounts for Sir Charles's knowing him and inviting him to the house-party. Last of the important guests—important from the point of view of the crime, that is—is a C.I.D. man (not Metropolitan, Sussex County) called James Wilburn. He's important because the evidence he provides is quite certainly reliable—there has to be a *point d'appui* in these affairs, and Wilburn is it, so you mustn't exhaust yourself doubting his word about anything."

"I won't," Fen promised. "I'll believe him."

"Good. At dinner on Christmas Eve, then, the conversation turns to the subject of the Rydalls ghost—and I've ascertained that the person responsible for bringing this topic up was Otto Mörike. So far, so good: the Rydalls ghost was a bait Sir Lucas could be relied on to rise to, and rise to it he did, arranging eventually with his rather reluctant host to go down to the pavilion after dinner and keep watch there for an hour or two. The time arriving, he was accompanied to the place of trial by Sir Charles and by Wilburn—neither of whom actually *entered* the pavilion. Wilburn strolled back to the house alone, leaving Sir Charles and Sir Lucas talking shop. And presently Sir Charles, having seen Sir Lucas go into the pavilion, retraced his steps likewise, arriving at the house just in time to hear the alarm-bell ringing."

"Alarm-bell?"

"People had watched for the ghost before, and there was a bell installed in the pavilion for them to ring if for any reason they wanted help. . . . This bell sounded, then, at shortly after ten o'clock, and a whole party of people, including Sir Charles, Jane Welsh and Wilburn, hastened to the rescue.

"Now, you must know that this pavilion is quite small. There's just one circular room to it, having two windows (both very firmly nailed up); and you get into this room by way of a longish, narrow hall projecting from the perimeter of the circle, the one and only door being at the outer end of this hall."

"Like a key-hole," Fen suggested. "If you saw it from the air it'd look like a key-hole, I mean; with the round part representing the room, and the part where the wards go in representing the entrance-hall, and the door right down at the bottom."

"That's it. It stands in a clearing among the trees of the park, on a very slight rise—inferior Palladian in style, with pilasters or whatever you call them: something like a decayed miniature classical temple. No one's bothered about it for decades, not since that earlier murder put an end to its career as a love-nest for a succession of squires. What is it Eliot says?—something about lusts and dead limbs? Well, anyway, that's the impression it gives. A *house* is all right, because a house has been used for other things as well—eating and reading and births and deaths and so on. But this place has been used for one purpose and one purpose only, and that's exactly what it feels like. . . .

"There's no furniture in it, by the way. And until the wretched Sir Lucas unlocked its door, no one had been inside it for two or three years.

"To get back to the story, then.

"The weather was all right: you'll remember that on Christmas Eve none of this snow and foulness had started. And the rescue-party, so to call them, seem to have regarded their expedition as more or less in the nature of a jaunt; I mean that they weren't seriously alarmed at the ringing of the bell, with the exception of Jane, who knew her father well enough to suspect that he'd never have interrupted his vigil, almost as soon as it had begun, for the sake of a rather futile practical joke; and even she seems to have allowed herself to be half convinced by the reassurances of the others. On arrival at the pavilion, they found the door shut but not locked; and when they opened it, and shone their torches inside, they saw a single set of footprints in the dust on the hall floor, leading to the entrance to the circular room. Acting on instinct or training or both, Wilburn kept his crowd clear of these footprints; and so it was that they came—joined now by Otto Mörike, who according to his subsequent statement had been taking a solitary stroll in the grounds—to the scene of the crime.

"Fireplace, two windows, a crudely painted ceiling—crude in subject as well as in execution—a canvas chair, an unlit electric torch, festoons of cobwebs, and on everything except the chair and the torch *dust*, layers of it. Sir Lucas was lying on the floor beneath one of the windows, quite close to the bell-push; and an old stiletto, later discovered to have been stolen from the house, had been stuck into him under the left shoulder-blade (no damning fingerprints on it, by the way; or on anything else in the vicinity). Sir Lucas was still alive, and just conscious. Wilburn bent over him to ask who was responsible. And a queer smile crossed Sir Lucas's face, and he was just able to whisper"—here Humbleby produced and consulted a notebook—"to whisper: *'Wrote it—on the window. Very first thing I did when I came round. Did it before I rang the bell or anything else, in case you didn't get here in time—in time for me to tell you who——'*

"His voice faded out then. But with a final effort he moved his head, glanced up at the window, nodded and smiled again. That was how he died.

"They had all heard him, and they all looked. There was bright moonlight outside, and the letters traced on the grimy pane stood out clearly.

"Otto.

"Well, it seems that then Otto started edging away, and Sir Charles made a grab at him, and they fought, and presently a wallop from Sir Charles sent Otto clean through the tell-tale window, and Sir Charles scrambled after him, and they went on fighting outside, trampling the glass to smithereens, until Wilburn and company joined in and put a stop to it. Incidentally, Wilburn says that Otto's going through the window looked *contrived* to him—a deliberate attempt to destroy evidence; though of course, so many people *saw* the name written there that it remains perfectly good evidence in spite of having been destroyed."

"Motive?" Fen asked.

"Good enough. Jane Welsh was wanting to marry Otto—had fallen quite dementedly in love with him, in fact—and her father didn't approve; partly on the grounds that Otto was a German, and partly because he thought the boy wanted Jane's prospective inheritance rather than Jane herself. To clinch it, moreover, there was the fact that Otto had been in the Luftwaffe and that Jane's mother had been killed in 1941 in an air-raid. Jane being only eighteen years of age—and the attitude of magistrates, if appealed to, being in the circumstances at best problematical—it looked as if that was one marriage that would definitely not take place. So the killing of Sir Lucas had, from Otto's point of view, a double advantage: it made Jane rich, and it removed the obstacle to the marriage."

"Jane's prospective guardian not being against it."

"Jane's prospective guardian being an uncle she could twist round her little finger. . . . But here's the point." Humbleby leaned forward earnestly. "Here is the point: windows nailed shut; no secret doors—emphatically none; chimney too narrow to admit a baby; and in the dust on the hall floor, only one set of footprints, made unquestionably by Sir Lucas himself. . . . If you're thinking that Otto might have walked in and out on top of those prints, as that page-boy we've been hearing so much about recently did with King Wenceslaus, then you're wrong. Otto's feet are much too large, for one thing, and the prints hadn't been disturbed, for another: so that's out. But then, how on earth did he manage it? There's no furniture in that hall whatever—nothing he could have used to crawl across, nothing he could have swung himself from. It's a long, bare box, that's all; and the distance between the door and the circular room (in which room, by the way, the dust on the floor was all messed up by the rescue-party) is miles too far for anyone to have jumped it. Nor was the weapon the sort of thing that could possibly have been fired from a bow or an air-gun or a blowpipe, or any nonsense of that sort; nor was it sharp enough or heavy enough to have penetrated as deeply as it did if it had been *thrown*. So ghosts apart, what *is* the explanation? Can you see one?"

Fen made no immediate reply. Throughout this narrative he had remained standing, draped against the mantelpiece. Now he moved, collecting Humbleby's empty glass and his own and carrying them across to the decanter; and it was only after they were refilled that he spoke.

"Supposing," he said, "that Otto had crossed the entrance hall on a tricycle——"

"A tricycle!" Humbleby was dumbfounded. "A——"

"A tricycle, yes," Fen reiterated firmly. "Or supposing, again, that he had laid down a carpet, unrolling it in front of him as he entered and rolling it up again after him when he left. . . ."

"But the dust!" wailed Humbleby. "Have I really not made it clear to you that apart from the footprints the dust on the floor was undisturbed? Tricycles, carpets. . . ."

"A section of the floor at least," Fen pointed out, "was trampled on by the rescue-party."

"Oh, that. . . . Yes, but that didn't happen until after Wilburn had examined the floor."

"Examined it in detail?"

"Yes. At that stage they still didn't realise anything was wrong; and when Wilburn led them in they were giggling behind him while he did a sort of parody of detective work, throwing the beam of his torch over every inch of the floor in a pretended search for bloodstains."

"It doesn't," said Fen puritanically, "sound the sort of performance which would amuse me very much."

"I dare say not. Anyway, the point about it is that Wilburn's ready to swear that the dust was completely unmarked and undisturbed except for the footprints. . . . I wish he weren't ready to swear that," Humbleby added dolefully, "because that's what's holding me up. But I can't budge him."

"You oughtn't to be trying to budge him, anyway,' retorted Fen, whose mood of self-righteousness appeared to be growing on him. "It's unethical. What about blood, now?"

"Blood? There was practically none of it. You don't get any bleeding to speak of from that narrow type of wound."

"Ah. Just one more question, then; and if the answer's what I expect, I shall be able to tell you how Otto worked it."

"If by any remote chance," said Humbleby suspiciously, "it's *stilts* that you have in mind——"

"My dear Humbleby, don't be so puerile."

Humbleby contained himself with an effort. "Well?" he said.

"The name on the window." Fen spoke almost dreamily. "Was it written in *capital* letters?"

Whatever Humbleby had been expecting, it was clearly not this. "Yes," he answered. "But——"

"Wait." Fen drained his glass. "Wait while I make a telephone call."

He went. All at once restless, Humbleby got to his feet, lit a cheroot, and began pacing the room. Presently he discovered an elastic-driven aeroplane abandoned behind an armchair, wound it up and launched it. It caught Fen a glancing blow on the temple as he reappeared in the doorway, and thence flew on into the hall, where it struck and smashed a vase. "Oh, I say, I'm sorry," said Humbleby feebly. Fen said nothing.

But after about half a minute, when he had simmered down a bit: "Locked rooms," he remarked sourly. "Locked rooms. . . . I'll tell you what it is, Humbleby: you've been reading too much fiction; you've got locked rooms on the brain."

Humbleby thought it politic to be meek. "Yes," he said.

"Gideon Fell once gave a very brilliant lecture on The Locked-Room Problem, in connection with that business of the Hollow Man; but there was one category he didn't include."

"Well?"

Fen massaged his forehead resentfully. "He didn't include the locked-room mystery which *isn't* a locked-room mystery: like this one. So that the explanation of how Otto got into and out of that circular room is simple: he didn't get into or out of it at all."

Humbleby gaped. "But Sir Lucas can't have been knifed before he *entered* the circular room. Sir Charles said——"

"Ah yes. Sir Charles saw him go in—or so he asserts. And——"

"Stop a bit." Humbleby was much perturbed. "I can see what you're getting at, but there are serious objections to it."

"Such as?"

"Well, for one thing, Sir Lucas *named* his murderer."

"A murderer who struck at him *from behind*. . . . Oh, I've no doubt Sir Lucas acted in good faith: Otto, you see, would be the only member of the house-party whom Sir Lucas *knew* to have a *motive*. In actual fact, Sir Charles had one too—as I've just discovered. But Sir Lucas wasn't aware of that; and in any case, he very particularly didn't want Otto to marry his daughter after his death, so that the risk of doing an ex-Luftwaffe man an injustice was a risk he was prepared to take. . . . Next objection?"

"The name on the window. If, as Sir Lucas said, his *very first* action on recovering consciousness was to denounce his attacker, then he'd surely, since he was capable of entering the pavilion after being knifed, have been capable of writing the name on the *outside* of the window, which would be nearest, and which was just as grimy as the inside. That objection's based, of course, on your assumption that he was struck before he ever entered the pavilion."

"I expect he did just that—wrote the name on the outside of the window, I mean."

"But the people who saw it were on the *inside*. Inside a bank, for instance, haven't you ever noticed how the bank's name——"

"The name Otto," Fen interposed, "is a palindrome. That's to say, it reads the same backwards as forwards. What's more, the capital letters used in it are symmetrical—not like B or P or R or S, but like A or H or M. So write it on the outside of a window, and it will look exactly the same from the inside."

"My God, yes." Humbleby was sobered. "I never thought of that. And the fact that the name was on the *outside* would be fatal to Sir Charles, after his assertion that he'd seen Sir Lucas enter the pavilion unharmed, so I suppose that the 'contriving' Wilburn noticed in the fight was Sir Charles's, not

Otto's: he'd realise that the name *must* be on the outside—Sir Lucas having said that the writing of it was the very first thing he did—and he'd see the need to destroy the window before anyone could investigate closely. . . . Wait, though: couldn't Sir Lucas have entered the pavilion as Sir Charles said, and later emerged again, and——"

"One set of footprints," Fen pointed out, "on the hall floor. Not three."

Humbleby nodded. "I've been a fool about this. Locked rooms, as you said, on the brain. But what *was* Sir Charles's motive—the motive Sir Lucas didn't know about?"

"Belchester," said Fen. "Belchester Cathedral. As you know, it was bombed during the war, and a new one's going to be built. Well, I've just rung up the Dean, who's an acquaintance of mine, to ask about the choice of architect; and he says that it was a toss-up between Sir Charles's design and Sir Lucas's, and that Sir Lucas's won. The two men were notified by post, and it seems likely that Sir Charles's notification arrived on the morning of Christmas Eve. Sir Lucas's did too, in all probability; but Sir Lucas's was sent to his home, and even forwarded it can't, in the rush of Christmas postal traffic, have reached him at Rydalls before he was killed. So only Sir Charles *knew*; and since with Sir Lucas dead Sir Charles's design would have been accepted. . . ." Fen shrugged. "Was it money, I wonder? Or was it just the blow to his professional pride? Well, well. Let's have another drink before you telephone. In the hangman's shed it will all come to the same thing."

THE GOLDEN MEAN

IT WAS IN THE village of Çhigfold, isolated on a corner of one of the Devon moors, that Gervase Fen encountered the only man who has ever seemed to him to be definitely evil.

A word like 'evil' needs (he will tell you) to be used with precaution: the descent of Avernus has no milestones which mark out for the traveller—or for others watching him—the stages of his journey. And yet at the same time there is, perhaps, somewhere along it a Point of No Return. On the maps of infamy it is never shown, since for each individual its location will be different. Moreover, the setting foot across it, in the downward direction, involves a spiritual crisis so acute, and an effort of will so intolerably degrading, that it is only very rarely passed. But that young St. John Leavis had passed it, Fen never for a moment doubted. It was not the attempted parricide which produced this overwhelming conviction; that, horrible though it was, seemed to Fen merely the ratification of a treaty already concluded. Rather, it was a wholesale reversal of normal personality which you scented the instant you met the man, and which made even the dullest-witted of ordinary wholesome sinners inexplicably uneasy in his company.

Yet there was nothing you could put your finger on, saying '*This* is the mark of the beast'. In all externals St. John Leavis was charming; and even if he were now and again petulant, that petulance so closely resembled the petulance of a child that it took you off-guard, compelling you to assume, against your better judgment, that there was a child's innocence underlying it. At the time when Fen met him, at Chigfold, he was just twenty-five years old—a good-looking young man with crisp, curly fair hair and big light-blue eyes. Laziness, and self-indulgence, had thickened his neck, had fattened his cheeks and chin, blurring, like a gauze, their original fineness, but he remained unusually personable in spite of that. His tastes were literary; his conversation was witty; his manners were impeccable. And by the end of the first five minutes of their acquaintance, Fen detested him.

It was irrational, of course—quite irrational and unfair: in discussing the matter(which he is oddly reluctant to do), Fen confines himself to a simple statement of the fact, making no attempt to justify it. Spiritual issues are irrelevant, in any case, he says, so long as a story is all you want: the act of violence was unquestionably an act of self-interest, and you are quite at liberty to rest content with that—which is a perfectly adequate explanation in itself—and to refuse to delve deeper. The fact remains, however, that to an actual participant the overtones were infinitely more impressive than the note which produced them; and it appears that the only person who was altogether deaf to those overtones, until the terror at last unstopped his ears, was St. John's victim, his father.

This—in Fen's opinion—was to be expected. The mere temperamental contrast between father and son was a formidable barrier to mutual understanding in itself, even if you left aside the natural blindness which goes with kinship and over-familiarity. For George Seymour Leavis differed from St. John in every important particular. At forty-seven he was boisterous, 'sporty', an open-air man; red in the face, active, a faddist in his diet, an unconquerably simple mind. He had made money, a good deal of it, out of steel. St. John, on the contrary, had never made any money out of anything, and avowedly had no intention of trying. And of this attitude, his father, as a self-made man, very definitely disapproved, with the result that St. John's allowance was exiguous, and he was forced, if he wanted a change from the great sooty Victorian-Gothic house in the midlands, to take his holidays—as on the present occasion—in company with Leavis senior. In this circumstance lay the more superficial explanation of the attempt to kill: Mrs. Leavis had died years before, and St. John was his father's sole heir.

The inn at Chigfold had three guest-rooms; and during that last week of April 1949 they were all occupied, two of them by the Leavises and the third by Fen, who was filling in time before returning to Oxford for the Trinity term. St. John drank, and read, and complained inoffensively of boredom; his father, and Fen, walked—together, for the most part, in the companionable silence which both of them liked better, while exercising, than conversation. Thus uneventfully the first part of the holiday went by. But there came a day when Fen found himself obliged to go walking alone: Leavis *père* had taken the bus into Tawton, twelve miles away across the moor, in order to attend a Rotary luncheon, and since he had decided to return to Chigfold on foot, would not be in until nightfall. St. John was no walker, even if Fen had had the slightest wish for his company, and in any case was proposing to drive into Barnstaple for the afternoon and evening, and see a film. After an early tea, therefore, Fen put on a mackintosh, recovered his stick from the teeth of the over-exuberant wolf-hound which was supposed to protect the inn against burglars, and thus equipped, set out on his own. Outside the inn, he hesitated. The road running through the little stone-built village beckoned impartially in either direction. But it was on Barnstaple that he turned his back, towards Nag's Tor and Tawton that he went. Leavis senior had hitherto shown a marked preference for the Barnstaple direction; and this fact, by provoking in Fen a natural reaction as soon as he was left to his own devices, was destined to save Leavis senior's life.

From Chigfold to Nag's Tor is a matter of some seven miles across deserted, wind-swept moorland. There is a road, of course—a white road which dips and rises, following the contours of the land like a stretched tape; but except in summer, pedestrians are as rare on it as vehicles, and Fen reached his goal, towards twilight, without having encountered a single living soul. He paused, staring up at the prominence—turf- and heather-covered, with outcrops of flaky-looking rock—in whose shape, viewed from the proper angle by a strenuously imaginative man, something dimly equine was said to be discernible. Then he began to climb. It was a longer and steeper ascent than it had seemed from the road; and the rocky gullies, when you actually came to them, were revealed as tolerably deep and dangerous. Fen reached the summit safely, however. And it was not until he was descending again—by the slopes *away* from the road—that he happened on the elder Leavis's body.

It lay sprawled and still at the foot of a high pile of rocks—hands clutching, left leg twisted. The drop was a big one, so that Fen, scrambling down circuitously, had little hope that Leavis would be still alive. Pulse imperceptible, he found. But when, after polishing his cigarette-case on his sleeve, he applied it to the pale, sagging lips, it grew ever so faintly misty; with the result that on hearing the distant drone of a car coming up the road he turned and ran, stumbling hurriedly down the lower slopes of the Tor to intercept what proved to be a baker's van. Having given urgent instructions to its driver, he made his way back to Leavis; and since it would obviously be more risky to move the man, and try to apply first aid, than to leave him as he lay, Fen occupied himself, while he waited, in studying the scene.

His examination was unrewarding, however. That Leavis had fallen from the top of the rocks was plain enough—but as to whether the thing had happened by accident or by design, there was no evidence, for the ground was too dry to take footprints. A gleam of gold, in a tuft of grass immediately beside the body, led to the discovery of a watch which might well have dropped from Leavis's waistcoat pocket as he fell. But Fen refrained from touching it, for fear of obliterating fingerprints (a precaution which was eventually nullified by the Tawton Inspector of Police, who apparently felt no such qualms); and when he came to consider the problem of whether it belonged to Leavis or not, he found he could remember no occasion in their brief acquaintance on which any question of watches, or the time of day, had arisen. . . . Presently, the light having become too poor for such work, Fen abandoned his search of the area, perched himself on a rock, and lit a cigarette. That mere motive is no proof of attempted murder, he was well aware; yet the feelings which St. John had aroused in him were such that the possibility of accident scarcely even crossed his mind. Proof was the problem—*proof*. And he was still pondering it, still vainly, when the police and the ambulance arrived.

Three days more, and the injured man was sufficiently recovered to be able to talk to visitors.

He had been fairly badly damaged—a broken leg, a broken finger, two broken ribs; and if he had been left to lie out on the moors all night, shock would certainly have finished him. Once that was remedied, however, the doctors pronounced him out of danger, for there was no injury either to the skull or to the internal organs. And if he still looked sick and pale and withdrawn when Fen went to see him at the Tawton Cottage Hospital—well, there was perhaps another reason for that. Entering, Fen had passed St. John who was on his way out, and the rage and fright which he had glimpsed in that plump young face, before the shutters dropped and the expected commonplaces passed between them, had appalled him. It was as well, Fen reflected, that he had succeeded in badgering Inspector Waycott into leaving a man on guard, night and day, in the patient's room.

The patient himself was making a gallant attempt to appear normal. "Damned stupidity," he whispered hoarsely, "losing my balance like that. High time I packed it up, if I'm going to nearly kill myself every time I go out alone. . . . I was wanting to see you, though, because they tell me it was you who found me. Lucky you happened along. . . . Thanks, anyway: thanks a lot."

For a minute or two they talked constrainedly. Then Fen noticed, on the bedside table, the watch he had discovered lying beside Leavis's body, and picked it up. Flipping it open, he noted idly that it was an English watch with a fourteen-carat gold case: plain but expensive. "I'm glad this didn't come to any harm," he said. "It's a nice thing."

Leavis nodded in a superficially casual manner; but now he was watching his visitor warily. "I'm glad, too," he answered. "It was my father gave it me, for my twenty-firster, and I shouldn't have liked to have it damaged."

"Ah." Fen returned the watch to its place. "Well, I'd better leave you now, I think, or the nurse'll start nagging me." But as he turned to go, a defect in the little room, of which subconsciously he had been aware since his arrival, suddenly took substance in his mind. "I thought you had a policeman on guard here," he said sharply. "What's happened to him?"

Leavis smiled feebly. "All a lot of nonsense," he said. "When the Inspector came to see me, earlier on, I told him to take the chap away. Anyone'd think someone had tried to murder me."

"Yes, well, someone might have, you know," Fen countered. "We couldn't be sure about that, till you came round."

"Nonsense." Leavis spoke with a throaty vehemence which verged on anger. "Utter nonsense." And with that Fen was obliged to be content.

Outside the hospital he paused, unsure of his next move. It was a moral certainty, he thought, that St. John had pushed his father off the rocks at Nag's Tor; but even if Leavis had been prepared to denounce his son—which patently he was not; and with the tutelary policeman removed from the room at the hospital they had now had the opportunity to patch up a story between them—even then, there was no *proof* of that odious young man's guilt. A second attempt? Fen thought it by no means impossible: no man can be on his guard *all* the time, even if he knows in what quarter the danger lies. Moreover, Leavis now possessed a knowledge so dangerous to his son that, even if he were sensible enough to disinherit the boy immediately, he would still remain in constant peril on account of his knowledge alone. On the other hand, if the police were to find some definite indication that St. John was responsible for the Nag's Tor affair, and he *knew* that they had found it, then the father would be relatively safe, in that another suspicious incident would be too big a risk to be worth taking. Some definite indication. . . . But what?

Fen is not, as a rule, much impressed by the operations of chance. But he thinks it at least vaguely portentous that during these reflections he should have been wandering aimlessly into the little town of Tawton; and that on asking himself the crucial question stated above he should have returned to awareness of his surroundings to find himself gazing blankly at the watches displayed in a jeweller's window. *14ct. gold,* he read on a label, *as new*. And reading it, he remembered something he had once encountered in a book. And remembering, he did a simple sum in his head. And when that was accomplished, he walked with a light step to Tawton police-station and asked for Inspector Waycott.

It cannot be said that Waycott was pleased to see him, for Waycott was a choleric man with a streak of real viciousness in his make-up, who had all along made a point of keeping Fen at arm's length. This had not perturbed Fen greatly, other than at the moment when the Inspector's carelessness had obliterated the fingerprints which might have established the watch's ownership; the only matter on which he had insisted had been the posting of a man in Leavis's room at the hospital. But in that he had got his way only by employing crude threats concerning his influence at the Home Office (which as a matter of fact was non-existent), so that he was scarcely surprised by the unfriendly welcome he received now.

"No, sir," said Waycott irritably. "It's finished, I tell you. Tied up and done with. Mr. Leavis has said it was an accident, and there's no reason, to my mind, for thinking anything different. Admittedly there's no proof his son went into Barnstaple that afternoon, but then, there's no proof he didn't, either. And now, my time's valuable even if yours isn't, so if you'll kindly let me get on with my work . . ."

"You're ordering me out, are you?" said Fen mildly. "You're not prepared to listen to what I have to say?"

With his clenched fist Waycott struck the desk a blow which rattled the ink-pots. "I'm telling you to get out and stay out, d'you hear? And to stop poking your superior nose into what doesn't concern you."

"Yes. Yes." Fen regarded him with interest. "Just get your Chief Constable here and repeat that in front of him, will you?" His tone altered. "Listen to me, Waycott, and try not to be more of a fool than you have to. There was a watch—as even you will remember—lying beside Leavis when I found him. It's in his room at the hospital now, and he's just stated definitely to me—no, don't interrupt—that his father gave it to him for his twenty-first birthday.

"But, d'you see, Waycott, it's an English watch with a fourteen-carat gold case. And the fourteen-carat standard wasn't introduced here till 1932, when it replaced the twelve-carat and fifteen-carat standards as a sort of compromise, a mean, between them. What follows? Well, this is 1949, and Leavis is forty-seven years old. And if you'll do a little sum on your blotter, you'll find that Leavis must have celebrated his twenty-first birthday in 1923, or 1924 at the latest. In other words, he's lying about that watch. It isn't his at all. And you can guess *why* he's lying, Waycott, can't you?"

The Inspector, whose first reaction to this lecture had been to deflect or stifle it at any cost, had grown quieter as it proceeded, and by the end was visibly shaken, with all the fight gone out of him. He sketched a gesture of defeat and slumped back into his chair. "You mean the watch is really the boy's, and it was the boy's pocket it fell out of?"

"That is indicated, yes."

Waycott considered the implications of this. "Well, if it *is* the boy's," he said, "there oughtn't to be much difficulty about proving it. . . ." Then he frowned. "But so long as the father insists it was all an accident, there's no *case*. He can just say his son *lent* him the watch, or something like that."

"Only that isn't what he's just told me," Fen pointed out. "Of course, the danger is that he'll retract that particular lie about the watch as soon as he gets a hint of where it's leading us—that he'll say he was tired and ill and bored and in pain, and simply mumbled the first thing that came into his head in order to get rid of me. . . . On the other hand, if we could get him to *repeat* the lie, we really should have something. I say, Waycott, how about you going along to the hospital now, on some pretext, and seeing if you can induce him to tell you the same story? It's a pity to *use* the poor man so ruthlessly, when he's trying to shield his ghastly son, but it'd be for his own protection." And Fen explained just how he believed it would be for the elder Leavis's protection.

Without another word, Waycott got up and went; and in under twenty minutes he was back again.

"Yes, he did repeat it," he said. "So if it's ever needed, it'll be pretty awkward to explain away. But there's still no *case*, mind. All we can do now is go to that young devil and tell him what we know, and hope that that'll keep him quiet for the future." He hesitated. "I suppose that's *my* job, really, but unless I'm actually *charging* him with something. . . ."

"No," said Fen. "Not your job at all. I'll do it."

And so it came about that on that same evening, in the inn at Chigfold, Gervase Fen paid a visit to the bedroom of the only man who has ever seemed to him to be definitely evil. In the public bar below they heard voices raised, and presently the landlord saw Fen coming away with a sweat and a pallor like sickness on him. What was said in that bedroom no one has ever learned. But the landlord will tell you that Fen got precious little sleep that night, to judge by the look of him when he paid his bill next morning and left.

OTHERWHERE

SEVEN O'CLOCK.

The gathering darkness was accentuated by a fog which had appeared dispiritedly at about tea-time. Looking across the river, you could no longer make out the half-demolished Festival buildings on the far side; and although October was still young, the sooty trees on the Embankment had already surrendered their stoic green to the first spears of the cold, and there were few homekeeping folk hardy enough to resist the temptation of a fire. Presently, to a servile nation-wide juggling with clocks, Summer Time would officially end. In the meanwhile, it seemed that Nature's edict had anticipated Parliament's by a matter of several days; so that more than one belated office-worker, scurrying to catch his bus in Whitehall or the Strand, shivered a little, and hunched his shoulders, as he met the cold vapour creeping into London from the Thames. . . .

In a room high up in a corner of New Scotland Yard, a room where the lights had had to be turned on more than two hours ago, Detective-Inspector Humbleby produced a sherry dedecanter and two glasses from a filing-cabinet implausibly marked 'Jewel Thefts', and displayed them to his visitor, who said: "I didn't know you were allowed to keep drink on the premises."

"We're not." Humbleby poured the sherry without any special sign of perturbation. "And I," he added, "am the only officer in the entire building who does. There's discipline for you. . . . But look here, Gervase, are you sure you wouldn't like to go on to the club, or wherever we're dining, and let me join you as soon as this call has come through?"

"No, no." And Gervase Fen, Professor of English Language and Literature in the University of Oxford, shook his head emphatically. "It's perfectly comfortable here. What's more, your sherry"—he sipped experimentally, and his face brightened—"your sherry is too good to leave. But what is the call? Anything important?"

"A routine report. From a pleasant though rather ponderous colleague called Bolsover, of the Mid-Wessex C.I.D. They dragged me in to work with him on a case," said Humbleby without relish, "arising out of primitive rustic passions. Tuesday and Wednesday I was on the spot where the thing happened, but then yesterday I had to travel back here so as to give evidence this morning at the Elderton trial, and Bolsover promised to telephone me here this evening and let me know if there was anything new."

"What sort of a case?"

"Murder. It makes my twentieth this year. There are times when I wish I'd specialised in art forgeries, or something peaceful and infrequent like that. Lloyd Jones, who's our best man for that kind of thing, has done practically damn-all for the last six months. . . . However, it's no use moaning, I suppose."

"Will you have to go back to Wessex?"

"Yes, tomorrow—unless in the meantime Bolsover's solved the thing on his own. I'm rather hoping he has, and that that's why he's late with his call." Humbleby raised his sherry-glass to the light and contemplated its contents with solemn gloom. "It's been an exasperating business, and the sooner it's done with, the better I shall be pleased. I don't like Wessex, either. I don't like any sort of bucolic place."

"Well, but what is the problem?"

"An alibi. We know who *did* the killing—we're morally certain, that is—but the wretched fellow has an alibi and I can't for the life of me see the flaw in it."

A little superciliously, Fen sniffed. His long, lean form was sprawled gracelessly in the office's only tolerable chair, his ruddy, clean-shaven face wore an expression of incredulity, and his brown hair, ineffectually plastered down with water, stood up, as usual, in mutinous spikes at the crown of his head. "Perhaps there isn't a flaw in it," he suggested. "It wouldn't be the first time a moral certainty had turned out to be a total delusion. What sort of a moral certainty is it, anyway?"

"It's a question," said Humbleby, "of fingerprints. A certain man's fingerprints were found on the weapon with which the murder was committed. The prints were slightly blurred, I'll grant you; someone wearing gloves *could* have used the gun subsequently, and left them intact. But then, this man's explanation of how they came to be there is a demonstrable lie—and what's more, he has a strong motive for the crime. So you see how it is."

"I'm not sure that I do," said Fen. "Not so far. But since we've got to wait for our dinner, we may as well pass the time usefully: tell me about it."

Humbleby sighed, glancing first at his wrist-watch and then at the telephone which stood mute by his elbow. Then, abruptly reaching a decision, he got up, pulled the curtains to across the windows, dispensed more sherry, and finally settled himself back into the desk-chair with the air of one who is now prepared to stand a long siege. Groping for a cheroot, "Cassibury Bardwell," he began suddenly, "is the scene. I don't know if you've ever been there?" Fen shook his head. "Well, it's a hybrid sort of place, too big to be a village and too small to be a town. The houses are almost all built of a damp-looking grey stone, and the rain-water pours down the surrounding hill-slopes into the main street from all points of the compass, all year round. The nearest railway-station is miles away, and the people are in every sense inbred. They're chiefly occupied with—well, *farming*, I suppose," said Humbleby dubiously. "But it's not, in any event, a very prosperous locality. In the countryside round about there are, apart from the farms, a few remote, inaccessible, horrid little cottages, and in one of these, tended only by a sister of advancing years, lived the protagonist of my tale."

"More matter," said Fen somewhat restively, "with less art."

"Unconscious of his doom"—Humbleby had at last found a cheroot, and was applying fire to it from a desk lighter—"unconscious of his doom, the little victim, aged about thirty and by name Joshua Ledlow, which goes to show the potency of the tradition of Biblical nomenclature in these less accessible rural places—the little victim. . . . What was I saying?"

"Really, Humbleby . . ."

"Here is this Joshua, then." All at once Humbleby abandoned frivolity and became business-like. "Thirty years old, unmarried, of a rather sombre and savage temperament, socially a cut above the farm labourer and living modestly on money left him by a farmer father. He is looked after by his sister Cicely, five to ten years older than he, who shows no particular fondness for him and who would in any case prefer to be looking after a husband, but who remains unwooed and, having no fortune of her own, housekeeps for Joshua as a respectable substitute for earning a living. Joshua, meanwhile, is courting, the object of his fancy being a heavily-built girl called Vashti Winterbourne, who appears to have cast herself for the role of Cassibury Bardwell's *femme fatale*. She didn't seem to me, when I met her, to be physically very well suited for this task, but the local standard of female beauty is extraordinarily low, so I suppose. . . . Well, anyway, you see what I mean.

"Now, as you'd expect, Joshua isn't alone in his admiration for this rustic charmer. He has a rival, by name Arthur Penge, by vocation the local ironmonger; and it is clear that Vashti will soon have to make up her mind which of these suitors she is going to marry. In the meantime, relations between the two men degenerate into something like open hostility, the situation being complicated latterly by the fact that Joshua's sister Cicely has fallen in love with Penge, thereby converting the original triangle into a sort of—um—a quadrangle. So there you have all the ingredients for a thoroughly explosive mixture—and in due course it does in fact explode.

"With that much preliminary," continued Humbleby rather grandly, "I can go on to describe what happened last Saturday and Sunday. What happened on *Saturday* was a public quarrel, of epic proportions, between Joshua, Cicely and Penge. This enormous row took place in the entrance-hall of *The Jolly Ploughboy*, which is by just a fraction the less repellent of Cassibury's two pubs, and consisted of (*a*) Penge telling Joshua to lay off Vashti, (*b*) Cicely telling Penge to lay off Vashti and take her, Cicely, to wife instead, (*c*) Penge telling Cicely that no man not demonstrably insane would ever dream of marrying *her*, and (*d*) Joshua telling Penge that if he didn't keep away from Vashti in future, he, Joshua, would have much pleasure in slitting his, Penge's, throat for him. Various other issues were raised, apparently, of a supplementary kind, but these were the chief items; and when the quarrellers at last separated and went home, they were all, not unaturally, in a far from forgiving frame of mind.

"Note, please, that this quarrel was quite certainly genuine. I mention the point because Bolsover and I wasted a good deal of energy investigating the possibility that Penge and Cicely were somehow in cahoots together—that the quarrel so far as they were concerned was a fake. However, the witnesses we questioned weren't having any of that; they told us roundly that if Cicely was acting, they were Dutchmen, and we were forced to believe them, the more so as one of them was the local doctor, who had to be called in to deal with Cicely's subsequent fit of hysterics. No chance of collusion in that department, then. Mind you, I'm not saying that if Penge had visited Cicely afterwards, and abased himself and asked her to marry him, she mightn't have forgiven him: she's not, poor soul, of an age at which you can afford to take too much umbrage at the past behaviour of a repentant suitor. But the established fact is that between the quarrel and the murder next day he definitely didn't visit her or communicate with her in any way. With the exception of a single interlude of one hour (and of the half-hour during which he must have been committing the crime), his movements are completely accounted for from the moment of the quarrel up to midnight on the Sunday; and *during* that one hour, when he *might* (for all we know) have gone to make his apologies to the woman, she was occupied with entertaining two visitors who can swear that he never came near her."

"I take it," Fen interposed, "that this hypothesis of Cicely and Penge working together would have solved your alibi problem for you."

"It would have, certainly, if there'd been evidence for it. But in actual fact, the evidence completely excludes it—and you must just accept that, I'm afraid. . . . But now let me get on with the story." ("I haven't been stopping you," Fen muttered.) "The next event of any consequence was on Sunday morning, when Cicely broke her ankle by falling out of a tree."

"A *tree*?"

"An apple-tree. She'd been picking the fruit, it seems. Anyway, the effect of this accident was of course to immobilise her and hence, in the event, to free her from any possible suspicion of having herself murdered her brother Joshua, since his body was found some considerable distance away from their cottage."

"You think the killing was done at the place where the body was found, do you?"

"We're certain of it. The bullet went clean through the wretched man's head and buried itself in a tree-trunk behind him—and that's a set-up which you can't fake convincingly, however hard you try: it's no use just firing a second bullet into the tree, because it's got to have traces of human blood and brains on it. . . . Cicely, then, is in the clear, unless you feel inclined to postulate her hobbling a couple of miles on crutches with a view to doing her brother in.

"The crime was discovered at about ten o'clock that evening by several people in a party, one of whom fell over Joshua's corpse in the dark: none of these people features in any other way in the affair, so I needn't specify them at all. The *place* was a little-frequented footpath on the direct route between Joshua's cottage and the centre of Cassibury, approximately two miles from the former and a mile from the latter. And I may as well say at once, to avoid describing the scene in detail, that all the obvious lines of investigation—footprints, position of the body, threads of clothing on brambles and so forth—led absolutely nowhere. However, there was just one substantial clue: I mean the revolver—a great cannon of a thing, an old .45—which Bolsover found shoved into the hedge a little distance away, with a fine set of prints on it.

"Now, we haven't, I'm afraid, so far discovered anything

about this gun—its ownership and history and all the rest of it. It may belong to the Prime Minister or the Archbishop of Canterbury, for all we know. But in view of the fingerprints we could afford to defer the problem of the gun's origin for a few days anyway; our immediate plan of action was of course to uncover possible motives for Joshua's death, get by guile the fingerprints of anyone suspicious, and compare them with the prints on the gun—and that led us straight away to Penge, because it was impossible to be in Cassibury five minutes without hearing about the Penge-Vashi-Joshua triangle in all its sumptuous detail. Penge, then, had this motive of jealousy—Vashti isn't the sort of girl I personally would do murder for, but then, I've known a *crime passionnel* be committed for possession of a penniless old lady of sixty-eight, and statistics show sex to be the motive for quite half the murders committed in this country, so that in that particular department I try not to be surprised at anything—Penge had this motive, then. And a comparison of his fingerprints with those on the revolver showed the two sets to be the same.

"When eventually he was asked to explain this circumstance he told, as I've mentioned, a demonstrable lie: saying that he'd handled the gun three days previously when Joshua (of all people!) had brought it into his ironmonger's shop to ask if a crack in the butt could be repaired. On its being pointed out to him that Joshua had quite certainly been in Dorchester during the whole of the day mentioned, and so couldn't possibly have visited the Cassibury ironmonger's, he wavered and started contradicting himself and eventually shut up altogether; in which oyster-like condition he's been ever since—and very wise of him, too.

"However, I'm anticipating: we didn't ask him about the gun until after we'd gone into the problem of the time of Joshua's death. There was delay in getting a doctor to look at the body, so that the medical verdict was too vague to be helpful—between six and ten was the best reckoning we could get. But then two women came forward to tell us that they'd seen Joshua alive at seven. They said that on hearing of Cicely's accident they'd visited the cottage to condole with her, and had glimpsed Joshua on arrival; though he'd disappeared almost at once (having met the two ladies, I can see why) and they hadn't set eyes on him again. So clearly the next thing to do was to talk to Cicely herself. By early on Monday morning—the morning after the murder—Bolsover had taken over; and the local Sergeant, an intelligent lad, had the sense to warn him before he set off for Cicely's cottage that she was a hysterical type who'd have to be handled carefully if her evidence was to be of any use—a diagnosis which the event confirmed. However, it turned out that by a great stroke of luck she hadn't heard of the murder yet; the reasons for this being (*a*) the fact that Joshua had planned to be away from home that night in any case, so that his absence had not alarmed her, and (*b*) the fact that the local Sergeant, a temperamentally secretive person, had sworn everyone who knew of the murder to silence until a higher authority should release them from the vow. Consequently, Bolsover was able to put his most important questions to Cicely *before* telling her his reason for asking them—and a good thing too, because she had a fit of the horrors as soon as she heard her brother was dead, and the doctors have refused to allow her to talk to anyone since. Anyway, her testimony was that Joshua, having seen her settled for the night, had left the cottage at about eight-fifteen on the Sunday evening (a quarter of an hour or so after her own visitors had gone), with a view to walking into Cassibury and catching a bus to Dorchester, where he was to stay with friends. And that, of course, meant that he could hardly have reached the spot where he was killed much earlier than a quarter to nine.

"So the next thing, naturally enough, was to find out where Penge had been all the evening. And what it amounted to was that there were two periods of his time not vouched for by independent witnesses—the period from seven to eight (which didn't concern us) and the period from eight-thirty to nine. Well, the latter, of course, fitted beautifully; and when we heard that he'd actually been *seen*, at about a quarter to nine, close to the place where the murder was committed, we started getting the warrant out without any more ado.

"And that, my dear Gervase, was the point at which the entire case fell to pieces.

"Penge had lied about his whereabouts between eight-thirty and nine: we knew that. What we didn't know was that from twenty-past eight to ten past nine two couples were making love no more than a few feet from the place of the murder; and that not one of those four people, during the time they were there, heard a shot.

"It's no use talking about silencers, either; even a silenced report would have been heard, on a quiet night. And so that, as they say, was that. Penge certainly shot Joshua. But he didn't do it between eight-thirty and nine. And unless Cicely was lying in order to help him—which is inconceivable; and in any case, Bolsover's ready to swear on the Book that her brother's death was an unspeakable shock to her—unless that, then he didn't do it between seven and eight, either."

Humbleby stubbed out his cheroot and leaned forward earnestly. "But he worked it somehow, Gervase. His lies alone would make me certain that he's guilty. And the thought that he's invented some ingenious trick or other, which I can't for the life of me see, makes me writhe."

There was a long silence when he had finished speaking. In Whitehall, the traffic had diminished from a continuous to an intermittent roar, and they could hear Big Ben striking a quarter to eight. Presently Fen cleared his throat and said diffidently:

"There are lots of things one wants to ask, of course. But on the evidence you've given me so far the trick looks fairly simple."

Humbleby made an incoherent noise.

"If Penge's alibi is watertight," Fen went on, "then it's watertight. But just the same, it's easy to see how he killed oshua."

"Indeed." Humbleby spoke with considerable restraint.

"Yes. You've been looking at it upside down, you see. The situation, as I understand it, *must* be that it isn't Penge who has the alibi. It's the corpse."

"The *corpse*?" Humbleby echoed, dumbfounded.

"Why not? If Cicely was lying about the time Joshua left the cottage—if in fact he left much earlier—then Penge could have killed him between seven and eight."

"But I've already explained——"

"That it's inconceivable she'd lie on Penge's behalf. I quite agree. But mightn't she lie on her brother's? Suppose that Joshua, with a revolver in his pocket, is setting out to commit a crime. And suppose he tells Cicely, if any questions are asked, to swear he left her much later than in fact he did. And suppose that a policeman questions Cicely on this point *before* she learns that it's her brother, and not the man he set out to kill, who is dead. Wouldn't that account for it all?"

"You mean——"

"I mean that Joshua intended to murder Penge, his rival in this young woman's affections; that he arranged for his sister (whom Penge had just humiliated publicly) to give him, if necessary, a simple alibi; and that then——"

"Ah yes. 'Then' . . ."

"Well, one doesn't *know*, of course. But it looks as if the plan misfired—as if Penge struggled with Joshua, got hold of the gun, and killed his assailant in self-defence. Behold him, then, with a watertight alibi created—charming irony—by his enemy. If the lovers hadn't been hanging about, he would have spoiled that alibi by going back afterwards—and one wonders why he *did* go back, though I imagine——"

"Morbid attraction," Humbleby interposed. "I've seen it happen time and time again. . . . But good God, Gervase, what a fool I've been. And it is the only explanation. The one trouble about it is that there's no *proof*."

"I should think there will be," said Fen, "as soon as Cicely ceases to be incommunicado and learns what's happened. If what you say about her dislike of Penge is true, she won't persist in the lie that exonerates him from killing her brother." All at once Fen was pensive. "Though come to think of it, if I were *Penge*——"

Shatteringly, the telephone rang, and Humbleby snatched it from its cradle. "Yes," he said. "Yes, put him on. . . . Bolsover?" A long pause. "Oh, you've seen that, have you? So have I—though only just. . . . Allowed to talk to people again, yes, so you—— *What?*" And with this squeak of mingled rage and astonishment Humbleby fell abruptly silent, listening while the telephone crackled despairingly at his ear. When at last he rang off, his round face was a painter's allegory of gloom.

"Bolsover thought of it too," he said sombrely. "But not soon enough. By the time he got to Cicely's bedside, Penge had been there for hours. . . . They're going to get married: Cicely and Penge, I mean. She's forgiven him about the quarrel —I told you she doted on him, didn't I? Bolsover says he's never seen a more obsequious, considerate, dutiful, loving bridegroom-to-be. And of course, she's sticking to her story about the time Joshua left the house. Very definite about it, Bolsover says, and if she weren't, there are always Penge's *beaux yeux* to make her so."

And Fen got to his feet. "Well, well," he said, "you'll never put him in the dock now. And yet I suppose that if he'd had the courage to tell the truth, he'd probably have got away with it."

"All I can say is"—Humbleby, too, had risen—"that I hope it really was self-defence. In the interests of justice——"

"Justice?" Fen reached for his hat. "I shouldn't worry too much about that, if I were you. Here's a wife who knows her husband killed her brother. And here's a husband who knows his wife can by saying a word deprive him of his liberty and just possibly—if things didn't go well—of his life. And each knows that the other knows. And the wife is in love with the husband, but one day she won't be any longer, and then he'll begin to be afraid. And the wife thinks her husband is in love with her, but one day she'll find out that he isn't, and then she'll begin to hate him and to wonder what she can do to harm him, and he will know this, and she will know that he knows it and will be afraid of what he may do. . . .

"Justice? My dear Humbleby, come and have some dinner. Justice has already been done."

THE EVIDENCE FOR THE CROWN

INSPECTOR GEORGE COPPERFIELD was of that enviable minority of policemen who have, as a rule, rather too little to do. In Lampound, where the peace of our Sovereign Lord the King was in Inspector Copperfield's charge, traffic offences were few, drunks fewer, serious crimes virtually unknown; and the Inspector was wise enough not to make his relative inactivity a pretext—as more zealous if less sagacious officers sometimes do—for tightening the reins in connection with licensing hours, parking of vehicles and so forth. Instead he devoted his spare time to improving the prose style of his reports with the help of a volume entitled *How to Write Good English*: an innocuous occupation which in his more buoyant moments led him to suspect that he had missed a profitable vocation as an author of realistic crime-fiction in the manner of M. Simenon.

Lampound is one of those towns whose *raison d'être* is unexpectedly difficult to explain. It has not grown up round an intersection of main roads, or a good defensive position. It is not situated at some strategic point on a river. It is not a Resort, nor a Beauty Spot. It is not a dormitory town, and there are no factories in the district worth speaking of. It is not, and never was, a market town or a see. In short, you cannot discover any consideration of a military sort, or an ecclesiastical, or a commercial or an industrial, which would adequately account for Lampound's existing at all. And yet there the place is: neither particularly new nor particularly old; neither specially big nor specially small; neither notably rich nor notably poor; neither lively nor dull, neither attractive nor ugly: a mediocrity among towns, a waste-product of southern prosperity, without any particular interests for its fortunate Member to defend in the Commons, without any particular aim other than the universal aim of survival. 'What then,' it may be asked, 'do its inhabitants *do*?' The answer is simple: they live off one another. The solicitor pays for his groceries by giving legal advice to the grocer, the grocer pays for his medicines by supplying sugar to the chemist—and so on. Lampound is not of course entirely self-contained; there are certain goods and services—to use the economists' jargon—which it takes from the outside world. But these are paid for, ultimately, by the large number of retired Civil Servants who rediscover in Lampound, on the plane of idleness, the unexacting moods of their working lives—are paid for, not to put too fine a point on it, by you and by me. A ponderable part of our taxes, reissued in the form of pensions, goes to prevent the economic disintegration of this inexplicable, useless township.

Useless, that is, except as contributing to the happiness of its natives: they like it. Inspector Copperfield, who had been born and bred there, liked it. And only if you had asked him where Blanche Binney figured in the leisurely ceremonies of exchange which were Lampound's main preoccupation would he have been brought to admit that the place had its black spots. Accordingly, the murder of Blanche did not, to him, represent unalleviated tragedy. It had the double merit of removing a long-standing source of nuisance and at the same time giving the Inspector something substantial to do—for he was a conscientious man who liked to give value for his wages, and it was useless to pretend that Clarity of Expression or Avoidance of Jargon were among the things which, in consideration of those wages, he had contracted to promote. The murder shocked him, of course: as an ordinarily humane person he held no brief for violence. On the other hand, if someone had *got* to be murdered in Lampound, then Blanche Binney was undoubtedly an excellent choice. The scandalous goings-on of this young woman had disrupted more than one home, and the number of men who had fallen victim to her blowsy charms was, after ten years, quite beyond computation.

This latter circumstance looked like presenting a difficulty, in that Blanche Binney, throttled shortly after lunch one May day on her own sitting-room hearth-rug, was clearly yet another instance of that favourite species of English homicide, the *crime passionnel*: and there were so many males in Lampound, married and unmarried, young and old, overt and secretive, who might have resented the catholicity of Blanche's affections, that the field of suspects seemed at first to be formidably large. Luckily, there were contributory factors which narrowed it drastically, chief of them the Clue of the Ring.

Once, and once only, Blanche had got herself engaged—to Harry Levitt, who lived alone in an old house out on the Twelford road, subsisting on inexplicit 'independent means'; he had naturally given her a ring—an expensive platinum one with diamonds encircling a large dark ruby; and she had not, when the engagement was broken off, returned it to him. Latterly, indeed, she would have been unable to return it even if she had wished to do so, for her sins had been rewarded with a sudden abnormal growth of flesh, and the ring was no longer, at the time of her death, capable of being removed except with the aid of a file.

Herein lay Inspector Copperfield's clue: for the hand which bore the ring had been hacked off, very horribly, after Blanche's death, and taken away by the murderer—and who more likely to want the ring than Herry Levitt, whose property it morally was? Moreover, Levitt had been observed by several witnesses lurking near Blanche's house at about the time of the murder, and the only business he was likely to have in that particular neighbourhood was with her. Nevertheless, Inspector Copperfield was not the man to act prematurely; enjoining silence on his witnesses (since experience had taught him that publicity assists the criminal more often than the police) he set forth to trace Levitt's movements during the day, so far as possible, before interviewing him. And thus it was that Barney Cooper came into the affair.

There are plenty of would-be amateur detectives in the land; but to few is it given, as it was given to Barney, to provide the authorities with conclusive proof of guilt in a murder case. The thing came about by accident rather than by expertise, for Barney was a day-dreamer, not a serious criminologist; but this was one instance where a day-dreamer rather than a serious criminologist was what the police required. For the rest, Barney was a small brown hen-pecked man, incurably doggish, incurably absent-minded; liked by his colleagues, tolerated by his superiors, given to mildly boastful pontificating on the unsolved crimes in the newspapers; one of those average people whom you never notice, who leave no perceptible hiatus even when they die or disappear. All ignorant of his exalted destiny, he arrived back at the bus-station terminus in the High Street, after the first trip of the afternoon shift on Route 18, punctually at three forty-seven. And thus was initiated the melodramatic train of events which was to end three months later in the hangman's shed.

Lampound would not be Lampound if there were anything in the least notable about its bus-station; and in fact you may find the pattern reduplicated in a hundred other places concrete façade with gilt letters, a tall archway into which red double-decker buses lurch like drunken elephants, the boom of voices under a glass roof, a cheerless waiting-room, an incompetent enquiry-office, and an administrative department housed in shrunken square boxes of rooms overlooking the yard. It was in one of these—the Superintendent's—that Inspector Copperfield was awaiting the arrival of Number 18. And Barney had scarcely set foot on the ground, and was still groping in his pocket for the apparatus on which he rolled himself damp, sprouting cigarettes, when a fellow-Conductor named Crittall hailed him.

"Hi, Barney!" called Crittall. "You're wanted. Inspector wants to talk to you."

"Copperfield?" Barney stared. "What the devil for?"

"Dunno. But 'e's waiting in the office now. You'd better 'ave a lawyer with you, 'adn't you?"

"Oh, shut up," said Barney, disgruntled, and made for the Superintendent's room—in which, now that he came to look, the massive blue-clad form of Copperfield was just visible behind the rather grimy window.

The Inspector was affable, however, thereby allaying Barney's vague qualms, and as soon as the Superintendent had taken himself off, in an almost overwhelming aura of discretion, they got down to business. Lord, yes, said Barney, he knew Harry Levitt all right: who didn't? And what about him, anyway? Not got himself into trouble, had he?—not that Barney'd die of surprise if he had, he having said all along that Levitt——

Copperfield cut this rigmarole short by asking, with considerable abruptness, the question he had come to ask. But Barney's reply was disappointing. It was on his bus, which did the Twelford trip, that Harry Levitt would probably have ridden if he had returned to his house immediately after the murder. Only unfortunately he had not ridden on it, not that day anyway. And with that the interview might have ended, but for the fact that the Inspector, who had long been aware of Barney's armchair-detective ambitions and who rather liked the little man, unbent so far as to offer a concise account of what had occurred; the consequence of which was that Barney went on to operate the remainder of his shift in a haze of criminological speculation which he interrupted only in order to stare ferociously whenever the bus passed Levitt's house.

His meditations were not fruitful, however, until the evening; when, having eaten his supper—liver, a dish which his wife knew him to detest—and being on the way to the local, he encountered the Inspector again, this time outside the police-station, and ventured, greatly daring, to ask if there were any developments. There were, it transpired—but exclusively of a negative sort.

"You keep all this under your hat, mind," said the Inspector. "I didn't ought to be saying anything about it, not rightly, but still, seeing as it's a hobby of yours. . . . What Levitt says to account for being near Blanche's house is that he went there to ask for the ring back for the umpteenth time, and then at the last moment thought better of it. That's *possible*, I suppose, but it sounds a bit thin to me."

"M'well," said Barney judicially, "you never quite know, do you? We all of us behave a bit queer at times. . . . No fingerprints, I suppose?"

"None that are any good, not even on the coal-axe that did the chopping."

Barney nodded. "Premeditation," he observed. "You don't wear gloves indoors, do you, not unless you've got a good reason for it. . . . I'm taking it the axe and so forth hadn't been wiped."

"Then you're taking it wrong," said Copperfield good-humouredly. "Because they had. No, it was done on the spur of the moment, if you ask me, in a sudden passion. And Harry Levitt——"

"Levitt's got a temper all right," agreed Barney. "Still, so's others."

"Always investigate the obvious first," said Copperfield didactically, "and you can't go far wrong. Which is what *I've* been doing. For instance, I got a search warrant for Levitt's house and garden—almost the first thing I did, that was."

"Any luck?" asked Barney eagerly.

But Copperfield shook his head. "Nope. Not a sign of the hand *or* the ring."

"Ah," said Barney. "No secret panels, eh?"

"No secret panels. And now I must be off." The Inspector squared his shoulders in a policemanly manner. "Mind you don't say nothing, Barney, not to anyone. We haven't got enough evidence yet, not for an arrest, and in the meantime there's such a thing as slander to reckon with. . . . We'll be searching the house again tomorrow, and I'll let you know if anything runs up. But remember—mum's the word." He went, and Barney very thoughtfully resumed his interrupted progress towards *The Pheasant*.

'*No secret panels. . . .*' He had spoken facetiously, without thinking, but it now occurred to him, as he drank his evening pint, that he might have spoken truer than he knew. For Barney's grandfather had been a builder; had built, among others, the house Harry Levitt occupied; and had made something of a speciality of secret hiding-places—in part because, prior to the invention of modern safes, such *caches* had been genuinely useful, and in part because of a naturally rather infantile mind Barney was unable, off-hand, to remember if any such theatrical feature was incorporated in 'The Elms', where Harry Levitt lived; but at least it was obvious, from what the Inspector had said, that the police had overlooked the possibility of such a thing, while at the same time there was a good chance that Levitt, after ten years' residence, had discovered it, if indeed it existed.

That evening Barney left *The Pheasant* earlier than usual. The bar was humming with the news of the murder, and more than once he was requested, half-frivolously and half in earnest, to give his opinion of it; but he waved these demands aside with so obviously genuine an air of abstraction that his silence created a greater impression than any amount of talking could have done. It impressed his wife, even, when eventually he got home. Where Barney was concerned she was not normally at all an impressionable person, but on this particular evening there was, as she said later, Something About Him, and she remained as nearly mute as she was capable of being while she watched him climb the stairs to the attic.

Now, it was one of Mrs. Cooper's recurrent grievances that the house was too large for them; and in this matter she had fairly good reason to complain. Barney, however, clung to his home, in spite of the inordinate rates he was obliged to pay, from an obscure sense of family piety which he would have found it difficult to justify or explain but which was none the less one of the very few things he was ever obstinate about. His grandfather had built the house, he said. his *grandfather* had built it. And that—he seemed to feel—was explanation enough. His grandfather had not as a matter of fact built the house very *well*; but he had certainly built it big. And the attic being correspondingly sizeable, not to mention crammed with the accumulated rubbish of three generations, it took Barney almost half an hour to locate his forebear's business papers, and another twenty minutes to disinter from among them the faded, yellowing plans of 'The Elms'. The search proved well worth while, however, for it turned out that 'The Elms' really did possess a *cache*. The rosette mouldings to right and left of the study fireplace were movable, it seemed; turn one clockwise, and the other anti-clockwise, and you released an iron centre-panel with a cavity behind it. Just the thing, Barney reflected, if you wanted to hide an amputated hand. And that being so....

By the time he got downstairs again his wife had made a full recovery from her pristine awe of him, and the news that he was proposing to leave the house once more was ill received. It is interesting to speculate about what would have happened if her indignation had prevailed. But it did not prevail: for once Barney was too excited to reckon the domestic consequences of argument and disobedience, and he had slammed out of the front door before Mrs. Cooper had got really into her stride. Outside, his excitement waned slightly. Harry Levitt was notoriously a tough customer, and to burgle his house with him in it would be, for little Barney, a very risky undertaking indeed. Luck was with him, however: a neighbour whom he met outside the gate told him that Levitt had just been brought in to the police-station for further questioning. Barney retraced his steps and fetched his bicycle. Copperfield wanted evidence, did he? Well, he, Barney Cooper, would see to it that he got it.

Some forty minutes later, standing before the fireplace in the left front ground-floor room of 'The Elms', with only a pocket-torch for illumination, he felt rather less confident. For one thing, he was still slightly breathless after his hectic ride. For another, it had turned unexpectedly chilly, with an unseasonable wind which blustered distressingly at the window through which he had entered. For a third, there was a dog howling somewhere close at hand; a dog whose voice rose and fell on the night air with a monotonous persistence which became, after a few minutes, extremely trying. . . Levitt's dog? There hadn't been any barking, but that was no guide. And whatever noises there might be outside the house, *inside*, by an irony, it was much too quiet for comfort. Funny, the atmosphere of an empty house. Funny how——

A switch clicked and the light went on. Shotgun in hand, Harry Levitt stood in the open doorway.

He was a big man, and in middle age he had lost none of his native vigour. The light shone harshly on his pitted, weatherbeaten face, and his small eyes were pitiless. From Barney, immovable with fright, his gaze shifted slowly to the fireplace. Then, without speaking, he crossed the room, twisted the rosettes and opened the iron panel. Groping inside, he produced the stiff, bloated hand of a woman, with the end of one finger cut away.

"So you thought you'd keep the ring, did you?" he said. "You thought the hand would incriminate me enough without it. What a fool. What a greedy fool. What a stupid murdering little bastard."

From behind the curtains in the corner Inspector Copperfield emerged. He said: "Barney Cooper, you're under arrest for the murder of Blanche Binney. And it's my duty to warn you that anything you say will be taken down and may be used in evidence at your trial."

But Barney said nothing. He had fainted.

"Yes," said the Inspector, when a Sergeant and a Constable had at last taken Barney away: "I'm sorry about all that pantomime of pulling you in for questioning. The only thing was, I was afraid he'd never dare come here unless he thought you were out of the way. I'd planted the idea earlier on this evening, see, by telling him that we hadn't got enough evidence against you, and that we were going to search the house a second time. And when he talked about secret panels, joking-like, of course I didn't mention this one you'd already showed us of your own accord. So now he's cooked his own goose by trying to frame you: done to a turn."

Levitt grinned, and spat into the fireplace.

"It's a laugh, isn't it," he said, "me helping the cops out, at my time of life. I've been inside once or twice—as you'll know—and you don't forget about that sort of thing in a hurry. But murder's something different. I'm not saying that bitch didn't deserve it, mind. But just the same, she was the only girl ever took me seriously, and I owe her something for that, even if she did double-cross me when it came to the point. . . . Ah well. That's all over and done with now. Did he kill her for the ring, d'you think? It wasn't worth all that much."

"I doubt it. Taking the ring was an afterthought, if you ask me. No, jealousy's why he killed her. He kept his affair with her pretty secret——"

"Affair!" Levitt interrupted. Blanche! That shrimp!" He spat again, contemptuously.

"Ah. That shrimp, yes. But you know what sort of a home life he had. . . ."

"I don't know. And I don't want to." Suddenly Levitt guffawed. "Barney Cooper in bed with Blanche—my God, what a thought! But then, Blanche never did have any taste. . . . You've got your evidence he was fooling around with her?"

Copperfield nodded. "You can't ever hide that sort of thing

from anyone as is really *looking* for it, so I didn't have too much of a job digging it all up."

"There's one thing I don't see, though," said Levitt. "And that is, what put you on to him in the first place. After all, half the men in Lampound have mucked about with Blanche one time or another. So how did you come to suspect *him*?"

"Just a bit of luck," said Inspector Copperfield with unconvincing modesty. He collected his cap, finished the beer Levitt had offered him, and stood up; in his mind's eye he was already conscientiously substituting *when I got there* for the more natural-seeming *on proceeding to the scene of the occurrence* in the wording of the report which he must write when he arrived back in town. . . . "Just a bit of luck," he repeated. "A *lapsus lingui*, as you might say—not but what the best authorities regard it as pedantic to use foreign words and phrases when an English equivalent is available. However . . . Point is, I called in at the bus-station this afternoon, see, so as to find out if you'd been on Barney's bus. So I'm up there in the office, and I hear one of his pals shout to him, *'Hi, Barney!'* this chap says, *'Inspector wants to talk to you.'* And *'Copperfield?'* says Barney, straight off. . . ."

The Inspector moved towards the door. "Well, I ask you. A busman, chap who has officious blokes in uniform looking at his passengers' tickets every day of his life, saying a thing like that. 'Barney's expecting me,' I said to myself. 'He's got something on his mind. . . .'

"And he had."

DEADLOCK

CAPTAIN VANDERLOOR HAD never understood the English licensing laws, and on the evening in question he came rattling at the bar door of the *Land of Promise* at a quarter past six, quite unaware that since his previous visit we had changed to the summer hours. He got his drink, however (as always, it was gin and bitters) because my father sent me to see who it was, and of course I took the Captain round to the back door and my father served him in the kitchen. That often happened—at any rate, with people my father approved of. Strictly speaking, it was against the law, but the Hartford police hardly ever visited us at the Basin, and the local folk, and one or two of the yachtsmen, had been used to drinking in the kitchen for so long now that we had all more or less forgotten there was anything wrong about it.

The *Vrijheid*—Captain Vanderloor's ship—had berthed that afternoon. Her monthly visits from Harlingen always provided an agreeable break in the routine of our tiny community. She was a grey, square-built, smallish craft, Diesel-driven, and she carried her cargo of eels alive in the hold (from the Basin they were shipped inland through the canal, and so eventually reached London). She would come up the Estuary on the tide, and then would follow the ticklish business of getting her into the lock, which was only just large enough. Like all the other craft, she moored on the west bank of the canal. She was manned by a mate, an engineer, and three hands, all of whom regularly took the bus into Colchester the evening after berthing, and there got drunk. And equally regularly, Captain Vanderloor stayed at the Basin and visited the *Land of Promise*.

He was a small, stocky man, with a close-cropped bullet head and an apparently permanent expression of gentle melancholy on his face, and he spoke English well, though in a decidedly guttural way. As a seaman he had rather come down in the world. He had been master of a large merchant vessel, the *Liverpool Gem*, which went down, it was said through his negligence, off the coast of Java. Plainly there was some doubt about what actually occurred, for he never lost his master's ticket. But in any case the Company brought him back to Europe, and he was relegated to the comparatively humiliating position he now held. Very occasionally he spoke of the old days, but he never welcomed questions, and I think he was anxious to forget as much as he could. Certainly he seemed a good seaman—though in those days I knew little about the handling of larger craft, and know even less now.

A kind of ritual had grown up which always followed his arrival. My father would hand him the gin and bitters and say: "Good crossing?" And he, even if it was blowing a gale, would say: "Very fair," and offer my father one of the thin black cigars he habitually smoked. This my father invariably refused.

There was no variation in the procedure on the Saturday evening I have in mind—except, perhaps, for the presence in the kitchen of our new maid, Anne, who was peeling the potatoes for supper. She was a plump, cheerful girl, with red face and hands, and she was already inclined to take a far too critical interest in my goings-on. But, as my father remarked, she was a good worker—and all things considered, it was just as well, for my mother had died when I was very young, my father had his work cut out looking after the bar and the Yacht Club gear, and Aunt Jessica was of no more practical use than Papo, the parrot, who sat squawking and whistling all day in the parlour. Aunt Jessica padded about in a pair of ancient carpet slippers—I don't remember ever seeing her without them—and was subject to mysterious 'attacks', the significance of which I didn't understand until later. Anyway, she was no help in our domestic economy, and to all intents and purposes the house was run by Anne.

The fact is, I never liked or trusted Aunt Jessica. For one thing, her appearance vaguely disgusted me (she was about sixty, with a good deal of straggling grey hair, thin, and with an extraordinarily long and pointed nose). And for another thing, the way she talked seemed to me unreal and ridiculous. She was my father's sister, and my grandparents hadn't been well-to-do people at all, but to listen to Aunt Jessica one would imagine them the flower of the Edwardian *haut monde*. Moreover, Aunt Jessica seemed quite unaware that the world had progressed—or, at any rate, changed—a certain amount since those days. In her insistence on out-of-date conventions she was somewhat of a museum piece. No lady, in her opinion, would do so-and-so; no well-bred child would say such-and-such. Please don't misunderstand me; our own age isn't such a model of courtesy and decorum that we can afford to laugh at the manners of other times. But Aunt Jessica's maxims were purely unintelligent and mechanical—and in addition, she had, as I now realise, views about sex which were positively diseased.

I seem to be a long time in arriving at the events of that night. But before I do, two more things remain to be explained: the relation between Murchison and Helen Porteous; and the topography of the Basin, which you will have to understand if you are to follow what happened.

Murchison was a member of the Hartford Yacht Club. The club-house itself is about a mile farther down the Estuary, but a good many of the members keep their boats in the canal, the moorings by the club-house being very limited in number. Murchison had two craft—a fine thirty-foot power launch and a sixty-foot Bermudian ketch. I may add that the use to which he put this last did not endear him to genuine yachtsmen. He would get a party on board, switch on the motor, pass through the lock, run a couple of miles down the Estuary, anchor, produce a case of gin, and after an hour or so return the same way. To the best of my knowledge he never went farther, and to the best of my knowledge he never set a sail.

He was well-to-do, unmarried, between thirty and forty, tall and powerful, with a black moustache, an aggressively loud voice, and a total lack of consideration for anyone not of his own financial standing. At the time of which I am speaking his chief interest in the Basin was his attempt to seduce Helen Porteous—an attempt in which, for all I know, he may have succeeded.

Naturally at the age of fourteen I didn't think of the matter in just those terms. It was a 'love affair' such as one saw on the films. But I well remember the night when Margaret Porteous and I crept along the canal bank and looked in at the porthole of the cabin in which Murchison and Helen Porteous

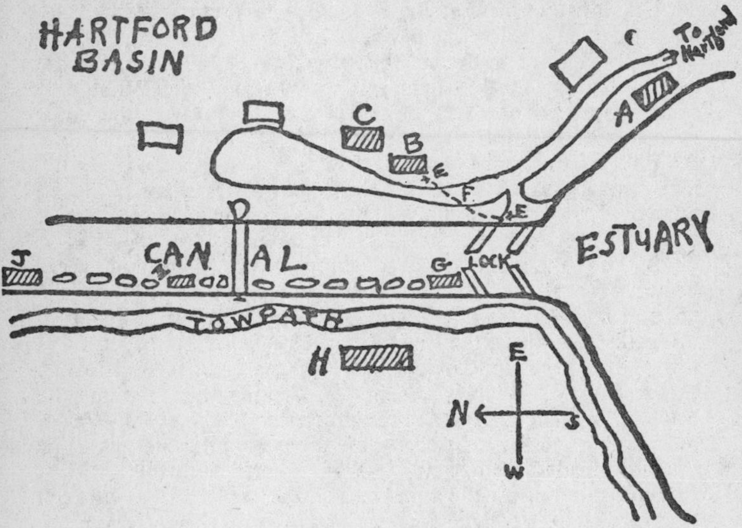

were sitting. The tiny curtains hadn't been properly closed, and we could see something of what was going on. It wasn't very scandalous, I suppose; but at the same time it wasn't quite the sort of thing two young children should be allowed to witness. Margaret whispered to me, in her queer, husky voice:

"I think that's horrid."

I said as casually as I could: "It's quite normal, you know." But I must admit that fundamentally I agreed with Margaret.

Margaret and Helen were both daughters of Mrs. Porteous, who lived next to Charley Cooke, the lock-keeper. Margaret was thirteen and Helen eighteen. Their father had died some years before. Helen was thin but pretty, and fair-haired; she dressed well and appeared to me to use too much make-up. (At the time I was inclined to be puritanical about such things.) Shortly after my father opened the bar that evening I saw her get off the bus from Hartford, where she worked. She generally stayed in Hartford for the evening unless there was some good reason for her to be back at the Basin, and I wasn't surprised when later on Murchison came into the *Land of Promise* with a couple of friends and announced that he proposed to spend the night on his boat. My father disliked Murchison (though, being employed by the Yacht Club, he couldn't afford to show it). So did I. So did Aunt Jessica. So did Captain Vanderloor. So, in fact, did everybody—which no doubt accounts for what happened to him.

You will have gathered that the lock is more or less the central feature of the Basin. The canal joins the Estuary at right angles, and the lock has to be a specially deep one, since even at high tide the river water is still six to eight feet below the level of the canal, while at low tide (when, of course, the lock can't be used) there is nothing but a stretch of sand and mud over which the gulls wander, scavenging. Along the west bank of the canal stretches a line of boats—boats of all ages, kinds, and sizes, one or two falling to pieces through sheer neglect, others painted and polished and cared for like the idols of some pagan tribe. Their mooring-ropes create a series of death-traps along the tow-path. There is nothing beyond this tow-path except some fields, in which the grass is kept brown and scanty by the salt winds, and the wooden hut in which the Yacht Club gear is kept. On the other side of the canal (which, by the way, can be crossed by the inner or outer lock gates or by a footbridge farther up) are the houses, with the *Land of Promise* standing a little apart on the road which comes in from Hartford. This road ends in a kind of gravelled car-park in front of Mrs. Porteous's house and the house of Charley Cooke, the lock-keeper. Finally, I ought perhaps to say that although the Basin can be warm enough in summer, at other times of year it's often bitterly cold, for it catches the east wind which blows up the Estuary. Just such an east wind was blowing on the afternoon three years ago when I . . .

But you will hear of that in its proper place.

As usual, I was sent to bed at half-past nine. I climbed the stairs to my room with a feeling of pleasant anticipation, for I had arranged to meet Margaret Porteous unlawfully at midnight, when we proposed to do a little innocent detective work. This involved climbing out of my bedroom window, and also—

what from experience I knew to be a far more difficult job —keeping awake until the appointed time.

We intended to investigate the Maoris—two women and two men—who lived amid indescribable squalor in a broken-down house-boat some way up the canal. Their bickerings and beatings were a perpetually interesting topic of conversation to the local people, as was also the problem of their livelihood, for they would disappear for months at a time, and then return to resume their existence in the house-boat as though they had never been away.

Probably the police knew all about them, but they were a complete mystery to us. I had some notion, I think, that they worshipped their native gods, with fearful rites, in the watches of the night, and it seemed to me important that Margaret and I should witness these proceedings.

At half-past ten I heard my father lock the door of the bar and retire, with one or two favourites, into the kitchen (it was another part of the Vanderloor ritual that he and my father should play a game of chess some time during his visit). Shortly after eleven, the mate, engineer, and crew of the *Vrijheid* emerged somewhat noisily from the taxi which had brought them back from Colchester, crossed the lock gates, singing a sentimental Netherlands ditty, and boarded their ship. After that I must have dozed, for the next thing I remember is hearing the Hartford church clock strike midnight.

I splashed some water from the jug on to my eyes, and then opened the window and climbed out. This brought me on to a sloping roof of grey tiles, and from there I could slip down easily enough to the penthouse roof, which overlooked the kitchen garden and was tarred—with the deliberate intention, I always suspected, of making my foothold on it precarious. Here I was held up for a short while, as old Charley Cooke, the lock-keeper, chose just this moment to depart for home. I wasn't worried, however. Charley was a sober enough man during the week, but every Saturday night he was in the habit of drinking as much beer as he could carry, and generally a bit more on top of that. So *he* wasn't likely to notice anything

When he had gone I jumped down from the penthouse roof. I didn't like doing this, as it was a six-foot drop, and you got rather a jar when you landed.

Margaret was waiting for me in the garden.

"I was afraid you weren't coming," she whispered.

"Don't talk here, idiot," I whispered back.

We made our way towards the lock. A fresh, cold wind was blowing, and the night sky was full of clouds, so that the weak moonlight came and went spasmodically. It was clear enough when we reached the lock, however, for us to be able to see that no one was about, though we could hear Charley Cooke singing as he approached his house. We crossed by the inner gates of the lock, and walked along the tow-path, feeling our way carefully among the mooring-ropes. Then, by the Yacht Club hut, Margaret stopped.

"I'm frightened," she whispered.

I was surprised. Margaret was a nervous child, but nervous in the way which welcomes rather than avoids an adventure. She was quite unlike me in that respect: I was unimaginative in the normal way, but prone to deep and sudden panics.

"What are you frightened of?" I asked.

"Suppose they don't like being watched?"

This consideration had also occurred to me, but at the moment I was not prepared to admit it.

"They won't know we're there," I said.

"They will if one of us coughs or sneezes or anything . . . You go and look, Daniel, and then come back and tell me if there's anything interesting."

I was annoyed. The Maoris' pagan sacrifices seemed considerably less fascinating now than they had in prospect. But male honour could hardly admit defeat—at any rate, in front of a girl.

"All right, I'll go," I said shortly. "You stay here. Shan't be long."

"Be careful." She was shivering a little, but that may have been only the wind.

It had taken us, I suppose, three minutes to get to the Yacht Club hut. In another five I had reached the Maoris' house-boat, passing Murchison's launch on the way. The cabin was lit up and I could hear voices, but I didn't delay. As it turned out, my precautions in investigating the house-boat were needless. It proved to be completely deserted. Either its occupants had not yet returned, or they had chosen this day to decamp.

I admit that I was relieved, but at the same time it made our truancy rather pointless. The Hartford clock struck a quarter past midnight as I left the house-boat. I had only gone a yard or two when I met Margaret, who had come to meet me.

"Mummy keeps opening the door," Margaret said. "Do you think she knows I'm not in bed?"

"I expect she's waiting for Helen," I said. "Helen's out tonight, isn't she?"

"Yes."

"There's no one in the house-boat," I explained. "We'd better go home, I suppose."

"I *can't* go home now Mummy's on the watch. . . . *Oh, Daniel. . . .*" She sounded so miserable, and she was shivering so much, that I put my arm round her shoulders—and the next moment, embarrassed, hastily withdrew it.

"You can get in round the back," I said encouragingly. "You'd better not go over the foot-bridge, though, or you might be seen. Come on. We'll go the way we came."

We returned along the tow-path as far as the Yacht Club hut. We had no sooner arrived there than, across the canal, Mrs. Porteous's door opened, and I could see framed in the oblong of light Mrs. Porteous herself, Anne, and my father. Almost at the same moment someone left Murchison's launch and crossed the canal by the foot-bridge.

"They *do* know we've gone, then," I whispered. "Come on—I'm going to try and get back before Dad does."

We continued on our way, and crossed the lock, this time by the outer gates. Here I unchivalrously left Margaret to her fate. But I had only just got inside the garden when Anne and my father caught up with me.

"So *there* you are," he said.

I was expecting to be punished, but he seemed unusually preoccupied, and simply ordered me to get off to bed, and stay there. He himself remained for some time downstairs, talking to Anne in the kitchen. And I just heard him say, as I closed the door behind me: "Curious about that blood. . . ."

I would have liked to stay and listen, but I didn't dare. I went upstairs and undressed, congratulating myself on my escape, feeling slightly ashamed of having deserted Margaret, and yawning as though I'd not slept for years. Then, when I came to take off my shoes, I found stains on them—dark red patches, sticky in places, but for the most part almost dry.

I assumed at once that this was blood, and although such romantic guesses are not often correct, this one was. I wondered whether this was what my father had been referring to, and then rejected the idea, for he would certainly have asked about it. I wondered, as I crawled into bed, whether I should go down and tell him. I was still wondering when I fell asleep.

As it was holiday-time, I was allowed to stay in bed until half-past eight if I wanted to, but the following morning was so gloriously fine that I got up at half-past seven. As soon as I looked out of my window I could see that something unusual was afoot. A little knot of men were looking at something at the edge of the lock—among them were Charley Cooke and my father. And when one of them moved aside I was able to make out what had drawn their attention—a dark, broad, irregular stain. You may imagine that I got downstairs and outside as soon as I could, and the general preoccupation was so intense that I was able to go quite close without being noticed. My father had sent for a long pole; now he was pushing and dredging with it in the water of the lock. And in a little time a face, white and curiously peaceful, rose towards the surface and sank again. The drowned do not float until five or more days after they are dead, and Murchison had been in the water only seven or eight hours.

After the body had been taken away, it was not at all easy to keep me out of the proceedings which followed. For one thing, I could hardly be confined to my room; for another, I was by way of being a witness, since I had been out and about somewhere around the time when the murder occurred. That it *was* murder, there seemed little doubt. And, as I realised at the time, the police were going to have no difficulty in ferreting out motives for it. There were motives everywhere; at one time or another, Murchison had succeeded in falling foul of a number of people at the Basin.

When breakfast was over I managed to slip out and inspect the bloodstains. From the pool (I call it a pool, though by now, of course, it was dry) at the edge of the lock, a trail of blood led almost to Charley Cooke's doorway. And here there was a second pool. I inspected these things with interest, but wasn't able to deduce much from them. Subsequently I went along to Mrs. Porteous's house and discovered Margaret in the garden. She had been soundly slapped on her return the previous night, and moreover had suffered from nightmares; so she was decidedly subdued. I made some attempt to enlist her co-operation in making a search round the lock—for what, I wasn't clear—but she had been forbidden to go out. I saw nothing of Helen; as it was a Sunday, she was pretty certain to be still in bed.

I wandered back to the canal side. Hardly anyone was about; a sort of expectant hush hung over the Basin. Captain Vanderloor was on the deck of the *Vrijheid*, but doing absolutely nothing; in the usual way, unloading would have started by now. I suppose he anticipated that it would be interrupted in any case by the arrival of the police, and was not sorry for an excuse to delay putting to sea again. A colony of jackdaws were quarrelling in the tall pine tree near the *Land of Promise*.

The sun shone brightly. I felt oddly purposeless and impatient.

Then I saw the weapon. It was a long, black, wooden stave, carved in loops and whorls at the top, and it was floating in the canal almost within arm's length of the bank. I called to Captain Vanderloor, and he seemed, for a moment, startled.

"What is it?" he shouted back in his heavy, guttural voice.

"Look!" I called. "Come and look!"

I heard him descend the creaky wooden gangway of the *Vrijheid*, and then, unable to wait until he arrived, I got down on my stomach and began fishing for the stave; after considerable effort I managed to pull it ashore, just as Captain Vanderloor came up to me.

He inspected it carefully.

"H'm," he said. "There are still traces of the blood on it."

"It means the Maoris must have killed him," I pointed out.

The Captain took out his cigar case; he did not reply for a moment. Then: "Yes," he said slowly. "It must mean that. Shall I keep this stick to give to the officials?" He must have glimpsed the disappointment in my face, for he added gravely: "I shall be careful to emphasise that it was you who found it."

Little mollified by this promise, I was preparing to argue the point when the police arrived from Hartford, in a rather dilapidated-looking car. There was an inspector and a sergeant and a constable, together with a doctor whom I didn't know. The Inspector was not impressive, and I was sadly disillusioned. He wore no uniform, and he was a weedy, undersized young man, with a marked Cockney accent, and fingers stained a deep brown by incessant smoking. His name was Watt, and he seemed to be totally lacking in any kind of method. On that Sunday morning he wandered about the Basin, talking to anyone he happened to come across, staring with vague interest at the scenery, and strolling in and out of people's houses more, it seemed, in accordance with some passing whim than for any definite purpose. I was at the age when I expected a detective to be hawk-eyed and ruthless, and I felt cheated.

The doctor and one of the constables hurried straight into Charley Cooke's house, to which Murchison's body had been taken. The Inspector strolled towards Captain Vanderloor and myself.

"Morning," he said. "Is that the weapon that did it?"

That was the first experience I had of his particular idiosyncrasy, which was to ask all and sundry for their personal theories about the crime. Most of what he heard must have been absolutely worthless, but I realise now that he did it partly in order to form a judgment about the person to whom he was speaking, and partly for the sake of the scraps of information which sometimes slipped out. He had, too, a disconcerting habit of silence, which sometimes forced one, from sheer embarrassment, to say more than one had intended.

"Polynesian," he said now, as he swung the stave between his fingers. "Ebony. Pretty heavy. Funny thing to have about."

"It belongs to the Maoris," I explained eagerly. "They live in a house-boat up the canal. Or rather they did. They weren't there last night."

"And you think they're the criminals?"

"I — I suppose so," I stammered. "That is, it looks like it, doesn't it?"

He seemed to lose interest in the subject. He stared about him. "Trim little ship," he said, nodding at the grey, unromantic bulk of the *Vrijheid* across the canal.

"I am her Captain," said Vanderloor.

"Eels," the Inspector commented. "Never liked 'em, I'm afraid." I realised now that he knew or noticed a good deal. "And what about you, Captain?" he went on. "Is your money on the Maoris?"

Captain Vanderloor shrugged. "I know so little about it," he murmured. I noticed that he was standing stiffly, and that his manner was defensive.

"Lot of blood," said the Inspector mildly. "He might have been knocked on the head outside that house there and then pulled to the lock and rolled in. . . ." He spoke slowly, as though inwardly preoccupied with some other matter. "Did you hear anything during the night, Captain?"

"I could not have," said Captain Vanderloor, "not in my cabin. I was on deck ten minutes or so before I go to bed, but I hear no sound then."

"What time would that have been?"

"Let me see: I return from *Land of Promise* about twenty to midnight. Then I talk to my mate and engineer till about five past. Then I go out for some air."

"You didn't step ashore at all?"

"No. I did not leave my ship."

"Can your people confirm that?"

"I think so. Several of them were awake."[1]

"Uh-huh." The Inspector flicked with the Maori stave at a blade of grass growing by the roadside. "I wonder what's the latest time it could have happened?" He turned to me "So

[1] I had better say at once that Captain Vanderloor definitely did not leave the *Vrijheid* after he returned to her from the *Land of Promise*.

you paid a visit to the Maoris and found 'em not at home?"

"Y-yes."

"And when would that have been?"

"About ten or a quarter past midnight. I wasn't supposed to be out, of course."

The Inspector grinned. "Let's hear about it just the same. You may be a star witness."

So I gave him a detailed account of the expedition—though unfortunately it was cut short, just as I was about to tell him of the blood on my shoes, by the doctor's coming out of Charley Cooke's house.

"Well, doc," said the Inspector. "What's the verdict?"

"Cause of death, drowning," said the doctor shortly. He was a plump, grey-haired, self-important old man. "The skull wasn't fractured, though the back of his head was pretty well battered."

"Could this have done it?" The Inspector held out the Maori stave.

"That's the kind of thing. I'll analyse the stains on it if you like and tell you if they belong to his blood group."

"Do that," said the Inspector, handing over the weapon. "Anything definite about the time of death?"

"Only within four hours or so."

"That's no good." The Inspector lit a fresh cigarette from the end of the one he was holding. "All right, doc. You'd better take a sample of this blood on the ground too, though I shouldn't think there's much doubt it's his." He spoke to the constable, who was hovering in the background. "Anything in the pockets?"

"Only a comb and a handkerchief, sir.

"No watch? No money?"

"He was sure to have been carrying money," I put in. "He was rich, you know."

"Uh-huh." The Inspector nodded. "Robbery with violence, eh? We must send out an S.O.S. for those Maoris. Who can give me a good description of them?"

"My father can," I said.

"Fine. We'll go and see him. You," he said to the sergeant, "find out where this house-boat is and give it the once-over." And to the constable: "You drive the doc into Hartford and bring the car back again."

"I'll send in an ambulance to take the body away," said the doctor.

"Fine," said the Inspector "It'll do where it is for the moment. Now let's go and see your father."

Captain Vanderloor went back to the *Vrijheid,* and the Inspector walked with me to the *Land of Promise*. We found my father limping about the bar, tidying it. He was a tall, weatherbeaten man of fifty, with short red hair, and he had been a seaman until an accident with a winch had made him lame.

"Hello," he said to me. "I didn't know you'd been out."

I introduced the Inspector.

"Pleased to meet you," said my father. "We may as well sit here. Will you have a drink?"

"It's a bit early," the Inspector grinned, "but I think I could manage a pint. Nice little place you've got here."

He gazed about him while my father drew the beer. There was only one bar in the *Land of Promise*, and I've seen nothing like it elsewhere. It served, really, as the family sitting-room, and Aunt Jessica, Anne, and I all sat there during the evenings. Consequently there were quantities of personal belongings—books, sewing, and whatnot—scattered about it, and they contributed to a much more friendly, informal atmosphere than is usual in such places.

"We like it," said my father noncommittally. He gave the Inspector a description of the Maoris, and the Inspector phoned it through to Hartford. While he was doing this Aunt Jessica shuffled in, wearing her carpet slippers and a curious, shapeless garment of grey and purple wool. She was insatiably curious and hated to miss anything, whether it concerned her or not. She settled down in a leather chair, sitting bolt upright, and began knitting.

The Inspector had finished with the telephone. "Well, Mr. Foss," he said, "have you got any ideas about all this?"

My father, who had not stopped his tidying, shook his head. "That'd be your job, wouldn't it?" he said doggedly. And since the Inspector made no answer, resuming his abstracted inventory of the room: "I'm not sorry he's dead," my father added. "I didn't like him."

Aunt Jessica looked up from her knitting. "We should speak no ill of the departed, George," she remarked.

I thought that my father was going to spit, but he restrained himself.

The Inspector drank his beer. "Any special reason for not liking the chap?" he said.

My father nodded. "You might as well know," he said. "You'd hear about it sooner or later. He said he intended to get me kicked out of my job here—looking after the Yacht Club gear. He could have done it, too."

"That would have been a nuisance?"

My father grunted. " 'Tisn't easy to make ends meet."

The Inspector turned to Aunt Jessica. "And were you fond of Mr. Murchison?" he enquired.

The click of my aunt's knitting-needles ceased abruptly. "He was impure. They say nowadays that the woman's as much to blame as the man, but I know it isn't so. *He was impure*," she repeated with sudden vehemence.

The Inspector accepted this comment with perfect equanimity. "Were both of you up and about round midnight last night?" he asked.

My father answered him clumsily, like one repeating a lesson inadequately learned. "I played chess with Vanderloor until about twenty to twelve. Charley Cooke left here at midnight. About a quarter past I found this kid had done a bunk, and Anne came along with me to Mrs. Porteous's house to see if Margaret had gone out with him. Jessica was there—weren't you, Jessie?"

"Since half-past eleven," my aunt supplied. "I often go along for a little gossip before bed." Her ball of wool rolled on to the floor, and the Inspector picked it up for her. She smiled graciously at him by way of thanks.

"Well, Margaret wasn't in bed, either," my father continued rather uneasily. "I knew they must be somewhere along the canal, so I decided to go after them."

"I saw you come out of Mrs. Porteous's house," I said audaciously, "about twenty past twelve."

"Oh, you did, did you?" There was a grimly humorous look in my father's eye. "Anyway, the moment Anne and me left Mrs. Porteous, we were held up by finding Charley Cooke clinging to his own door-post. We'd seen him, as a matter of fact, lying in a drunken stupor when we first went into the house, and I'd made a note to get him indoors as soon as I had a moment——"

"Uh-huh," the Inspector interrupted. "You didn't think it was very urgent, then?"

"No. That sort of thing's happened before. Anyway, he was on his feet again by the time we reached him."

"Just a minute. I take it that Charley Cooke's house and Mrs. Porteous's are next door to one another?"

"That's right."

"Are you sure the man you saw lying there when you went into Mrs. Porteous's house *was* Charley Cooke?"

My father hesitated. "I suppose I'm not, really, now I come to think of it. It was just a black huddle in the shadow of the house. But it never occurred to me it was anyone else."

"How long were you in Mrs. Porteous's house?"

"Four or five minutes, I'd say."

I was interested. For the first time the Inspector seemed to be asking definite questions with a definite purpose.

"And whereabouts," he went on, "was this person lying?"

"Just outside Charley Cooke's door."

"Where that pool of blood is?"

"Yes. Somewhere there."

"And after you'd pushed Charley Cooke indoors——" The Inspector stopped, looking at the oddly elusive expression which had appeared on my father's face. "Well?" he said.

"Well what?"

"Did you by any chance notice that Charley Cooke had blood on his clothes?"

"Yes," said my father slowly. "Yes, he had blood on his clothes."

"And after you left him?"

"Anne and I were just setting out to look for the kids, when we met Helen Porteous. She'd come across the foot-bridge from Murchison's launch."

The click of my aunt's knitting-needles ceased again.

"Uh-huh. And you talked to her?"

"Only for a moment. We left her with her mother."

"Then?"

"Then Anne heard these kids scuttling along the tow-path on the other side, so we went back to the *Land of Promise*."

"Did you pass the lock?"

"No. We went the back way, through Mrs. Porteous's garden. It's a bit quicker."

"Ah." The Inspector sighed deeply, as though exhausted by so many questions. "And you, Miss Foss?"

"When my brother came to Mrs. Porteous's house," said Aunt Jessica primly, "I saw that it was after a quarter past midnight—a very late hour for me—and so I returned here."

"With your brother?"

"No. I was ahead of him."

The Inspector lit a fresh cigarette as the black marble clock on the mantelpiece struck a quarter to ten. And then came the moment I had been dreading all morning. Every week my father sent me off on my bicycle to ten o'clock Sunday School in the Baptist Church at Hartford. At the best of times this was a misery. This particular Sunday, with the police at the Basin, I felt that it would be a monstrous imposition to be made to go, and I had been desperately hoping that in the general excitement my father would forget about it until it was too late Unfortunately he heard the clock.

"Well, Daniel, time for you to cut along," he said.

"Oh, but Dad . . ." I began.

"There's no 'but' about it, my lad. Off you go."

Protests were useless. I went, and I don't think I've ever passed a longer hour. I remember that we were given the story of Nebuchadnezzar, but even the exploits of my namesake failed to arouse the smallest spark of interest in me, and when asked for my view of the incident of the fiery furnace I expressed the opinion, very sulkily, that it was all a trick with chemicals. Needless to say, this theory wasn't well received.

However, even Sunday School must come to an end some time, and shortly after eleven I was back again at the Basin. Luckily I had not missed a great deal. It is true that the Inspector, by some means known only to himself, had succeeded in the interval in acquiring a good deal of general information about us all; true also that his interview with Charley Cooke had resulted in what the newspapers call 'dramatic revelations'. But as regards these last, Margaret Porteous had been enterprising enough to eavesdrop, and when I returned she told me what she had heard.

What it amounted to, in brief, was that on getting back from the *Land of Promise* Charley Cooke had found Murchison lying unconscious almost on his doorstep, had been seized with the fear that he would be implicated in the crime, and had dragged the body to the edge of the lock and left it there.

Unfortunately he was quite vague about the details of the affair—times and so forth. For instance, he was dimly aware that at some stage or other he had 'passed out', and again, he thought that he *might* have entered his house before moving the body, but could not swear to it.

"But what *I* don't see," said Margaret, "is why he moved the body but didn't try to hide all the blood."

The only explanation I could suggest was that he had been drunk—as to which there was no doubt whatever. Admittedly the story wasn't very plausible (I was half-inclined to think that Charley had not only dragged Murchison to the lock but pushed him into it as well), but at the same time it struck me that Charley's account corresponded pretty closely with what any drunken, timorous, not very intelligent old man might have done in the circumstances. He would consider the area round the lock a sort of no-man's-land; and in the darkness even a sober person might have failed to observe the blood.

I was asking Margaret for more details about the interview

when Mrs. Porteous called her indoors to talk to the Inspector. I'm sorry to say that the temptation to do some eavesdropping myself proved too strong for me. I knew that the Inspector would be in the sitting-room at the back, and I knew also that at the expense of a few wall-flowers I could listen beneath the window. Scarcely more than a minute after Margaret had left I was settled at my station.

I risked a look into the room. It was shabby and comfortable, with the big black stove along one side, and the kettle simmering on it, and Pip, the canary, sitting rather dejectedly in his cage. There were hunting-prints on the walls, and the glass and crockery gleamed on the dresser. The Inspector was sitting with his elbow on the oilcloth which covered the table. A cup of tea was in front of him. Mrs. Porteous was in a wicker armchair which creaked every time she moved. Helen, with her scarlet lips and large eyes, was propped up against the dresser, evidently sulking. And Margaret, thin, nervous, and slightly elfin, with her fair hair in a tangle over her eyes, was repeating the story of our night's expedition.

"Uh-huh," said the Inspector when she had finished. "And while you were waiting by the Yacht Club hut, you didn't hear anyone moving about on the other side of the canal?"

"No. Except for Mummy opening the door."

"Fine. And now perhaps the other young lady will tell me what she did last night."

There was a moment's pause before Helen replied. "I was on John's launch," she said at last. "John Murchison, that is. I was there from after supper till a quarter past midnight."

She stopped. In accordance with his habit, the Inspector said nothing. Finally Helen went on:

"John was there, of course, and two friends of his. Then—then some time around midnight, I can't remember exactly when, we ran out of gin, and John said he'd go to the *Land of Promise* and try and get some more. I—we waited a bit, and he seemed a long time about it, and at a quarter past I thought I'd better go home. I'd said I'd be in early, you see," Helen added spitefully, and I could visualise the look which she gave her mother.

"Yes," said the Inspector thoughtfully. "And as I understand it, you met Mr. Foss on your way back?"

"That's right. He asked if I'd seen the kids anywhere. I hadn't, so I came on home."

The Inspector's voice was placid. "You were up at the time, Mrs. Porteous?"

"Yes, Mr. Watt." Mrs. Porteous was plump, homely, and

slow-moving, and her speech mirrored her perfectly. "I was a bit worried, you know. . . ."

"Oh, *mother* . . ." Helen began impatiently.

"Yes, dear, I know. . . . Not of course that there was anything *wrong* in Helen's being out, Mr. Watt. But when it got to midnight, and I heard Charley come home singing from the *Land of Promise*, I thought I'd just have a look outside the door to see if there was any sign of my girl. It was then I saw that Charley had fallen down outside his door."

The Inspector spoke sharply. "You're sure it was Charley?"

"Of course it was. Who else would it have been?"

"But could you definitely *see* that it was?"

"No," Mrs. Porteous admitted. "But all the same I'm quite sure——"

The Inspector interrupted her—impatiently, I thought. "What time was this?"

"A minute or two after midnight."

"Uh-huh. And you just left him lying there?"

"I knew the night air would soon bring him round, Mr. Watt. And indeed it did. When I next looked out, he was gone."

"What time did you next look out?"

"It was close on ten past. Naturally I kept glancing at the clock, since I was anxious about Helen."

"And at that time there was no one lying outside Charley's house at all?"

"No, no one."

"After that Mr. Foss and Anne turned up?"

"Yes. A little after the quarter. I found Margaret wasn't in her bed, and Mr. Foss set out to search for her and Daniel. It was then that Jessica left. A minute later Helen arrived, and a minute after that, Margaret."

I don't think that anything further was said which had a bearing on the case. The Inspector thanked Mrs. Porteous for the tea and took his departure, and after a discreet interval I took mine. I didn't see him again until nearly an hour later. Eventually I found him standing near the lock and staring out across the Estuary, his hands pushed into the pockets of his untidy brown raincoat. It was low tide, and the horizon was unusually clear—a sign, I knew, of rainy weather in the offing. The wind was freshening, and clouds were beginning to obscure the sun.

I went up to him.

"Well, well," he said when he saw me. "With your talent for eavesdropping—*and* Miss Margaret's—you must know nearly as much about the case as I do."

I blushed.

"And what's your opinion of it all?" he asked.

"I suppose really it depends on the two bodies," I said, fearful of being thought a fool.

"It depends on the two bodies," he assented gravely. "Which was Murchison? The one lying outside Charley Cooke's door from 12.02 to 12.10? Or the one lying there from 12.16 to 12.20?" He paused. "Well?"

"I don't know," I said.

"There's no doubt it was the second one," he told me.

"Why?" I demanded.

"For the good and simple reason that if it was the first, Charley must have dragged it to the edge of the lock some time between 12.05 and 12.10. And in that case either Margaret or Captain Vanderloor would have heard. You can't perform *that* sort of operation in complete silence."

"I see," I said slowly. "Then Mr. Murchison's was the second body, and Charley took it to the lock between 12.16 and 12.20, when Anne and my father were in with Mrs. Porteous. And he'd just come back from doing that when Dad found him leaning against the door."

"You've got it."

"But in that case when did the Maoris attack Mr. Murchison?"

"Pretty certainly between 12.10 and 12.15."

"But Margaret and Captain Vanderloor would have heard *that*."

"I don't think so. Some of these natives have got the art of making a silent attack pretty perfect. The only thing that troubles me is whether Margaret and Vanderloor could have *seen* anything that was going on on the other side of the canal."

"No," I said definitely. "It was much too dark."

"There you are, then. Charley Cooke comes home from the *Land of Promise* just after twelve. He tumbles down on his own doorstep. Some time before ten past he recovers and goes inside, so that when Mrs. Porteous looks out, she sees no one there. Then along comes Murchison, heading for the *Land of Promise*. He left the launch *about* twelve—neither Helen nor the other two people could tell me anything more definite than that. The Maoris, who've had their eye on his bank-roll and have been lying in wait, follow him, strike him down, rob him, drop the weapon quietly into the canal, and do a bunk. Enter your father, who mistakes the body for Charley Cooke. While your father's in with Mrs. Porteous, Charley comes out of his house, sees Murchison, and drags him to the lock."

I considered this. "Yes," I said, "I suppose so. . . ."

"Vanderloor had gone below," he explained, "Margaret had run up the canal to meet you, and the others were indoors. So no one would have heard."

"No one would have heard," I pointed out, "if Charley had pushed him into the lock there and then."

"Ah, but look at the pool of blood," he said. "Murchison must have lain there at least five minutes."

"Oh, yes, of course." I was annoyed with myself for forgetting this.

"So that's the set-up, it seems to me. Charley left him there, and someone pushed him in. . . ." The Inspector paused, and there was an uncertain look in his eye. "I don't think I should be telling you all this. . . ."

He looked back over the Estuary. Down at the bend a sailing dinghy was visible, skimming across the shallow water. The gulls were quarrelling fiercely over a small fish stranded on the mud.

"You can't mean it was my father," I said boldly, "because he was with Anne from a quarter past twelve onwards."

I reflected, and realised what he was thinking. "Aunt Jessica?" I said in a small voice.

For a long time he was silent. Then:

"I've been looking into possible motives, you see," he said almost absently, "and she is the only person having a motive and lacking an alibi. She went back alone to the *Land of Promise*. . . . You don't like her, do you?"

"No," I answered slowly, "but all the same . . ."

"She's a bit cracked, you know." He tapped his forehead meaningly. "I don't think it'll get as far as a trial. They'll put her in a home, and she'll be quite well looked after."

I said: "She hated Mr. Murchison because of Helen."

"Uh-huh. And there he lay, unconscious and right on the edge of the lock. It couldn't have needed much strength to shove him in. . . . Well . . ."

He turned away, to gaze again at the Estuary. The wind was still rising, and the sailing dinghy had passed out of sight.

"Pretty view," he said. "I'd like to paint that some time."

"Paint it?"

"I turn out a daub now and again." The Inspector sighed, and I noticed that for the first time that morning he was without a cigarette. "Well, I'll have to be getting back to Harford."

We returned to the *Land of Promise* in silence, each of us

occupied with his own thoughts. My father was working in the kitchen garden, and the Inspector went to speak to him. I watched them for a moment. My father was leaning on his spade; he said nothing, and his expression hardly changed. Then I went slowly into the house.

Anne was not in the kitchen, but Aunt Jessica was. She sat swaying back and forth in the rocking-chair, and she was talking slowly and quietly to herself. The grey woollen dress had a damp stain down the front, and a broken tea-cup lay at her feet. Tiny drops of sweat stood out on the smooth yellow skin of her face, and her eyes were as blank as the windows of an empty room. What she was saying had no coherence or meaning at all. At first she didn't notice me, but when eventually she became aware of my presence she made as if to leave the rocking-chair and come towards me. I ran from the room in terror. She was still talking, in that gentle, insane monotone, when they took her away.

The Maoris were never found. Since Murchison's watch was discovered in a pawnbroker's shop in Liverpool, it was thought that they had taken ship and left the country. Certainly they never reappeared at the Basin. As the Inspector prophesied, Aunt Jessica did not come to trial. The death of Murchison had permanently turned her brain, and she was sent to a Home Office institution, where my father visited her regularly every month. She never spoke of what had happened, but the police were in no doubt about her guilt. My own apprehension subsided little by little, as I realised that she would not recover her reason. I suppose I ought to excuse myself for saying that, since, after all, Aunt Jessica was innocent of the murder. But I could not bear the thought that an interlude of sanity might reopen the case and direct the attention of the police to the person whom I knew to be guilty.

Nine years have passed since the events of which I have spoken. In that time much has happened. When Hitler invaded Poland, Captain Vanderloor was given the command of a large merchant vessel. He visited us, staying at the *Land of Promise* for a night, just after he had had the news, and we celebrated his return to bigger things. A month later he went down with his ship, torpedoed in mid-Atlantic. Helen Porteous became the mistress of a second-rate engineer (and a petty swindler into the bargain), and I believe had a child by him. There was much less yachting at the Basin. The eel-boats were replaced by small, fast vessels which brought engineering supplies from Sweden. There were sporadic bombing attacks.

And in one of these Margaret Porteous was killed.

I had been called up, and was far away in Yorkshire when it happened. My father wrote to me about it, and for minutes after reading his letter I sat in the crowded, noisy mess as though stunned. Margaret and I had drifted apart as we grew older, a shyness lay between us, intensified in my case by a sense of my obvious inferiority, for she, at seventeen, was a slender, almost ethereal girl, while I, a year older, was as clumsy and loutish as young men generally are at that age. My only comfort now—and it's so petty a consideration in the circumstances that I'm almost ashamed of mentioning it—is that she must have been aware of what I knew, and yet trusted me implicitly. To what happened during that night neither of us ever referred. And perhaps it was that, as much as anything else, which fixed such a gulf between us in the years that followed.

I had always thanked God that the doctor had interrupted us before I was able to tell the Inspector about the blood on my shoes. Now I'm not so sure. If they had put her in a reformatory, Margaret would be alive now. Alive. . . . I ought really to say, existing. Perhaps things are better as they are. I don't know.

Once I had begun to think about it, it was all obvious enough. The bloodstains on my shoes could not have been picked up on the way back to the *Land of Promise*, for Margaret and I returned by the *outer* gates of the lock, and there was no blood on the ground as far along as that. So I had stepped in it when we first crossed the canal, by the *inner* gates of the lock. That, you will remember, was just after midnight. By that time, then, Murchison had already been attacked. But Charley Cooke had only just set off for home, and so could not have had time to drag the body to the side of the lock. It seemed, then, that it must have been beside the lock that Murchison was originally attacked by the Maoris. He was not lying there, however, when Margaret and I crossed the canal, for it was light enough for us to see that no one was about, and consequently, as the blood trail showed, he must have been already by Charley Cooke's doorstep, where either he dragged himself in search of assistance or he had been dragged by the Maoris. So this was the *first* of the two bodies that were seen lying there—the one that was gone when Mrs. Porteous looked out at ten past twelve. Charley Cooke had taken it back to the lock, the second blood trail being superimposed on the first. Afterwards he returned, fell in a stupor, and was seen by my father.

There was only one difficulty about this theory: Charley Cooke could not have dragged Murchison to the lock in complete silence, and yet both Captain Vanderloor, on the deck of the *Vrijheid*, and Margaret, awaiting me beside the Yacht Club hut, swore that they had heard nothing at all. I knew, as soon as I had got this far, that they must be lying. Yet Captain Vanderloor had not committed the murder, for it was established that he had not left his ship. If he was lying it could only be because he knew that Margaret had pushed Murchison into the lock, and wished to shield her. And she, of course, was lying to save herself. After the thing was done, it was an easy matter for her to return along the tow-path and meet me by the Maori house-boat.

Why did she do it? Certainly, I think, because of her sister Helen. The night we saw Murchison making love to Helen—her mother's grief at the relationship—Aunt Jessica's sex-obsessed prejudices—these things, to a sensitive child of thirteen, would probably be more than enough to inspire the easy act which resulted in Murchison's death. She must have heard Charley dragging him to the lock, gone to investigate, and found him lying there, seen the easy way, and taken it. . . . I sometimes wonder if, as she grew up and discovered that what had so disgusted and horrified her was, after all, the merest commonplace, a sense of guilt deepened in her. Yet I am inclined to think, after all, that it was not so. Children and adults have very different values about some things—death, in particular. If you have read *A High Wind in Jamaica*, you will remember the indifference of the other children to the death of John. I believe that Margaret felt just such an indifference—amounting in the end almost to forgetfulness—about Murchison, and it remained with her until she was killed.

A week before the raid I was home on forty-eight hours' leave, and it was then that I saw Margaret for the last time. I was helping my father carry a sail from the Yacht Club hut to the *Land of Promise*, and she was standing at the very edge of the Estuary, gazing across it as the Inspector had done six years previously. The tide was full, and an east wind that whipped the grey water into millions of little wavelets was tangling her fair hair and moulding the old mackintosh which she wore against the lines of her body. She did not look round, and I, poor fool, hesitated to speak to her because of some trivial squabble we had had on my previous visit. She lies in Hartford churchyard. Now and again I put flowers on the grave.